REDRUM

I0609768

Selina's Way
1st edition
(First German edition)
Copyright © 2018
(First American edition)
Copyright © 2019
REDRUM BOOKS, Berlin
Publisher: Michael Merhi
Translated by Simon Kossov
Editor (American edition): Monica J. O'Rourke
Proofreading: Jasmin Kraft
Cover design and concept:
MIMO GRAPHICS by using an
illustration by Shutterstock.

ISBN: 978-395957-551-5

Mail: merhi@gmx.net

www.redrum-verlag.de

YouTube: Michael Merhi Books

Facebook: REDRUM BOOKS

Facebook Group:

REDRUM BOOKS—Nichts für Pussys!

SIMONE TROJAHN

SELINA'S WAY

About the Book

Do you have kids? Do you love them? Would you do anything for them?

Really anything?

Dan Meller once lived in a rundown trailer park. He was an alcoholic, addicted to drugs, and barely able to look after his little daughter, Selina.

Today, Dan is clean and sober and seems to have made it. Together with his wife and two daughters, he lives in a pretty house on the outskirts of town, has a job, and only has the best intentions.

The little girl from back then is now almost an adult. A pretty young woman.

Daddy's pride and joy.

And of course he does everything to make up for what he screwed up in the first years of her life.

But Selina looks at things a little differently.

A dark abyss hides behind her radiant façade, because deep in her broken soul, she is still a neglected toddler.

She needs her daddy so much!

And Dan will do anything to make his beloved daughter happy.

Really anything!

You don't want this girl to be your enemy!

About the Author

Simone Trojahn writes fiction that is terrifyingly realistic, profound, and ruthless. Her stories are mercilessly authentic. This exceptional author has been in the social work field for many years and knows the dark side of life. In a unique way, she shows what happens if we become the person we never expected to be.

Contact
t.simone80@googlemail.com
Simone Trojahn Fans at Facebook:
facebook.com/simonetrojahn

SIMONE TROJAHN

SELINA'S WAY
Hardcore Psycho-Thriller

She tied you to a kitchen chair
And she broke your throne and she cut your hair
And from your lips she drew the Hallelujah.
—Leonard Cohen

PREFACE

In 2016, I watched the first season of the American drama series *Secrets and Lies,* in which a family man discovers the corpse of his neighbor's son while jogging in the woods and is chased as the main suspect shortly after. His apparently perfect family idyll is put to the test, and a look into the abyss suddenly determines his life. In the end, he learns his own daughter is responsible for the boy's death. And it wasn't an accident.

While the season is slowly coming to an end, a nightmare begins for the family man. He realizes his daughter suffers from a mental disorder. Emotions like compassion or remorse are alien to her. But instead of seeking professional help for his child, he does something that gave me the idea for the novel, *The Princess*: to protect his child, he takes the blame and goes to jail, despite knowing she will always be a danger to others, perhaps even to her own family.

Out of love for his daughter he puts not only himself but the rest of his family in a desperate and dangerous situation. In the end, he only wants to protect his girl, but he loses every sense of reality.

This selfless as well as misguided fatherly love made me think: *Would I have done the same?*

Don't good parents do everything humanly possible for their children?

But where are the limits?

What would I do in an emergency?

What would you do?

In the series, this man goes to jail for decades, so that his daughter can live a blameless life. As one learns in the second season, he even dies in prison in the end—although he knows at that point that she is a psychopath who has selfishly and calculatingly killed someone.

Would your love for your children go this far?

Or is that not real love at all?

Wouldn't all parents say they would do everything for their children?

Through hell and back?

That's how it should be, isn't it?

Or can you overdo it?

The idea for *The Princess* was born from these thoughts.

Just like the girl in the series, Selina is a psychopath without compassion. She would do anything to get her way and protect her imaginary perfect world.

And her father?

Well, he does anything to make that possible for her. Just like the family man in the series, he also loses sight of himself and everything around him. But Selina acts even more vehemently and brutally to win her father for herself.

That was unfortunately the problem in the original version of *The Princess*. I came across a taboo issue that is regrettably often suppressed in our society. Most people prefer to look the other way rather than deal with it. Real offenders are often convicted with ridiculous punishments, or there are no sanctions against them at all.

But if you come up with a fictional story, it's probably a nuisance for those who don't have any more space left under their carpet.

Selina's behavior was already set in her earliest childhood, when she became a victim of abuse and her father deserted her.

This not only leads to broken child souls but to psychopathic and sociopathic behavior, as displayed by the precocious Selina. So this is not just fiction or an author's excessively violent fantasy, it's dark reality—hidden, suppressed, locked away.

But since many don't want to know anything about it, the book was no longer allowed to be sold.

In the new version we now have a likewise disturbed and precocious Selina, who, however, is ready to seduce her father by every trick in the book only after she turned eighteen. Which doesn't mean that she was tame before.

The people who like to sweep the dirt under the carpet are certainly not satisfied with it either, but I don't care about that, because whoever likes to suppress it should keep their hands off my books anyway.

We all know how ugly reality can be.

The media report about it every day.

If you need a fictional story to realize that, I'm a little sorry. Above all, it's a great pity for the many real victims of violence and abuse. It's not of any help for them that their environment acts as if nothing has happened.

For their sake, I will continue to look closely and come up with stories that are as dreadful as the reality we live in.

The Princess became *Selina's Way*, but the message remains the same: look, empathize, and understand!

There is no more formative time than childhood, and everything that is screwed up comes back like a boomerang sooner or later. The results are destroyed souls and brutalized people.

Selina's Way is hardly the right way, but for people like Selina, it may sometimes be the only possible one. Because our world doesn't offer the same opportunities for everyone, and a wrong start in life can sometimes screw up all the rest.

We should never forget this before we judge.

—Simone Trojahn, November 2018

A TOUCH OF NOTHING

He loved those moments early in the morning, just before getting up, when he wasn't fully awake but wasn't sleeping, just lying there listening to the noises in the house.

In *his* house.

Noises coming from his wife and children.

In the end, everything had turned out fine. Hadn't his mother always predicted it would? Everything would be good, she'd say. Sometime and somehow. The only thing you couldn't give up on was hope. It was the only thing that remained in a person's darkest hours. You had to hold on to it, even if it was the last thing you did.

His mom had been right. Had he ever thanked her for that? Dan wasn't sure.

But as he turned from his side to his back and sleepily blinked into the dull gray daylight, he decided to do it very soon. He'd call her. Tonight or tomorrow at the latest.

Dan made a mental note, hoping he wouldn't forget. Life had been particularly good lately, but that also meant he had all sorts of things on his plate. His life was as beautiful as it was exhausting. He had a family and a job and commitments he would hardly have dared to dream a few years ago. As a result he had less time for himself, but he paid this price with a smile, because he now had Kate, his wife, whom he loved to bits.

Three years ago he wouldn't have believed he'd ever love again.

But now everything was fine.

They were now the proud parents of a wonderful little six-month-old girl. Whenever Dan held Leila in his arms and looked at her little face, he was so overwhelmed by feelings. Tears filled his eyes. This wonderful girl was the culmination of a wonderful relationship and the highlight of this wonderful life that had come upon him as suddenly as warm rain in August.

All these wonderful things had caught him by surprise and he'd never stop being grateful. Not only grateful for his own sake, but also for Selina, his sweet princess. Selina was now eighteen and not a little girl anymore, even though it still felt that way to Dan. Maybe it was because he'd missed so much when she was little. Most of her childhood he'd been present, but not really there.

These days this fact upset him.

Selina came from Dan's earlier relationship—if you wanted to call living in a rundown trailer with a drug-addicted hooker a relationship. But Dan hadn't been lost in the objectionable ambience at the time. At least he—unlike his then girlfriend Clara—had never injected drugs. That gave him a slight head start toward brighter moments, but it had never been enough to provide adequate care for a small child.

While Clara spent most of her time in semi-consciousness strung out with other addicts on the discarded patchwork furniture in front of the trailer, Dan tried to take care of little Selina inside the camper, ignoring piles of pot, meth, and alcohol.

Unlike Clara, he retained a basic understanding of what an infant needed to survive. He swaddled her (although he often had to wrap her in towels because there were no diapers) and gave her a bottle every few hours (more or less). Getting powdered milk wasn't always easy, especially in a household where the little money on hand had the annoying habit of liquefying in a flash. Sometimes Dan stole a carton from a nearby supermarket. Sometimes, little Selina only got lukewarm sugar water. Two or three joints, a bottle of booze, or a few noses of meth (preferably a little of everything) made his guilty conscience disappear.

Dan reluctantly had to admit there were days when he hung around for hours with Clara and the others in front of the trailer while inside, his poor girl screamed her heart out. The music and voices were loud enough to make a crying baby invisible or seem dull and unimportant.

And when Clara sat on his lap and thrust her tongue down his throat while she gently massaged his crotch, and he felt the wet hot spot under her miniskirt, which was rarely covered by panties, for a few hours he completely forgot the infant in the laundry basket who hadn't been diapered since yesterday and hadn't received a bottle for far too long.

Nevertheless, she was his little princess. Dan loved her with all the fervor a trashy junkie could muster—even though he didn't know (still didn't) whether she was his biological daughter. Although Clara hadn't cheated on him in the conventional sense, she liked to spread her legs for anyone who had something to offer—usually money, drugs, or alcohol. She sucked cock for a few dollars and let guys fuck her in the ass for a shot. Sometimes she disappeared with some stinking dealer in the trailer while Dan sat outside smoking and trying not to think. Since he didn't have much to offer, he knew he had to tolerate her escapades if he didn't want to lose her.

And he didn't want to lose her because he loved her.

For whatever reason.

At that time, a life without Clara would have been unimaginable. Dan still didn't understand the reasons, but by now he attributed his behavior to his love of drugs and alcohol.

Something had to be to blamed.

Or someone.

It sure wasn't the drugs or booze.

When Clara got pregnant, he was happy about the baby and never considered the possibility that a horny dealer knocked her up. It was clear to him that Selina was his daughter.

His little princess.

She had to be his daughter. Anything else wouldn't have been fair.

From the beginning, Clara had shown no great interest in the little girl who had slipped out of her. She went on like before, uninhibited and merciless.

Three long years went by, and Selina's survival was more a miracle than the result of parental care. Dan tried to be an acceptable father, but it was never much more than a feeble attempt.

Then Clara choked on her own vomit, which turned out to be a real stroke of luck. Selina probably owed her life to tragic circumstances.

One morning, Dan woke early with the sour smell of vomit in his nose and the taste of rotten meat in his mouth. He moaned and turned his head and found his face in a semi-dry puddle of puke. Still too stoned and wasted to feel disgust, he thought it was his own. The idea of a shower—rather, rinsing off outside using a hose—vaguely haunted his fuzzy brain.

He sat up and took a closer look at the lifeless woman beside him. Clara's naked body stank. The skin had already turned grayish and was strewn with dark spots of various sizes. She was lying on her back, her open mouth filled with vomit. Splashes of puke covered her face and her pale, flaccid breasts. A large puddle had stained the pillow under her head, and flies crept over it.

Dan had been sleeping there. Something like revulsion slowly rose in the pit of his stomach.

Or was it horror?

Urine and liquified feces soaked the sheet under Clara's body. Flies crawled between her spread legs.

Dan suppressed a scream and jumped out of bed.

How long had he been lying with her?

What the hell happened?

And *when* had it happened?

How long had he been spaced out?

And oh good God, where was little Selina?

Frantically Dan searched the garbage-filled camper.

No trace of her.

Totally naked and panic-stricken, he rushed outside and found her sitting on the filthy couch outside in the yard, playing with her doll. She was dirty, her hair matted. Selina looked like a larger version of the filthy doll in her arms. Dan lifted her and firmly pressed her cheek against his.

Then came the tears.

Neighbors called the police and an ambulance. Dan was taken into custody until the cause of Clara's death was determined. Selina was taken away without authorities giving him any information. Neither begging nor crying helped. In the end, he was quiet and did what they wanted.

After two days they let him go. They told him Selina was still in the hospital. She was malnourished and severely dehydrated. After the stay in hospital, she was to be sent to a foster family. Dan begged to see her.

But they hadn't let him and instead sent him home to the trailer that stank of Clara's corpse. They wanted him to undergo therapy, which Dan didn't understand. Why? Clara was dead, and they had taken his princess away.

He was alone.

Instead of therapy, he spent days blowing himself away with everything he could find. After all drug and alcohol supplies were used up, he slowly regained consciousness and realized he was still alive. For hours he'd been crying on the couch in front of the trailer, because he never wanted to go inside again.

He finally burned the damned thing down, and somebody called the cops again.

Dan was arrested again, this time for arson, and this time they didn't release him so quickly. They filed arson charges against him.

He kept asking about his daughter but got no answer—except for one sentence: "She's fine, and you don't need to know more."

After all this, he'd thought about his mother, with whom he'd once quarreled because she'd been against his relationship with Clara. She'd known what this bond would do to her son.

And she'd been right.

He'd hated her and never wanted to see her again.

Back then.

There'd been five years of silence, so his mother didn't even know Dan had a daughter.

Her granddaughter!

His mother was so different from Clara. She'd taken good care of him as a single parent and tried to give him a good life despite the financial limitations. He could have learned a profession and become a respectable member of society, just like she'd always been. Instead, he'd gone bad, and her efforts had been in vain. When Clara came into his life, his fate seemed to finally be sealed. His mother had given up on him and was probably finished with him. What else should she have done? He'd behaved like an asshole and had destroyed all bridges to her.

Nonetheless, she was his last chance at the time. Dan called her from prison and begged her like a little child when she didn't want to talk to him. Dan cried, apologized, and asked for help. He wanted her to try to get custody of Selina.

He didn't care about his pride. He just wanted his daughter to be well. Really well! In return, he promised to undergo therapy. He'd have done anything as long as she helped him get his little princess back.

And because Nora Meller's heart was soft and she secretly always waited for her son's remorseful return, she promised to help. His mother scraped her savings together to pay his bail, and then she brought him straight into a rehab clinic, a state institution where things were anything but comfortable.

While Dan fought his addictions there, Nora pulled out all the stops to get custody of little Selina. In the end, her persistence was a blessing. She won the case, and the nightmare finally turned into a beautiful fairy tale: Dan managed to get clean and was given a suspended sentence. He moved back in with his mother (one of the requirements), where his little girl had already settled in. She attended kindergarten and was a normal, healthy little girl. The dolls she played with still looked like her, but now they wore pretty clothes and had smooth, fragrant hair that shined in the sun.

Dan succeeded in regaining her trust. Just like his mother's. For this he fought like a tiger. He'd really changed, and everyone could see that. Best of all, when he looked in the mirror, the gray, haggard junkie face had disappeared. Instead, he saw a handsome young man with his life ahead of him.

He'd never again be able to drink a single drop of alcohol or smoke even the smallest joint, or the addiction would return—and with it, the descent into a hell that he never wanted to reenter.

But he was willing to live with these restrictions, as long as his daughter wasn't lacking anything and he was allowed to have her around every day. There couldn't have been a greater gift for his efforts. His guilt for what Selina had gone through during the first years of her life would forever remain, but he was ready to accept it.

Dan hoped that someday she could forgive him.

The years went by. Dan obtained a truck driving license and found a job in a freight moving company. He only saw Selina on weekends, and he showered her with love and gifts. She was allowed to sleep in his bed with him, her thin arms wrapped so tightly around his neck that it almost took his breath away. But that was fine. She probably needed it. She had to hold him and feel him to be sure he'd never leave her again.

Dan could never have refused her a wish. Instead of going out on his free evenings to meet new people, he stayed home with her. She didn't leave his side for a minute: she sat on his lap while eating and slept in his bed—even when she grew too old for that.

When he woke in the morning with the hands of his fourteen-year-old daughter on his body, it didn't feel right. She now had breasts and shaved her legs. When she pressed herself against him, it was no longer a child's body. But what should he tell her? She was a poor little lost child who could have died because of him. Should he admonish her or push her away?

No!

Unthinkable!

He could never treat her like that.

So everything remained the same.

And through the years, the little princess became a tall princess.

At some point he'd almost forgotten he wasn't only a father but also a man. He hadn't had a girlfriend since Clara.

When he was on the road with the truck, he sometimes picked up prostitutes at rest stops for a quick, impersonal fuck.

He was a man, after all.

When Dan lay in bed next to his teenage daughter's warm body on the weekend, he thought of those women: the moist red mouths and worn-out pussies he slipped into more for warmth than lust.

Warmth.

At home, Selina pressed her little breasts against his stomach. Sometimes, while sleeping, she put one leg over him or caressed his thigh until it pulsed—along with the middle of Dan's body.

It was wrong.

Somehow. But Selina wanted it that way.

She needed that.

She needed *him*.

On warm days she slept in her underwear, and on cold days, she pushed herself so close to him under the blanket, as if wanting to disappear into him.

And Dan let it happen—first when Selina was little, and later, when she was fourteen … fifteen … sixteen.

Sometimes he wondered if she had a boyfriend. But she never talked about the subject or went out when Dan was home.

Just like him.

Crazy!

Of course Dan's mother noticed this extreme closeness and asked him about it many times. But he only replied with a shrug. Selina was his daughter, and as long as she needed him, he'd be there for her. After all, she had a special past that couldn't simply be wiped away.

Whether or not his mother thought that was right was of little importance to Dan. After all, Selina was a kind and intelligent girl. She got good grades and would probably qualify for a college scholarship. During the week she met up with friends at the mall or for sporting events and was very popular.

So there was no need to worry. She preferred spending weekends at home, as most parents wanted from their pubescent children.

This time belonged to father and daughter.

Why the hell should that be wrong?

They loved each other and were very close.

What was reprehensible about that?

That Selina sometimes covered her father's naked chest with kisses? That she sometimes stuck out her tongue when they kissed good night?

That Dan often woke up with an erection next to his half-naked teen daughter?

What man didn't have morning wood?

Besides, things changed when Selina turned sixteen. She still slept in his bed, but when she crawled to him far after midnight, she often smelled of alcohol and sometimes of boys.

Dan had considered talking to her about contraception but hadn't managed to. He ignored his conscience by finding explanations for this as well. Selina surely knew what she was doing. His girl wasn't stupid, after all.

And Dan? His feelings varied between relief and jealousy.

Of course, he normally would have found a woman, having gone to parties or a bar. But at forty, he now felt too old for that. He figured he'd waited too long.

All for Selina's sake.

And now, it seemed his time had run out. When his daughter lay next to him and smelled of sex, he sometimes cried. On those nights, he hoped she'd be his little princess forever. He was ashamed of it, but he was also afraid of loneliness. Selina had changed. She'd grown up, and her kisses had become more daughterly.

The more she stayed out on weekends, the more he longed for a stable life. He was sick and tired of rest stops, and the smell the hookers left in his driver's cab disgusted him. He didn't want to spend his time on the highways any longer, where darkness and loneliness were on the agenda.

Now when he returned, often there was only Nora, his mother. Returning home just wasn't worthwhile.

So Dan looked found a new job in a local supermarket. The salary was bad, but now he'd be home every evening. He'd be able to participate in his daughter's life again.

Selina had seemed happy about it. She hugged her father and pressed a big, peppermint-tasting kiss on his cheek that sent a hot rapture flying through his body.

Was that wrong?

Of course!

But you're powerless against your feelings, and it was certainly only because he was so happy to finally have more time for her.

Right?

She wouldn't be living at home much longer. Selina was now seventeen and in her last year in high school.

Once she went to college, he'd only see her during the semester break.

If at all.

Dan's mother hadn't understood why he'd changed jobs and allowed his finances to get so bad. There was so much Nora didn't understand.

On the other hand, it was important to Dan that his little girl was doing well. Because of this he suffered with pleasure and waited alone in bed at night. At some point, he finally realized Selina was going her own way.

And one day, he went to a bar and flirted. He did it again. He thought it was meaningless, but it didn't seem as unimpressive as he'd thought. Maybe he'd learned to underestimate his effect on the opposite sex over the years. He was simply out of practice and had to warm up again.

Nevertheless, he spent most evenings alone or with his mother—until fate finally showed its friendly side again.

On a sunny autumn day, a pretty young woman dropped a huge bag of groceries in the supermarket parking lot. Swearing, she knelt down to pick everything up. A milk carton had burst open, and several eggs broke. Her groceries were scattered in a slimy mess.

Dan, who was busy pushing shopping carts into place, hurried to help the woman. She was a true beauty, with long, tanned legs and the same flaxen hair as his Selina.

Her cheeks were reddened. She looked up at Dan with sparkling eyes. "What a bummer!"

Dan smiled and squatted next to her. "We'll have that cleaned up in a minute."

He collected apples, a head of lettuce, a box of tampons, and various canned foods from the glop of egg and milk and wiped them clean on his shirt and pants.

The woman was impressed by his helpfulness. Their arms had touched as he put the gathered groceries in her car.

He smiled. He was covered in milk and egg slime and looked like an idiot.

The woman smiled back.

It was like a scene from a romantic comedy.

Dan said, "Wait—I'll be back in a minute." He hurried inside the store and grabbed a carton of eggs and two containers of milk.

She was still there when he came back to the parking lot. Yes, she'd been waiting for him. She smiled at Dan and gave him her phone number.

*

Her name was Kate, she was twenty-seven, a grade school teacher, and had been single for a long time. She came from an average middle-class family and led a similarly average life herself.

On their first date, they went to the movies and later had a drink. Dan didn't tell her about his past until months later, and Kate reacted with a lot of understanding.

It had been love at first sight for both of them.

Kate seemed to be the perfect woman. She was funny, beautiful, loving, and intelligent—and she got along great with his mother.

With Kate, Dan got to know a sexuality based on love and trust, not on insanity and dependence. And because this was a fairy tale without evil trolls and ugly witches, it got even better: Kate's grandmother left her favorite granddaughter a little house in a tranquil suburb. They immediately fell in love with the pretty house and its little garden. And because luck was still on their side, Kate and Dan found jobs in the surrounding area. Kate started as a substitute in the local grade school, and Dan found a better-paying position in an electronics store.

They settled in well in the new environment, and Selina quickly made new friends, although she hadn't been very enthusiastic at first.

A perfect life was completed by Kate's pregnancy and then, ultimately with Leila's birth.

The memories of his personal hell and the time in the stinking trailer with the crazy drug-addicted Clara faded. So did his guilty conscience.

Nowadays he woke up and heard the laughter of his wife and daughter preparing breakfast together, while little Leila chuckled happily in her playpen. There was no bad taste in his mouth (and certainly no smell like dead junkie bride). There was nothing but soft light and fresh, clean sheets that held the sweet scent of his beautiful wife.

The fact that his daughter had been in this place next to him for far too long didn't worry Dan anymore. It had been a phase, just like other things in life. After their traumatic past, Selina and he had simply taken a little longer to cut their cord. Their relationship was more intense than in other families, but there had never been anything bad about it. It had only seemed like that sometimes because he hadn't been at peace with himself.

But that was all over now.

They found their place.

Life was beautiful; it was perfect, and it should always be that way. Dan had been through bad times. He'd made many mistakes and had paid a price for them, but he'd also been richly rewarded—more abundantly than he ever dared hope. Dan knew it would have been a mistake to forget the gratitude he still felt after all these years.

At forty-one, he'd finally arrived, and he found it a good idea to look back with contentment. He preferred to do this in that short phase of silence in the morning that was so sweetly interrupted by the sounds from the kitchen.

By the people he loved.

Then he could remember how awful the awakening had once been, and he thanked God that these dark times were history.

Dan turned to his side one last time and pulled the blanket over his bare shoulders.

Just another minute …

He heard voices and then steps on the stairs.

He closed his eyes. He'd get up in a moment.

Just one more moment …

The scent of fresh coffee filled his nose. Steps echoed across the hall.

Then silence.

Dan tucked the blanket under his chin. In a moment he'd fall asleep again.

Suddenly, a scream cut the silence. Much too loud and shrill to be real. Dan kept his eyes closed. That was probably a dream …

Another scream.

Kate?

Dan opened his eyes and stared at the closed bedroom door. Out there, someone was running across the hall.

"Dan?"

It was Kate.

"*Dan!*"

He jumped out of bed. Not really awake yet. Fragmented thoughts, the smell of coffee and Kate's weird screams fighting his consciousness.

"*Dan!*"

The door burst open.

Dan flinched.

His heart jumped into his throat, throbbing badly. The spit dried in his mouth. He wanted to swallow but couldn't.

Kate stood in the door, still in her nightgown, a sweet little breath of nothing.

She held Leila in her arms.

Kate's face was a mask of horror.

Confused, he rushed toward her. "What's the matter, darling? Give me the baby."

He reached out for Leila, but Kate didn't want to let go. She pressed the baby firmly against her body. Dan could only see the blonde head.

Selina appeared at the door, looking worried.

"Leila!" Kate stammered, her voice trembling. She pressed the child to herself, wavering, about to collapse.

"Kate, what's wrong? Please give her to me!" Dan still smelled the damn coffee.

He stretched out a hand to Leila. And he flinched, pulling it back.

The little body in the pink blanket was cold.

Cold?

Dan looked his wife in the eye. There he read the answer.

"Oh my God, Dan." She burst into tears.

Why didn't she let go of the child?

Dan snatched the little body from her.

So cold!

Kate shrieked and sank to her knees, stretching her arms upward as if in prayer.

Dan held Leila in his arms, the way he'd done so many times so she could fall asleep or drink a bottle. He rocked her back and forth and sang to her.

But Leila was already sleeping.

Her eyes were closed. The long eyelashes cast dark, fan-like shadows on unnaturally pale skin. The small lips were purple-blue and slightly open. Behind it, Dan saw a tongue that seemed much too thick.

Was that the reason she couldn't breathe?

Without thinking, he pushed his thumb and index finger into the small dry mouth and tried to get hold of her tongue. He just wanted to pull it out a bit so Leila could breathe again …

"What are you doing?!" Kate yelled. She was out of her mind. Her nightgown had slipped so high that you could see between her legs.

He desperately tried to catch Leila's tongue but only pushed it further back until it disappeared completely in her throat.

Horrified, he stared into the waxy face of his dead child. He wanted to shake it, beat it, and shout at it … anything, so that his little daughter woke up.

In the end, he did none of that. He lay the little body on the floor and knelt beside it. His heart pounded in his throat, and the smell of coffee was everywhere.

Kate crouched next to him and kept touching Leila's cold face as she sobbed loudly.

Dan thought maybe he should take his wife in his arms. He should hold her and comfort her and say something. He should fucking do something!

But in the end he just sat there.

Apathetic.

Helpless.

And when he raised his eyes and looked into the face of the mute Selina, who had been standing in the doorway the whole time, he thought for a moment that she'd smiled.

Which, of course, couldn't be.

Dear God, why should she?

Actually, Selina looked very worried.

And distraught.

Nevertheless, she went to him and helped him to his feet. "We have to call somebody, Dad. I'll take care of that, if you want."

That's when Dan finally collapsed, into the arms of his daughter. Selina held him tight. She was astonishingly calm.

"Leila," he sobbed.

Kate lay on the floor, rolled up like a fetus, her little dead girl in her arms. Sweet Leila in her pink blanket, with wheat blonde hair and waxy cheeks that had still been rosy last night. Because she'd still been alive last night. The whole thing seemed as absurd as it was plausible.

Selina led Dan downstairs, while he left Kate alone with the dead baby. He barely knew what he was doing. The powerful coffee smell was far too overwhelming to concentrate on anything.

Only Selina seemed to be in her senses. She dialed 911.

Dan stood next to her, silent and stiff, freezing his ass off in his boxer shorts while barely noticing.

Selina spoke into the receiver. Dan heard her but didn't understand what she was saying.

When she hung up, his gaze pierced her face. But he said nothing. He couldn't.

Selina touched his arm. Her hand was warm. "You gotta get dressed, Daddy."

Dan nodded but didn't move.

Selina led him to the couch and helped him sit. Then she put a blanket over his shoulders, which he held on to because it was damn cold.

34

"They'll be here in a minute," she said. "I'll go back upstairs and check on Kate. She shouldn't be alone now with … she shouldn't be alone."

Dan nodded. He felt empty and numb.

Selina bent over him and kissed his forehead. "Everything will be fine, Daddy. I promise."

Dan looked at her. Tears filled his eyes. "Leila," he whispered.

"It'll pass, Daddy. Definitely," Selina said before she turned away.

Dan stayed seated. He thought he'd never get up again.

And part of him was right.

***

Everything that happened in the following hours remained shrouded in fog and the haze of coffee. The emergency doctor arrived, and shortly afterward, the police. Some went upstairs to take the dead child from the hysterical Kate, and a middle-aged officer stayed with Dan. He sat next to him on the couch and talked to him. But his words went unheard because of Kate's screaming.

Dan wanted to say something, but he just cried. A young female officer came downstairs with Selina and Kate. They had to support Kate on both sides so she wouldn't lose her balance. She screamed and whined. They gently placed her on the couch next to Dan. He just sat there stiffly.

He didn't look at his wife.

He didn't touch her.

It was impossible for him.

Nothing was possible.

Except for memories …

He thought of the sunny day in the supermarket parking lot. Of spilled milk and broken eggs …

The past was so much better than reality.

But the coffee odor was too strong, covering everything and everyone. Dan felt powerless.

Selina sat next to him and put her hand on his thigh. He couldn't touch her, but it was good that she was there.

Kate was hysterical and sobbed nonstop. Tears mixed with snot in her pain-distorted face. Her body radiated an unpleasant heat, and she smelled strange to Dan. Of course, she was unwashed on this terrible morning. Just like himself. The only one sitting here on the couch, freshly showered and dressed, was Selina, who should have been in school long ago.

But it wasn't the smell of sweat and unwashed skin that aggravated Dan. It was something else, something deeper. And was it right to think that way about your own wife now, who almost suffocated on her profound pain?

She isn't the only one, Dan thought. That was all he was capable of.

Selina pinched him gently, and he looked at her. Now she actually smiled. She probably wanted to help him with that.

Dan looked away quickly. It hurt too much.

A doctor suddenly appeared. Dan hadn't seen her coming. She gave Kate an injection, and she quickly became quiet. The doctor asked Dan if he needed anything to calm him down, but he shook his head.

He was calm.

At least on the outside.

Selina said something about her taking care of him, which put a compassionate smile on the doctor's otherwise rigid face. Dan caught himself dealing with the coffee smell again.

"Can somebody dump that coffee?" Did he really say that out loud?

Apparently he had, because the doctor and the policeman looked at him with confusion.

Selina, however, patted his thigh and rose with a smile. "I'll do it, Daddy. Don't worry."

She went into the kitchen, but when she came back, the coffee smell was still there. Dan knew it was in his head and might perhaps never go away again. The thought was unbearable.

Selina was immediately at his side again, and she touched him with her warm, tender hand. Dan was glad she was there because Kate was just a wreck, staring into the void.

And Leila?

Leila was somehow dead.

You could say the words, but you couldn't understand them.

Six-month-old babies don't just die!

Six-month-old babies drank milk, ate cereal, and chuckled in the playpen. But they weren't dead! Not in a normal world.

But in a world that drowned in coffee haze …?

Dan heard noises on the stairs. He turned around. Kate also looked in that direction, although her eyes were nothing but slits.

A man carried something down the stairs. Something very small, in a black plastic bag.

But it wasn't right to put Leila in a dark bag! She wouldn't be able to breathe in there. She'd be scared because it was so dark, and she wasn't used to sleeping without her night light.

Dan felt Selina's hand on his arm. She tried to hold him back, but he'd already jumped on his feet and ran to

Leila. He just wanted to take her in his arms and free her from this terrible bag. He'd make sure she could breathe. Even if it made her cry, because he was so upset. Her being upset wouldn't matter, because it would pass.

Dan reached the man who wanted to take his baby away from him. He grabbed the little body and pressed it to his chest. Hands gently but firmly held him back. Dan screamed something (his own voice was deaf to him), and he fought back, sobbing and thrashing as they stole his baby girl from him.

They pushed him to the floor and held him down until Leila was gone. Somewhere in the coffee-impregnated background Kate cried. Selina held her in her arms, and it looked as if she wanted to comfort her stepmother.

Dan only stopped fighting when a needle penetrated his upper arm. A dull warmth spread over him. He stopped sobbing, even though he didn't want to. Several people held him and led him back to the couch. They put the blanket over his shoulders again. He was still naked except for his underpants.

Little Leila had chosen a cold, gray day on which to die, so the sky could weep for her. Dan thought that was quite right. Then he remembered that none of this was right.

Only Selina's hand on his leg felt as if it belonged there.

***

The following hours were gray and thick and full of coffee haze.

Selina called Nora after they took Leila away. She called her school and explained the circumstances and was told that, despite all understanding for the difficult situation, the signature of a parent or legal guardian was needed to exempt her from classes. Selina then wrote a letter and presented it to Dan to sign. He scribbled his signature without reading it.

She stayed with him, sat next to him, and stroked his hand as he cried softly. Kate had raised her knees and wrapped her arms around them. She stared silently and flinched every time someone spoke to her or touched her.

Two officers and the psychologist stayed in the house after the others left. They asked all kinds of questions but got no useful answers from either Dan or Kate. Most of the time it was Selina who spoke.

She was so incredibly brave.

They were impressed.

The officers finally left and said they would report back later when the results of the autopsy were available. On hearing the word autopsy, Kate gave a short and sharp scream. Dan wasn't able to hold her. Selina took care of her while he sat there crying quietly and trying not to imagine what they would do with the sweet little girl during an autopsy. But he also knew that it was important to do it.

They had to find out what had happened.

They had to know in order to understand it, even if you could never really understand it.

A few hours later Nora's old Buick turned into the driveway. Selina saw her through the window and hurried to the door. Dan also rose. Dull and far away, he felt an unpleasant pressure on his bladder. He'd had to pee for hours. But who wanted to deal with such mundane things as urinating when a baby was dead?

The idea of going to the bathroom now was so trivial, just stupid and ridiculous.

Selina opened the door and threw herself into the arms of her crying grandmother. Nora wore blue jeans and a black parka because it had cooled down. Her blonde hair with gray streaks was combed back properly. She looked the same as always. Only the reddened eyes showed that she'd been crying.

"Mom!" He stood there like a little boy who'd been beaten up at school. After all those hours he still wore nothing but boxer shorts. He'd ignored the psychologist's advice to get dressed, just like Kate in her thin night-gown, that silken touch of nothing that had once been sexy.

Nora gently freed herself from Selina's embrace and went to him. Dan stretched out his arms like a drowning man.

"I'm so sorry, Danny."

When he sank to the ground, she got on her knees with him. Her chest smelled like home. Dan clung to her and vented his feelings.

Kate sat on the couch. Her family hadn't arrived yet. Dan couldn't give her any support or comfort, and again Selina took care of it.

From time to time there was a soft smile on her lips.

***

The following week consisted of hours that stank of cof-fee, tasted of salt and shit, and were smothered in tears and snot.

The officers ran out of questions at some point, and the psychologist was replaced by family members. Kate's parents had arrived about an hour after Dan's mother, and he was glad someone finally took care of his wife so that he could have Selina for himself again.

Dan ignored his conscience for the moment.

He stayed in the living room with Selina and Nora while Kate and her parents retreated to the kitchen. Suddenly, it felt as if they never belonged together. Dan tried to think of the day in the supermarket parking lot, but images of dead Leila with her blue lips kept showing up in between, and he finally gave up. He let his mother lead him upstairs.

In the bedroom, he stared at the unmade bed. Here he'd lain and imagined that life would be good while his daughter had died in her white crib a few feet away.

Was that irony? Fate? Goddamn fucking bullshit?!

Nora took a pair of jeans and a white hoodie out of the closet. Was that an appropriate outfit for the day your daughter died?

Dan stared at the clothes like he'd never seen them before. Was there appropriate clothing for such a day?

Probably not. But if there was, it should at least be black, right? Would he feel better if he wore something black?

Did he even have any black clothes? A T-shirt? Was he supposed to wear a white hoodie on the day his child died?

What did people do in such moments? Did they go shopping for black clothes? Or did everyone—except for him— have something like that in their closet? Maybe you should prepare for it all your life and set up a black corner in the closet, just in case?

Dan stared helplessly at his mother. He couldn't put his thoughts into words. He let her help him dress. Now he was a little boy again. He wanted that. Never before had he wanted to be less grown-up than at that moment.

When he was dressed, he fell on the bed. He was barefoot, and Nora brought him socks. She even put them on his feet. Wasn't that crazy? Then she sat with him and stroked his hair, which was blond and curly. As a little boy, he'd looked like an angel.

That's what his mother called him then. Angel.

She said that now. It was good that she was there. The smell of home that surrounded her covered up the coffee stench a bit.

A little while later Selina came and lay down with him. Finally again. It seemed to Dan as if he'd been waiting for it. She also smelled good. She snuggled up to him and stroked his thigh. Her hand was soft and warm.

A touch of nothing.

She stroked him until he fell asleep. He hardly noticed that her hand was no longer lying on his thigh, but a little above it.

***

The autopsy revealed that Leila had died of SIDS— sudden infant death syndrome, or crib death. She must have stopped breathing sometime during the night, somewhere between midnight and two a.m., and suffocated from a lack of oxygen. There were no external symptoms, except for her tongue, which had slipped back inside. But it was clear that this had happened hours after her death—during Dan's last desperate attempt to save his daughter. According to the forensic pathologist, there had been no external influences.

Nothing indicated that.

The parents' state of shock seemed more than just credible. There was no motive for killing. Why Leila had fallen victim to this nightmare of all parents, however, remained inexplicable. According to the latest findings, Kate and Dan had heeded everything that could be done

42

to prevent SIDS. Leila had slept in a pleasantly tempered room, in a nonsmoking household, without blankets, pillows, or stuffed animals in bed, only in her blanket. She'd been lying on her back when Kate found her. The only thing they might have been accused of was moving Leila from their bedroom to her own room two weeks ago, and one of the guidelines to avoid SIDS was to keep children in their parents' bedroom for at least a year. The breathing sounds of the parents may have a positive effect on the child's breathing activity and may also make it easier to notice when something was wrong at night.

Of course, these were speculations, and even the experts didn't know whether infant death was avoidable. Although the number of crib deaths had decreased significantly in recent years, nobody was able to say for sure why.

Kate and Dan had decided to let Leila sleep in her own room, after she'd been sleeping through the night for several weeks. They had installed a baby monitor and thought nothing of it. Kate slept very lightly and tended to wake up with every tiny noise coming from the nursery.

They blamed themselves for leaving Leila alone, but they were told they couldn't have prevented what had happened. In fact, it was assumed that babies who slept through the night very early and also slept a lot during the day and screamed little had an increased risk of dying of SIDS, as they often slept particularly sound and deep, and parents didn't notice if their breath stopped for too long.

You could drive yourself endlessly crazy, which Dan and Kate did, but it didn't make any difference. Basically, they had done everything to be good parents for Leila. They loved her and took good care of her. She'd been a healthy, happy baby—until that night when she suddenly forgot to breathe. It was painful and pointless to keep thinking about possible causes. That didn't help anyone and especially didn't bring back any dead children.

A week after her death, Leila's body was released for burial. Nora and Kate's parents, Stefanie and Bill, had taken care of everything. There was a white coffin and pink flowers. It was heartbreaking to look at this tiny white box that couldn't possibly hold a little human.

Selina held Dan's hand throughout the ceremony. Nora stood behind him and touched his shoulder from time to time. Kate was at his side, but they didn't touch each other. Instead, Kate held on to her father while her mother supported her from behind. Kate wore a black outfit that was almost too elegant for a funeral. Dan wore a black suit that was too big on him. Nora bought it, and he hadn't tried it on. It didn't matter. He didn't intend to ever wear it again.

Even during the funeral, that damn coffee stench didn't go away. Dan had hardly eaten anything in the last few days and only drank because his mother forced him to. His stomach was an angry, aching lump that turned somersaults at that disgusting coffee aroma. Again and again he was afraid of vomiting, but in the end, nothing happened. He just stood there until it was over.

The priest's words didn't mean anything to him. The sight of the white coffin slowly disappearing into this dark hole made his heart bleed. He could no longer cry. His tears had dried up.

Again and again there was this completely banal need to pee. His bladder and abdomen hurt, but somehow he always forgot to go to the toilet. It was as if he didn't know what to do there anymore—in a life where everything had become so pointless, why shouldn't he keep the poison in his body to gradually be killed by it?

Why bother to stay alive and well?

Why?

But there was a reason. It stood right next to him and held his numb hand.

Selina.

For her he would eat, drink, and go to the toilet. For her he would get up every morning and put on some clothes that would never fit the occasion.

She pressed his hand, and Dan felt too weak to return her touch, but he was glad she was there.

Selina and his mother, of course. But Nora had to return to work; she'd go home in a few days.

And Kate?

Kate was suddenly so insanely far away. He just couldn't get hold of her. Her pain was as huge as his. She lacked the strength to stand by him, just as he was too weak to give her the necessary comfort. So it was better that she stayed with her parents for a while. Dan hadn't protested when Kate's mother, Stefanie, told him about this plan. They wanted to help Kate get back on her feet. They knew Dan wasn't able to help her right now.

He knew that too, and he was grateful that this burden was taken from his shoulders. His own pain was simply too much to take care of his wife's misery.

The memories of the afternoon in the supermarket parking lot didn't change anything about it. Kate was no longer the pretty, sexy woman with the long legs he'd fallen in love with. And he wasn't that cool, funny guy anymore, who got over the death of his (junkie bride) ex-girlfriend so well and took care of his daughter so devotedly. Now they were both just two sad, frightened creatures in numb bodies with broken hearts, trapped in their grief, incapable of giving another person even a touch of the comfort they needed so desperately themselves.

It was good that Kate left for a while, because when Dan looked at her, all he saw was the dead Leila in her arms and this terribly desperate emptiness in her eyes.

That hurt too damn bad.

But when he looked into Selina's eyes, he saw comfort, hope, and understanding. Selina gave him strength. She knew exactly how he was doing and how she could help him. Soon, Dan could only sleep if he felt her hand somewhere on his body. It didn't really matter where, because it was only about the touch itself, that little warm touch of nothing, which had now become more important than anything else.

SIP BY SIP

Selina was back at school for two days now, and Leila's death was almost two weeks ago when Nora finally said goodbye on a sunny October morning to drive back to Tennessee in her old Buick. They hugged each other in the driveway, and Dan inhaled that inimitable fragrance of home that only mothers and grandmothers could have.

The thought drove new tears into his eyes, which were so sick of crying. At least this farewell was much more emotional than Kate's two days ago. She hadn't been able to give him more than an awkward hug and a dry kiss on numb lips. Now she was with her parents, and Dan didn't know when he'd see her again. They planned to talk on the phone but hadn't done so yet.

Maybe it was better that way.

Maybe they had to deal with the pain in their own way first.

Was it possible that they subconsciously blamed each other? Secretly and unspoken, but still there? Dan didn't believe so, but he wouldn't know what to accuse her of. In his eyes she'd done everything right and had been a good mother. So that wasn't what it was about, at least for him.

But what about Kate? Did she blame him? After all, he'd been the one who had suggested moving Leila into the nursery after he'd finished painting it. She slept so well, and somehow it felt wrong for him to have sex when she was in the bedroom—asleep or not. Kate seemed to have a similar opinion, because since the little one was born, they'd had sex only once, and as expected, it was over quickly. But after Leila moved into her own room, things went well again in bed. Almost better than before, as if motherhood had stolen her last inhibitions. It was horny and fun.

If a relationship worked so well in this respect, even after the birth of a child, there was no need to worry. Life had been good to them.

Dan would never understand why it had to punish them so badly shortly afterward.

It didn't seem fair.

He wondered how Kate felt about it. He should have talked to her before she left, but he hadn't said a word.

Just like her.

What if she blamed him? Because he'd been a horny asshole who banished his daughter from the room so that she could die alone in her bed, while he banged her mother in the next room? Did that match the facts? Basically yes, because they'd had sex that night, maybe even the very moment Leila took her last breath. Strange noises on the baby monitor? They could have easily ignored it when they were shagging. Leila had died between midnight and two in the morning, according to forensic medicine.

Bingo!

Exactly at that time, her stupid parents had been screwing like rabbits. Like there's nothing more important in the world, dammit! And so it seemed they were to blame for Leila's death. Only now did it dawn on Dan that Kate's rejecting behavior was not solely because of her grief. She did this quite intentionally because she wanted him to feel the guilt. Just because he wanted to fuck like a damn teenager, his little daughter had died. They should have kept Leila in their bedroom for the first year, even if it wasn't always optimal. It might have saved her life. Instead, Dan had been selfish. Horny and driven by testosterone. And now Kate had left him. Not because she was sad that he couldn't comfort her, and not because she wanted to spend time with her parents—but because she blamed him!

That's why she didn't want to see him anymore and certainly didn't want to touch him!

She was disgusted with him.

Yes, that was the explanation for her behavior.

Why didn't he think of it before?

"Danny? Are you sure I can leave?" Nora asked worriedly. She'd probably noticed him stiffening in her embrace.

She noticed everything.

Dan nodded. Of course he wanted her to stay, but he knew she couldn't afford to. She worked as a hotel chambermaid and needed the job to keep her apartment. Unfortunately, he didn't earn enough to support her financially. He wouldn't earn anything if he didn't make it back to work soon. He'd been allowed two weeks, but two weeks weren't much. Kate had better luck, because she was still on maternity leave and wouldn't have to work until next September.

Or was that invalid now that Leila was dead?

A strange thought.

Dan had forced himself not to think about it.

"Of course you can leave," he replied to his mother. "I'm not alone."

"Selina's such a good girl," Nora said.

Dan nodded. "Without her, I'd have gone crazy long ago."

Nora took his hand and squeezed it firmly. "That'll all be fine, Danny. You'll get through this, for sure. You just have to give Kate a little time. The shock is still too deep."

Tell me about it! Dan thought. Suddenly it occurred to him that he'd be alone in the house now—alone with a dead girl's room that looked like she was still alive. His stomach tensed up, and his face contorted.

"Are you sure you'll make it?" Nora asked.

"Yes, Mom. It'll be all right. Selina will be home soon."

"I'll call as soon as I arrive. Okay?"

Dan kissed her forehead. "Okay, Mom. Thank you. For everything."

The last word almost got stuck in his throat. Suddenly there was a lump that he swallowed before he could continue.

"I've wanted to tell you that for so long, Mom. I just wish something so bad hadn't happened to remind me of it."

Nora hugged him again. "I wish that too, Danny. But I'm here for you. No matter what happens. Hear me?"

He nodded again. Then he gently released from. It was time. The traffic wouldn't lessen the longer they stood around.

"We'll talk on the phone later, Mom. Drive carefully!"

She gave a restrained smile. "See you later. Give Selina a kiss for me."

Dan watched her drive away. He waved and tried to smile, but when she was gone and he slowly turned around, everything (inside and out) collapsed, and he barely made it into the hallway before he broke down trembling and sobbing.

Now he was alone.

There was no one to hold him.

He was alone in this once-cheerful house, which now only served as a cover for a dead girl's cold room.

Selina came home at five, two hours later than usual. It was a warm day, and she wore hot pants and a tight top. The thin jacket she'd put on in the morning was now in her backpack. She'd tied her long blonde hair to a cheerfully bobbing ponytail. She knew her grandma had gone back to Tennessee today, but her heart didn't get heavy when she thought of it. It didn't make her sad to walk up to the quiet, lonely house where they had all lived so happily together recently.

On the contrary!

At the moment, she felt fresh and pleasantly exhilarated. She looked forward to coming home. The butterflies danced in her belly, because this afternoon Dad would finally be alone in this big empty house. She assumed he wasn't feeling well. He'd be completely desperate, weak, and helpless, overwhelmed by all the grief and loneliness.

So he'd probably make it pretty easy for her.

Since Leila's death, he'd always done that.

Since then they slept in the same bed again, and he'd tolerated all their touches.

Just like in the past. Before Kate had shown up and so brazenly pushed herself into their life.

When Selina started sleeping with boys and leaving her dad alone at night, he'd become pensive and sad. She knew he'd never admit how much he missed her. But it was the proof she wanted.

He was crazy about her.

Back then, he'd even quit his job to be with her more often. But Selina had never intended to make it easy for him.

He didn't deserve that.

Before she got involved with boys, Selina had researched online. Nowadays, this was the easiest thing in the world. Some of the stuff she'd seen there almost took her breath away her and left her speechless. The idea of doing something like this with *him* had almost made her lose her mind. At that time, she'd decided to take it slowly.

It required composure and patience.

First she had to gain experience and turn her back on him for the time she needed. He'd be all the hungrier and more willing when she finally came back to him.

Back into his bed and his arms.

If she did it right, he wouldn't reject her. He'd never done that. She just had to wait—and practice. She already knew at the beginning of puberty that she wasn't allowed to be a child anymore. Otherwise he'd never touch her as she wished. She'd tried that before.

The first time was when she was twelve.

Back then, she'd brushed his penis again and again with her knee. As if by accident. Until there was a bulge in his boxers. But he'd behaved as if nothing had happened, pretended to be asleep and just turned away. That had made Selina very angry. But she'd also understood that it wouldn't work like that.

Not so soon.

Daddy's seduction was a long-term project. She'd have to grow older and become more skillful. And because she loved him, she'd accept that. She'd accept *anything*. Just like the disgustingly sweaty bodies of the guys she'd been doing it with in every imaginable way over the last few years to prepare herself for the one and only. To know exactly how to touch and stimulate him and which buttons to press to make him lose his mind.

Most boys appreciated it, but for others it was too much. So Selina had to find some real men who didn't know any inhibitions. She'd had them fuck her in dirty toilets in pubs. She couldn't remember how many greasy cocks she'd sucked and how often she'd come home with sperm in her hair.

She wondered if Daddy had ever suspected anything.

Definitely not *that*.

He was probably just thinking of teen parties with weed and too much alcohol. Selina went there as well. You had to keep up appearances, but she rarely had sex on these occasions. Very few guys her age had what she needed to learn to win over her father by every trick in the book. She wanted to be able to offer him more than he'd ever dreamed of.

More than any other.

She wanted him to freak out and be so crazy about her that he couldn't think clearly. That was the goal. Since all those years ago, when Selina sat on Daddy's lap as a little girl and thought he was the greatest guy ever. She knew he hadn't always been there for her, even though she couldn't remember it consciously. But then he'd fought for her like a lion. He would have died for her in the blink of an eye, would have done everything possible and impossible for her.

Because he loved her so much.

He hadn't looked at another woman since she'd been with him. Selina was sure of that. He'd never mentioned a woman or even brought one home. Her daddy was faithful, and it hurt a little to tantalize him like that. But she had to do it to prepare for what really mattered: their final and complete union, not only as father and daughter, but as man and woman. She had to push him away in order to finally have him completely.

But then the unpredictable happened: Dad met a woman.

So much for Selina's plan.

This damn bitch!

Fucking slut!

Now there was Kate, Kate, and Kate again.

Selina didn't have a chance to get to her daddy anymore. Every night this damn woman lay by his side and got everything Selina was supposed to have.

Why had Selina been so stupid? She shouldn't have waited so long. Surely he would have been ready years ago if she'd done it right.

But now it was too late.

Kate was here, and she wasn't leaving anytime soon.

Dad seemed to love her.

And then she got pregnant.

That fucking slut!

Despite her hatred, Selina had put a brave face.

All those years.

Now she was almost grown up and living her own life.

This is what it should look like.

Everyone should believe that.

Of course, she granted her father his happiness and would never have opposed it. And she'd been looking forward to her little sister.

Of course!

Most of all for Dad, who finally found his happiness after all.

Wasn't that wonderful?

A dream come true.

And then this baby!

Leila was a rosy, sugar-sweet little thing.

Just to cuddle.

And to be eaten alive …

Who was the princess now?

Dan had sworn to be there for Selina forever.

And now?

What the fuck …?

He needed neither a wife nor a new daughter.

She'd been enough for him before. And she could be anything for him.

Everything he wished for.

It might have been a bit strange since he was actually her father, but Selina wasn't too sensitive when it came to "funny" feelings. She saw her father as a man and completely hid this fatherly thing (if necessary). As a man, he was pretty hot, actually. He looked really good and had a decent body for a guy in his mid-forties. Some guys her age couldn't compare. Must be because of his good genes. Her grandmother also looked great—in contrast to Kate's mother, on whom the ravages of time had gnawed, although she was much younger. Selina had apparently also received a good portion of these genes. In September she'd turned eighteen, and she developed into a pretty hot babe.

Can't Daddy see that anymore?

He called her his princess ever since, and he certainly considered her a sweet girl, but his goodnight kisses had always been chaste, and he'd never reciprocated her nightly touches.

Selina was a daddy's girl and had always been crazy about him. She knew he'd saved her from hell and had had to fight for a long time to get her back. He'd even been in prison.

For her.

He'd given everything so they could be together, and Selina appreciated it. She loved her dad, which was part of it. Now she was old enough. Someday he'd see the woman in her, and then they could finally be truly together. Selina had never doubted it. Everything seemed to be in her hand.

But now it was Kate whose hand he held while watching television in the evening or on family trips. Kate had entered the picture and hadn't just destroyed her plans, she'd taken everything Selena cared about. Now this filthy woman was doing everything with him that Selina had prepared herself so doggedly for in recent years.

Sometimes she'd sneak into the bedroom when Dan and Kate were having sex. They never noticed. The silhouette of her father's naked body had burned itself into Selina's brain. She knew he was fond of blowjobs. He loved to be spoiled with the tongue. During sex, he often lay below and kneaded Kate's breasts while she moved on him, slowly at first, and then faster. Their smells were absolutely fascinating.

The intermingled bodily fluids.

The noises.

The clapping of meat on meat.

The wild moaning.

The whispered tones.

Selina knew all that. She'd done it dozens of times, but it had never felt right because it hadn't been with him.

Leila's death had now provided the desired move.

It was happening much faster than Selina would have dared hope. It was clear that the death of the baby would cause a deep rift. But she never guessed it would drive the two apart so quickly.

When she'd put the pillow over the little face of the sleeping baby, she thought it would take months to get Dad where she wanted him.

Instead, it would perhaps be today, barely two weeks after Leila's death.

The idea made Selina's stomach do somersaults. Nevertheless, she reminded herself to be patient and careful. Dan was still paralyzed with shock and deeply trapped in his grief. She couldn't make any mistakes now, otherwise she'd probably screw things up until the end of time.

After all, he was supposed to belong to her.

Completely.

Forever.

A hostage of love.

Well, a little bit of fear and coercion would probably help move things along, but first and foremost it would be love, because she knew her dad idolized her and would die a thousand deaths for her. Now he just had to understand that she couldn't only be a daughter but also his wife. Who still needed a family and babies?

Smiling, Selina put her backpack on the kitchen table. She pulled out her jacket and threw it carelessly on the ground. She pulled out two bottles wrapped in brown paper bags.

Red wine. Medium price range.

With the bottles in her hands, Selina became aware again of the wet feeling in her panties. Her thoughts revolved around her dad and how to get him to drink the wine.

Besides the price, she'd invested a lot in it. Selina had approached a man of about fifty in front of the supermarket. She'd seen him there before, sometimes accompanied by similarly sad figures, but mostly alone. He wore shabby clothes and a dirty full beard. Most of the time he sat on the ground, leaned against his faded backpack, and drank cheap booze from a crumpled paper bag. Selina wasn't sure whether he was homeless or just broke. She didn't care. The main thing was that he understand what she wanted.

"Hi," she said, standing right in front of him. She was well aware that from this position, he could stare between her legs.

The guy grunted something incomprehensible and lifted the bottle again. Selina was lucky he was alone today. This gave her the necessary calm and time to talk him into her plan.

"Could you do me a little favor?" she asked with a wanton look.

"Hm?" The guy was puzzled and stared with a glassy gaze.

"I need two bottles of wine from the supermarket, and I'm not twenty-one yet. They're supposed to be a gift for my dad. I want to surpri—"

"And you want me to get them for you now, right?"

Selina was annoyed because he interrupted her, but whatever. She nodded. "Of course, I'll give you something for your trouble."

He coughed disgustingly before he could speak again. His rough voice now sounded even scratchier. "Like what?"

"Ten dollars," Selina promptly replied. Buying wine hadn't been a spontaneous idea but had been planned out.

The guy didn't react as she'd intended. He laughed disgustingly, until he coughed again.

Selina looked around nervously as she waited for him to calm down. No one seemed to have noticed her yet, but it was only a matter of time.

"Well?"

"You gotta be kidding me with your ten bucks, girl!"

Selina, who had more important things in mind than to fool any bums, shook her head. "Not really, mister."

This had caused another guffaw of laughter.

"You can call me Pete, baby."

"All right, well, Pete, I'm not kidding you. The offer is serious. Unfortunately, I don't have much money …" She hoped dear Pete would somehow be familiar with this problem.

And something else …

His glassy eyes wandered over her body like slimy snails. She'd dressed up extra-sexy today. Nora and Dan had still been much too disturbed in the morning to notice this. Usually she didn't walk around like that. After all, it was a matter of preserving a reputation.

"You can't get me with that little bit of money," Pete finally said. "But I have another idea." He grinned lecherously, so Selina didn't have to think long about what the answer would be.

Yet she remained silent and waited for what would come next. To her own horror, she felt she was willing to do quite a lot just to get a decent amount of alcohol into her father's dry throat as quickly as possible. She knew he was highly at risk of addiction because of his past. Just a few drops could trigger a relapse. And when would be a better time to start drinking again than shortly after the death of your own child? Selina was sorry to tempt him to drink, but she had to think of herself (as always). As soon as he was back on the bottle, it would be much easier to make him submissive.

"Don't panic, honey, I haven't been able to get a hard-on in years. But I'd like to lick some pussy again," Pete said with a rapturous undertone. "A tender one like yours."

"That would be all?" Selina asked—happy that he didn't want more.

"Well, I'd also love to stick my finger in your cunt …
on that occasion." He laughed and stretched his dirty,
nicotine-stained index finger upward.

"All right, then. But only one finger." Selina had been
anything but eager to get groped by this stinking guy, but
for Daddy, she'd do it. He'd finally done enough for her
too.

"Okay. Where can we do it?" she finally asked and noticed after looking around the supermarket parking lot
that everyone here was busy with themselves.

Pete had gotten on his feet with a moan. He smelled
disgusting of old sweat and fresh shit.

"The car I sleep in is right over there." Pete pointed
with a vague gesture toward the main street.

"Is it far?" Doubts gnawed at her, but then Pete was already on his way.

Selina followed at a distance that seemed appropriate
and thanked God that this creep only wanted to finger
her.

They walked for ten minutes, during which Selina
struggled not to change her mind.

*What if he rapes and kills you? He could easily do that. Nobody
will hear you scream back here.*

Selina knew she'd have to take the risk if she wanted to
seduce her father tonight. The time was just right. She
had to do it as long as he was weak and desperate.

Someday Kate would come back, and until then she
had to make him her man. She had to finish what she'd
started here. Selina had no choice if she wanted to get the
wine. She only knew young people under twenty-one.
The second option would have been to steal the bottle,
but the risk of getting caught definitely seemed too high
for Selina.

Daddy would be angry and disappointed.

That wasn't supposed to happen.

Not now.

So close to the finish line.

It was better to put herself in the hands of this stinking drunkard and hope for the best. After all, he'd claimed he couldn't get an erection. If that was true, it could be to her advantage.

But what if he can do it once he's tasted my cute, tender pussy? Maybe that'll bring everything back and he won't be able to hold back. Then he'll rape me ...

Even if ...

Selina thought it was worth it. Except for her life, she'd have given anything to seduce Daddy—as crazy as that sounded—and undoubtedly was.

She crossed the parched property of an abandoned warehouse littered with garbage. Although Pete wasn't the fastest, Selina tried hard to keep as much distance as possible, even though she knew she'd soon have to let that man get damn close to her.

From time to time he looked back, probably to make sure she was still there. "Watch your step! You can easily get hurt by all the shit that's lying around."

Selina nodded and found it quite decent of him to care about her. Maybe the alcohol (and who knows what else) had broken him and he was just a hostage to his addiction: lonely, disgusting, and stinking, abandoned by the world, a sad shadow of himself.

With a certain melancholy, Selina realized she wanted to turn her father into a similarly poor sucker. However, Dad would never be as miserable as Pete. He had her taking care of him and making sure he didn't crash completely. She'd also make sure he never drank too much, just the right amount to lead him in the right direction and dispel his concerns. Without any mind-altering substances it would be hard to do, and Selina thought alcohol was the most harmless method.

Pete finally stopped behind the weed-covered wall of the old factory ruin, and then in front of a rusty car wreck that someone had covered with a tarpaulin. The windshield of the decrepit Ford pickup was shattered. Inside she saw a moth-eaten blanket, filthy clothes, packaging waste, and something that looked like a rat. It smelled miserably of putrefaction and piss. Home, sweet home. Selina had suppressed a retching reflex and decided that no wild horses would drag her into this dirty cart.

"It's not exactly the Ritz, I know."

"I'm not getting in there. No way!"

Pete nodded understandingly, lifted his bottle for a final sip, and carelessly threw it into a dry bush that, judging by the smell, served not only as a dump but a toilet.

"I wouldn't get in there sober either." His laugh turned into another disgusting coughing fit.

"So, what now?" Selina had become impatient. She was running out of time and wanted to get this crap over with as soon as possible.

"Let's go to the truck bed. It's clean there," Pete suggested with a voice that trembled with excitement while he nervously licked his chapped lips.

"Okay." She had climbed onto the truck bed with Pete, put down her backpack, pulled down her skirt and panties, and sat on an old tire with her legs spread.

"Go ahead!" she prompted and closed her eyes to avoid seeing his wide open mouth with the brownish tooth stumps and the greedily twitching tongue.

Pete kneeled in front of her. He gasped, stroking his callused hands over her delicate inner thighs.

Selina kept her eyes closed. She was able to block out the touches to some extent, but not the stench that emanated from Pete's pores. She leaned back and thanked God for not having any olfactory organs in her pussy.

The rest wasn't a piece of cake either. Pete slobbered over her like a mangy dog. His stinking tongue slipped over her belly, along her thighs, and thrust like an eel into her pussy …

"Oh, baby, I wish I could fuck you. You're so hot." Pete groaned, opened his pants, and pulled out his encrusted cock, which looked and smelled like a dead animal.

For a second Selina felt the impulse to ram her foot right there, but then she saw the tears running down Pete's dirty cheeks. Yes, she felt sorry for him, but she wasn't public welfare.

"If you want to shove your finger in me, you put that thing away now. Got me?" She tried to sound tough, even though she was scared shitless, not to mention the disgust and that little spark of pity.

What if he shoves that sick rotten dick inside me now?

Selina had sent another quick prayer to heaven, while Pete put only his finger in her. Her eyes had been closed, her thoughts far away. She'd endured the moaning, the licking, the pricking for her plan.

For Daddy.

***

Pete kept his promise, even though he'd probably live off it for the rest of his life and never know why such a pretty girl had made such a bad deal.

But Selina was only interested in her plan. She had what she wanted: the wine she was now taking out of the paper bags. She showered and washed Pete's putrid saliva off her skin.

No big deal.

***

After he'd said goodbye to his mother, Dan spent a few hours in the living room watching TV without being able to concentrate on a program for more than a minute. Again and again his gaze wandered to the stairs, and he remembered the officers coming down that day, one with a bundle in his arms. His little girl. He could still hear Kate's screams and the psychologist's pointless chatter.

His senses were once again flooded with a disgusting coffee aroma, although since Leila's death, no one had made any.

He couldn't take it anymore. He left the TV on and dragged himself upstairs like a centenarian to the first floor. He hesitated at the landing and looked in the direction of the cold room of his dead child. Then he forced himself to go right into the bedroom. The bed hadn't been made, and clothes were lying around everywhere. It was hard to find anything to wear that would fit the mood.

Was there any company that made clothes for people on the verge of a nervous breakdown? Or did you just slip into your jeans as if nothing happened? And how crazy did you even have to be to rack your brains over such crap?

Dan didn't know. It was too exhausting to think about it. He let himself fall on the bed. Face down. The pillow smelled vaguely of laundry soap and strongly of his own hair.

That was okay.

As long as it wasn't coffee.

Dan took a deep breath and sobbed again. Tears that shouldn't have been there came out of the corners of his eyes.

At some point he fell asleep.

When Selina came home another hour later, he didn't notice. The girl arrived far too late, and something could have happened to her in the meantime, but Dan Meller wouldn't have known. He slept the sleep of the just, which would soon lead to the reality of injustice.

He still believed this misfortune was the most terrible thing life could punish him with.

He had no idea.

Not the slightest.

***

After Selina unpacked the wine and placed it on the kitchen table, she looked around the lower floor. The TV was on, but there was no trace of her dad. There were no dirty dishes around, so she figured he hadn't eaten anything yet. That was good, because the alcohol would work all the better then.

She took off her shoes and sneaked up to the first floor. The door to the bedroom was open. Dan lay across the bed in jeans and shirt. His white socks were dirty.

When was the last time he took a shower?

Selina would take care of it in due time. Dan's quiet snoring told her he was sleeping soundly. Perfect.

She moved quietly away from the door and went straight into the bathroom. That way led past Leila's room, but it didn't cause her the slightest emotion. Instead, she pondered her options. It would be smarter not to just serve him the wine. He'd want to know where she got it and why. He was sad and traumatized, not stupid.

While standing in the shower, Selina remembered what she'd learned in civics class: once you were an alcoholic, you remained an alcoholic. As long as you didn't drink, you were dry—a dry drunk—no more, no less. The smallest dose could be enough to change this. Selina knew Dan only ate foods if he knew the exact ingredients. In restaurants, he sometimes asked about it. He didn't even take cough syrup until he knew for sure it didn't contain alcohol.

But what would happen if he drank a drop of alcohol? Would he relapse on the spot? Would he notice it? Would he be able to control it, or would he become a helpless victim of his own addiction?

Selina rubbed shower gel between her legs and decided she wanted to find out. It was the perfect solution. Her poor, sad daddy hadn't eaten all day. As a good daughter, it was her duty to take care of him. And he loved her spaghetti with tomato sauce.

Freshly showered and dressed (she was now wearing a baggy T-shirt and leggings), her hair still wet, Selina took another look into the bedroom. Dan hadn't moved.

Smiling, she hurried downstairs. She left the TV on while she prepared everything in the kitchen. She found tomatoes in the pantry, and she sautéed chopped onions and a little garlic—and like the chefs on TV, she added a large shot of red wine. Was that enough? She added more, about the amount of a full glass.

It smelled delicious. Selina closed her eyes and sniffed. Except for the wine, she prepared the sauce exactly as she'd been making it for years, generously seasoned with Italian herbs and freshly ground pepper.

She hid the bottles in the cupboard.

Would he smell the wine?

She had to take the risk.

Selina poured off the noodles and set the table. She used the good Sunday dishware. There was orange juice to drink. Maybe (surely) he had no appetite, but would he be able to refuse to eat if his princess had cooked it especially for him and put so much effort into it? If necessary, she'd cry. After years of practice, she could do that at the push of a button.

When everything was ready, she put the pasta on two plates and added the sauce. Not much for her, a lot for Dad. His pasta was drowning in red sauce. He liked it that way.

Finally, she turned off the TV and turned on the radio. The local rock station played good songs at this time of day. Dan loved rock. Selina was more into hip-hop, but that's not what it was about now.

She ran her fingers through her wet hair and tried to ignore her wildly throbbing heart, and then she hurried upstairs to wake up her father.

***

Dan struggled hard to get out of the dense fog of sleep because someone was shaking his shoulder. He moaned and tried to push away the hands, which just wouldn't leave him alone. He didn't want to wake up.

Waking up meant thinking.

And thinking meant feeling.

And feeling meant pain.

He absolutely wanted to avoid it. He'd already overdosed.

Unfortunately, the hands wouldn't stop. Then there was a voice that he knew so well and loved so much that in the end, he forced himself to shake off his sleep and rub his eyes.

"Selina … how long did I sleep?"

Selina stood above him, smiling. She took his hand and stroked it. "Don't worry about it, Daddy. Do you feel better?"

Dan pulled his hand away and rubbed his face. His eyes were swollen, and a scratchy, three-day beard grew on his cheeks. He laboriously sat up. Selina stood before him in a sloppy outfit and with scented wet hair. She was so pretty, so loving. He was infinitely sorry that he couldn't be there for her.

"You gotta hurry," she said. "Otherwise, the food will get cold."

Food? Dan could have puked at the thought of it, although he was actually terribly hungry. Only the appetite was missing.

But his girl had cooked for him after he'd left her alone all day. He couldn't possibly say no.

"You cooked?"

"Yeah, right after I was done with my homework. I wanted to let you sleep, but now you have to get up because everything is ready downstairs."

The scent of sautéed onions permeated the air. Much better than that goddamn coffee stench.

"Okay, sweetie, give me a minute. I'm just going to the bathroom."

Selina nodded but looked disappointed. "Will you really come downstairs then, Daddy?"

He stood up, bent over to her, and kissed her on the forehead. "I promise, Princess. I'll be right there."

A pleasant tingling sensation shot through Selina from her forehead to her toes. "Okay. I'll wait downstairs."

***

Selina was sitting at the table when Dan entered the kitchen. In the background, quiet rock music was playing Don Henley's "Boys of Summer." Dan liked the song. He also liked spaghetti piled high with tomato sauce.

He just couldn't get that coffee stench out of his nose!

The aroma of the sauce got lost in it again and again. His stomach cramped, yet he took a seat. He forced a smile and sipped juice. His throat craved the cool refreshment, but his stomach didn't like it and clenched like an angry fist.

"That's so sweet of you, Princess. I just don't know if I can eat anything."

"But you have to eat, Daddy. I know how bad all this is, but if you don't eat, you'll get sick, and then …"

The tears came.

Dan reached over the table for his daughter's hand and tightly enclosed it.

"It's all right, Selina. Please don't cry. I can't stand it. I'll eat, okay?"

He grabbed his fork, wrapped pasta around it, and stuffed it in his mouth. He chewed for a while, then swallowed and smiled. "Wow, that's delicious! You're a real cooking talent."

"Thanks, Daddy."

He let go of her hand and went on eating. With the food came the appetite.

Selina tasted her food. She had to force herself as much as he did. But she also had to eat something. That was important for both of them. And it was good to sit here with him at the table.

Dan kept eating. Now it was easier. He chewed automatically, and the pasta slid down his gullet without any resistance. The more he shoved into his mouth, the greedier he became and the bigger the chunks he swallowed. The sauce tasted fantastic—somehow extra special—and it made his taste buds explode.

Soon he concentrated completely on his plate. He shoved the food into his mouth, chewed a little, and swallowed. In between he reached for his glass again and again. Soon the juice was gone. He didn't notice that his daughter was watching him. Her plate was still full.

When all the pasta had disappeared into his mouth, Dan grabbed the spoon and scratched the sauce from the plate to the last remnants. It was far too delicious to waste any of it.

He looked up for the first time. His mouth was smeared a toddler's. "That was great."

Selina nodded. "I'm glad to hear that."

He licked his lips and thoughtfully looked at the empty plate and wondered if he should lick the last remnants of the tomato sauce.

"If I didn't know any better, I'd almost think there was wine in the sauce." He smiled pensively and then shook his head. "But it can't be. We don't have any alcohol in the house."

"Hm," Selina hummed. "Would it be bad?"

Dan looked at her in confusion. What about her plate? She'd hardly eaten anything.

"What did you put in the sauce, Selina?" he asked sharply. He should have stopped eating as soon as he noticed this special taste, but he'd simply continued. He knew he had to avoid consuming alcohol.

Not a single damn drop!

Did she do it on purpose?

No, impossible!

Why should she?

***

Selina was innocently picking at her food. The smartest thing now was to act naive. Dad had to believe she hadn't done that on purpose. She was his daughter, after all, and would never want to harm him. She was in shock and unable to cope with the situation.

Who would blame her?

She'd lost her little sister and had to watch her father's life falling to pieces. It was impossible to keep a clear brain under these circumstances.

Wasn't it?

After all, he had no idea how long and closely she'd studied his behavior.

Normal daughters didn't do that.

Normal daughters wouldn't even think about a few sips of wine in tomato sauce turning their father back into the drunkard he'd been so long ago.

That's why it was so important for her to act stupid and ignorant. She seemed desperate and confused—just like him.

Dan's eyes widened. "Selina, what was in that sauce?"

He rubbed his hand nervously over his mouth, as if he could eliminate what he'd just eaten.

Selina's feigned insecurity reached Hollywood-level acting. "There were two bottles in the cupboard. I thought the sauce would taste even better if … I saw that in this cooking show. Wine gives such a special aroma—"

Dan jumped up. "Where? In which cupboard?"

"In the pantry. Two bottles. Maybe Kate put them in there …"

Dan rushed to the cupboard and opened the door. He paused for a moment and then reached in and grabbed the opened bottle. He stared at it as if it was the most amazing and unbelievable thing a person had ever found in a kitchen.

He turned to Selina again. "And they were just here in the cupboard?"

His hand trembled, and Selina prayed he wouldn't drop the bottle. She'd take care of that.

"We never have alcohol in the house!" His voice broke and he started to cry.

Selina was silent.

This situation would play out the way she wanted without any interference on her part. It wasn't important for Dad that she answered. Where these bottles came from and why she'd used the wine was irrelevant. This wasn't about her and any explanations. It was all about him and that bottle.

The fight had begun.

And he was weak.

Selina didn't believe he could defend himself against it. "I don't know why Kate did that. What was she thinking?"

Dan leaned his back against the wall next to the open cupboard and slowly slid down until he sat on the floor, his legs stretched out.

The bottle was in his hand.

Selina sat at the kitchen table in front of the plate with the cold pasta and watched her father.

"I can't drink, you know? I have no idea why someone would bring wine into the house."

Selina kept silent and waited.

She could be very patient.

Weeping, Dan pulled the cork from the bottle. She'd put it back in after cooking.

He looked at Selina and then at the bottle. His broken gaze even touched her cold heart, but she had to be hard. It was for his own best interest.

"I'll drink this now, Princess. Although I know it's wrong. Forgive me."

He closed his eyes and raised the bottle to his mouth. Selina watched silently the movements of his Adam's apple as he greedily swallowed the wine. The radio played "Losing My Religion" by REM.

Selina found this title more than fitting.

When Dad finished drinking, she sat beside him on the kitchen floor. His eyes were dry, his lips red from the wine. Selina reached for his hand and held it in her lap as she leaned her head against his arm.

He smelled of alcohol.

A smell she'd get used to.

"I'm sorry," Dan whispered.

Selina straightened up a little and pressed her mouth against his lips. She kissed him without tongue, but with a fervor that wasn't very daughterly.

Did he notice?

He let it happen. Selina pressed her head against his chest and put her arms around his waist. His breathing was deep and heavy and smelled of wine. Selina lifted her head and kissed him again. With the tip of her tongue she tickled the gap between his lips. He gave way and opened his mouth a bit. He flinched briefly and stiffened when her tongue penetrated his mouth, but in the end he gave in.

For the first time.

He gave in.

Simple as that.

It was much easier than she'd expected.

Selina's kisses were demanding.

She knew she had to savor the moment.

Her hand slipped into his crotch.

Dan flinched again, but the kiss continued.

He didn't resist.

Not against the wine and not against Selina.

His tongue had now found hers. Heat exploded in her guts and spread to her abdomen. Her dad tasted of wine and salt; his tongue was firm and gentle. She pushed herself even closer and massaged his penis through his pants.

It got hard.

It was like in her dreams. Only better!

But then he suddenly pushed her away. Selina screamed in surprise and landed on her butt.

"Shit, no!" Dan pressed his hand to his mouth as if he'd tasted something disgusting. He kept shaking his head and didn't look at his daughter.

"I'm so sorry, Selina! I don't know what's going on! I'm sorry! I'm sorry!"

He punched his forehead with his fist. Again and again. Selina still saw a slight erection between his legs.

"Nothing happened, Daddy. We have to stick together now, and that's okay."

Dan didn't stop hitting his forehead.

Selina approached him on all fours. She wanted to hug him, but he pushed her away.

"I'm not allowed to do this!"

"You need to calm down, Daddy."

She stood up and took the second bottle of wine out of the cupboard. Dan didn't see what she was doing, as he was still punching his fist against his head.

Selina opened the bottle above the sink. Then she went to her father and pressed the bottle into his hand.

Now Dan paused.

He looked at her without understanding.

Selina helped him raise the bottle to his lips.

"What are you doing?" He sobbed.

"Let me help you. You need to calm down. It's okay if you're weak now. Just let it happen, Daddy. I'm here."

***

Dan wanted to protest again, but then the neck of the bottle already touched his mouth, and it was as if every pore of his body opened to take in this delicious liquid. Everything felt warm and pleasant. Leila's face was gone, just like the coffee haze. Now everything smelled and tasted like wine and Selina. Wasn't that much better than before? At least that's how it felt.

What did Selina say? *Just let it happen …*

Didn't that sound good?

She wasn't angry with him, that was the main thing. And it wasn't bad when a father kissed his daughter. There was nothing to it. His princess had said it was okay. She didn't mind. She only wanted to be there for him. And she was everything he still had. He only had to allow it, and she'd forgive him.

His princess would forgive him everything.

Dan closed his eyes and opened his mouth. He drank, and Selina helped him by holding the bottle.

And then there was this exquisite flavor, the pleasant warmth, and the bittersweet music in the background. Music from his youth …

He drank and let himself fall into the almost-forgotten lightness of alcohol. How beautiful it was to feel no suffering, no pain, only the warmth of the wine and his princess.

Selina snuggled up to his less tense body.

She kissed him.

Caressed his senses.

This time Dan willingly opened his mouth.

He felt as if he was floating.

No questions were pounding in his head.

No fear.

Everything was soft.

Soft and sweet.

Like the wine and Selina.

She'd said it was all right.

Why shouldn't he believe her?

This kiss was long and passionate. Dan's hands found their way under Selina's T-shirt. She wasn't wearing a bra, and her breasts were tender and warm. Dan was gentle with them. Amazing how quickly his little girl had turned into this sexy woman. Her breasts were even bigger than Kate's. And they felt much firmer ...

While he emptied the wine, Selina undressed. Her skin was soft and tanned and smelled of vanilla. The little blonde hairs on her arms shined like gold. Dan wanted to stroke them. She helped him find the way between her legs. Her pubic hair was incredibly soft and nothing more than a narrow strip in the middle of her sweet crevice.

Not a little girl anymore, but a woman.

How could he have ignored that for so long?

His princess had grown up and had the body of a goddess.

Every man would have gone weak at that sight, wouldn't he?

So what could be wrong about it?

She was no longer a child. At age eighteen, she knew exactly what she was doing. And perhaps she wasn't even his biological daughter ...

Dan had never allowed himself to think about it, because he simply didn't want to let it happen. Selina was his little girl. He'd taken care of her because it was his job, and he loved her more than anything.

But had she really been fathered by him or by one of the many others who had visited Clara in the trailer at the time?

Wouldn't that explain everything?

All those not very fatherly feelings that had attacked him years before when she lay next to him at night?

Hungry for love!

Didn't that explain everything?

"Take me upstairs, Daddy," she whispered. "It's okay."

Maybe he hesitated for one last second, maybe not.

Maybe the alcohol had made sure there won't be any more hesitation that night.

Was that important?

After all, everything could be explained. Maybe she wasn't his daughter, and she was an adult anyway.

She knew what she was doing.

It was okay.

That's what she'd said.

Okay …

Dan Meller carried his naked princess into the bedroom.

***

After he lay her on the bed, he paused. But Selina was faster than any qualms. She sat up and grabbed his belt. With trained fingers she opened his pants and then grasped deep enough to blow away all doubts.

Dan frantically got rid of his pants and all other clothes. Then he climbed into the bed with her.

At last they were skin to skin and could melt into each other, as Selina had always wished. She took the lead.

Just as he liked it.

So he could accept it without a guilty conscience. A conscience that had dissolved in the wine.

As soon as Dan lay on his back and closed his eyes, she took his erect penis in her mouth, licked it, and sucked it as she'd done to other men dozens of times before.

Her father's moaning was like music to her ears. Impressive how his already-enormous erection continued growing in her mouth. A first drop of lust came out, and it didn't taste as bitter and salty as she was used to, but much sweeter and a little spicy. Selina forced herself to stop when Dan already reared up under her. She slid up and rubbed her wet vagina against his throbbing cock.

They looked each other in the eye.

Dan's lips twitched, but he remained silent.

It was better that way.

Selina put a hand over his mouth so he wouldn't change his mind. With the other hand she took his penis inside her. Her movements were timid and slow and became faster and more demanding. Dan grabbed her breasts, just as he'd done with Kate, while Selina had watched secretly and the jealousy had boiled inside her. Now other feelings were bubbling inside her. She screamed out her lust and rode like a cowgirl on her father's dick.

Finally!

He moaned and breathed hot air into her palm.

He reached his climax, only his screams of pleasure soon turned into sobs.

Selina took her hand away and kissed him. She bit his lower lip to make him open his mouth.

She kissed him passionately, smothering his sobbing until he slept like a baby. Satisfied, she cuddled up in the crook of his arm, enjoying his closeness while his semen seeped out of her. A part of him, as precious as it was fleeting. Now she was imbued with his smell, his taste, and his fluids.

Finally, they were one.

Close to her quietly snoring father, Selina fell asleep that night with a smile, while the radio in the kitchen tirelessly played songs from a time when Dan hadn't even guessed what a terrible turn his life would take.

THE AWAKENING

For the first time since Leila's death, Dan's first thought when he woke wasn't of his little dead daughter. Instead, he noticed something he probably hadn't felt since more than a decade ago: his mouth tasted like shit, and his head was about to burst. Groaning, he turned from his side to his back. Grayish-blue sunlight filtered through the tilted bedroom window. Rain dripped from the eaves.

So the weather had changed.

That matched the situation!

Dan put a hand in front of his eyes because even that little bit of light hurt. He carefully blinked through his fingers into the room. The walls were somehow wobbly and bent in all directions. He moaned again.

He'd been drinking.

How could that have happened?

He slowly turned his head, and the pain drilled into his brain like fine pinpricks. The other side of the bed was empty, but it looked used, which was no surprise, as Selina had mostly slept here since Leila's death. What was unusual, however, was the sperm stains on the sheet.

He threw back the blanket.

He was naked.

No normal father would lie like that with his daughter.

Most fathers don't fuck their daughters either!

The memory hit him like a sledgehammer. "Oh no!"

Dan shot up.

His skull seemed to explode.

The world spun like a merry-go-round, and his stomach cramped painfully. Puke rose in his throat.

Dan jumped out of bed and rushed into the bathroom. He had barely bent over the toilet bowl when the first hot surge of vomit shot out of him.

He sank to his knees and put his head on the toilet seat.

What had he done?

The next gush shot out of him, and he puked his guts out.

The world was spinning, and the coffee haze gradually returned.

The smell was starting again—only worse!

He'd done the unspeakable.

He'd abused his own child.

Dear God, could that be true?

That was so horrible.

He was so miserable!

At some point, he disgorged the bitterest bile. His stomach and throat hurt like hell. Dan considered banging his head on the toilet seat until his skull burst. But even for that he lacked the strength—and courage.

Suddenly he noticed movement behind him.

Selina?

Dan couldn't lift his head. There was a rushing in his ears, and water splashed in his face: Someone had flushed.

"S-Selina?"

It couldn't be anybody else. Dan didn't want her to see him like that: naked and in his own filth. What would he tell her? He'd abused her and destroyed her life.

She'd never forgive him for that.

His princess.

"I'm so sorry," he whined without looking at her.

Selina lay her hand on his hot neck. It felt pleasantly cool. "You don't have to be sorry, Daddy. I'm fine."

"Are you sure?" Dan whimpered.

"Absolutely sure. It was very nice with you."

What? What did she say?

Dan wanted to turn to her, wanted to look her in the eye, because he had to know if she was serious. She couldn't know what she was talking about!

But before he could stand, his stomach reared up again and he was shaken by another round of vomiting. Nothing came out but bile and slimy saliva.

He felt empty.

His guts had landed in the bowl.

Selina stood there as if nothing had happened, wearing clean jeans and a pink T-shirt, her hair tied in a ponytail. No girl who had been raped looked like that!

I didn't rape her! I'd never do that!

"I have to go to school now," Selina explained with a smile. "We'll talk this afternoon. You have nothing to worry about." Her smile grew wider. "I'm very happy now."

"You're what?" Dan stared at her in complete bewilderment. From his lower lip hung a thick thread of saliva, which Selina wiped away with her hand without hesitation.

"You don't have to say anything now, Daddy. I know you have to come to terms with that. Just get some rest."

Her facial expression seemed cool and insincere. Her eyes wandered over Dan's body as if she checking him over. "Go take a shower and then lie down again."

"What's all this about, Selina?"

"You love me, Daddy, don't you?" She pushed her lower lip forward and immediately looked like the worried daughter she'd been until yesterday evening.

"Was that on purpose ... the wine?" Dan couldn't believe what was coming out of his mouth. That wasn't possible! Where would she have gotten the wine from anyway? She wasn't twenty-one yet!

"Does it matter?"

"It does for me!"

"Then you can rack your brain about it if you have nothing better to do. I have to go." She blew him a kiss.

Horror crawled slowly but steadily through his entrails. Was it possible that his own daughter had gotten him drunk—and then seduced him? That only happened in bad porn! That couldn't be reality.

Nobody would believe him.

He didn't believe it himself.

She was his girl, his princess!

He loved her more than his life.

He would have done anything for her.

When Selina left, he crawled away from the toilet on all fours and curled up on the cold floor in a corner of the bathroom, his arms wrapped around his knees. He was freezing and had never felt so miserable, not even during the times living in the trailer park.

But he didn't want to change this condition so quickly, because it seemed to him an appropriate punishment for what he'd done to this girl. Seduced or not, he was her father.

His own flesh and blood!

Or not ...

She didn't even know that he'd always had doubts about fatherhood. So that wasn't an excuse for him fucking her like she was an obscure bitch. What he'd done to her was absolutely horrible and detestable. He should atone for it by lying on this hard cold floor until he froze to fucking death!

***

At some point Dan got up because he had to pee so badly that he couldn't take it any longer. He dragged himself to the toilet and took his hated dick in his hand. He would have loved to cut off the damn thing to flush it, together with his fucking soul.

He dug his fingernails into the miserable piece of flesh until the pain drove tears to his eyes. Bleeding and howling, he let go and went into the shower. Scorching hot water rained down on his skin. He rubbed his sore penis with shower gel until it burned like fire.

Red as a beet and half out of his mind from pain, he dried himself and took care to treat his penis as brutally as possible.

He refused to look in the mirror.

After getting dressed, he cleaned the toilet and the floor. Then he stripped the bed and stuffed everything into the washing machine. His penis was a hot throbbing lump in his underpants. But somehow that wasn't enough for Dan. In the kitchen (which was quite tidy because Selina had apparently cleaned up before school) he found a can of chili powder. With clenched teeth he poured half of it into his underpants and rubbed it on his sore cock.

Well done.

He wouldn't stick that thing anywhere soon.

Dan concentrated on the furiously burning pain between his legs. How he would have liked to undress and hold his dick under cold water, but he wouldn't do it.

Never!

He would endure this because he deserved it.

Every second of it.

At least he barely felt the rest of his scalded body now. Dan was terribly thirsty but refused to drink because he didn't want to allow himself any refreshment after everything he'd done. Again and again fragments of that night appeared in his brain, and he saw himself kneading his daughter's breasts, his cock disappearing in her mouth and then—loudly groaning—penetrating her hot, deep tightness, which had felt so incredibly good (dear God, please forgive me!).

At that moment he'd felt security and unbelievable gratitude because she was with him and stood by him.

How could he ever deal with her normally again?

Last night she hadn't been a girl or a daughter. Her feminine curves had made it easy for him to forget.

Maybe it'd be better not to have her around for a while. I could send her to my mother in Tennessee for a while. That could be good for both of us. We're all in shock.

That was an option, but what about school? Selina had just settled in. It would be a difficult break.

But for her own good. Right?

It's only about this one school year anyway. Then she'll go to college and all the problems will solve themselves. She's an adult and no longer needs to be treated like a child.

Last night he'd also managed very well not to treat her like a child …

It was his fault.

Not Selina's.

Why should he punish her?

No, he couldn't send Selina away now!

Nora would be happy to have her granddaughter back with her, but what would become of their father-daughter relationship?

Fuck the father-daughter relationship! It's better for both of us not to see each other for a while. It's better not to have a relationship than one in which an old man fucks his own child. That is so disgusting!

Dan still couldn't believe what he'd done. Even if she wasn't his daughter, Selina had grown up believing she was.

Until now …

Yeah, until now.

Dan rubbed his red face with both hands and kept thinking. He even forgot the pain in his penis.

The phone rang.

He flinched as if he'd been beaten.

Let it ring or answer it?

He currently felt unable to talk on the phone. Especially not with his mother or his wife!

What was he supposed to say? *Sorry if I sound a little strange, but I scratched my dick and rubbed it with chili so I won't get a boner anymore because of my daughter whom I fucked last night to stop thinking about my other dead child. It's all a bit complicated at the moment, I hope you understand.*

Good God! He better kept his mouth shut and just let the phone ring.

It took half an eternity until it finally stopped. Dan knew he couldn't ignore the calls forever. Nora would rightly worry and not rest if she couldn't reach him. Sooner or later, his mother would surely be standing at the door.

But first she'd call Kate's parents and ask them if they'd heard from him. Kate, who didn't want to know anything about him anyway, would of course say no. All in all it would kick up a fuss, which he didn't need at all. So the next time the phone rang he'd answer, whether he wanted to or not.

Dan decided to go to bed again until then. The hangover stuck deep in his bones. He didn't deserve to feel better, but he didn't know what else to do. Moreover, a bursting skull wasn't necessarily helpful in thinking.

So he dragged himself upstairs o the bedroom and lay on the stripped bed. At least it didn't smell of Selina and last night's juices anymore. While Dan believed he'd never be able to fall asleep, he sank into a dreamless sleep. Neither the chili in his pants nor the horror in his mind could keep him awake.

***

It wasn't easy to concentrate on classes with all the crazy pictures in her head. Selina still couldn't believe it. She'd actually managed to put all her hopes and fantasies of the past years into action in just one night.

They had slept together!

It was reality and finally no longer a dream. This morning she gave herself a quick "cat lick" to keep his smell and the sticky consistency of his sperm on her pussy as long as possible. Now she was sitting here in history class with that inimitable tingling sensation in her abdomen, and the memories of last night drove the heat into her face.

She loved him so much!

She could never have felt the same for another man. Dan was her father, whom she loved more than her life. The absolute highlight was to unite with him and feel him in her innermost being. The coronation of a love that was as intense as it was forbidden.

What did he think about it?

Daddy didn't look good this morning, but it was probably just the alcohol. Would this one time be enough to make him a drinker again? Maybe he'd long since gone out to get supplies? Selina had thought about visiting Pete again, but she had enough of the disgusting guy with his sick cock. If she were forced to continue providing Dan with alcohol, she'd have to think of something else. But the best thing would be to make Dan take care of it himself. Selina wasn't able to judge whether two bottles of wine would be sufficient for such a change.

Perhaps he was already hooked on the bottle again, which would make it easier to deal with him. But maybe he just sat like a lump in a pile of misery in some corner and regretted things that were not to be regretted. Whatever he did, Selina had to be prepared for everything when she got home. He certainly wasn't about to welcome her with open arms, however much she wished. She'd already achieved a lot, but he wasn't fully ready yet.

It was important to repeat it as soon as possible so he'd learn that there was no point in resisting. He needed to realize he needed it as much as she did.

Suddenly Mr. Willis, the history teacher, wanted to know something about the Trojan horse. Selina stammered an answer that turned out to be wrong. Mr. Willis looked at her pitifully. Of course, he knew about Leila. Her classmates gave her similar glances. Understanding and compassion. They had no idea. Otherwise, only horror and disgust would show on their stupid faces.

Selina grinned inside herself.

No, they had no idea.

Leila had died by her hand. Silently and completely unspectacularly. Death by soft covering, the experts called it. Selina had Googled diligently. That's why she knew that this type of death was usually not to be distinguished from SIDS—as long as you didn't make the mistake of putting any kind of pressure on the child's head. A little patience was required.

Selina was good at that.

She'd just stood there and waited ten minutes before taking the pillow off her sister's face. It was her own pillow, which she hadn't even cleaned since.

Why should she?

No one would come up with the idea of searching her room for Leila's DNA. There was no reason because they were all convinced the little girl had lost the desire to breathe all by herself.

Such things happened.

Nobody understood it, but you had to accept it.

Just like Selina's love for her daddy.

It couldn't have been any better for her.

Leila was dead.

Kate was gone.

And …

The shrill sound of the school gong ended her ponderings. As if in a trance, Selina gathered her things while her classmates hurried to the door. The babble of voices and giggling grew louder. Selina didn't pay attention. With stoic calm she pushed folders and notebooks into her backpack until everyone else had left the classroom. No one was waiting for her. They probably didn't know how to deal with her eerie silence.

Selina looked up.

Now only Mr. Willis was still here. A young, tall man with dark hair and black framed glasses. He actually didn't look so bad. Selina imagined taking his glasses off his face and messing up his accurately combed hair before kissing him and—

"Selina?"

She was about to leave. Her bus left in twenty minutes.

"Do you have a moment?"

Mr. Willis came up to her. He stopped so close that Selina could smell his aftershave. Not so bad at all. Did he have a girlfriend? He definitely wasn't married. No ring. In his white shirt and dark jeans he looked sexy. Again, Selina imagined taking off his glasses while massaging his cock. He wouldn't be the first to fuck his mind out of his head with her.

He laboriously cleared his throat and looked at her in a way Selina didn't know to read.

"I know it's not easy for you at the moment," he finally said.

Selina remained silent and waited while her eyes wandered to his crotch. What she saw was quite promising.

"I just wanted to tell you that you can come to me anytime you need someone to talk to. You know, I'm also a guidance counselor."

No, she'd forgotten that, but it suited her pretty well.

Selina nodded and smiled coquettishly. "Thanks, Mr. Willis. That's very kind of you."

"You know where my office is?"

She nodded again and was suddenly all too aware of the sticky milieu in her panties. What would dear Mr. Willis say if she told him that her own father's dried juice was sticking to her pussy?

Perhaps he'd even like it. Who knows?

"You can find me there every day after school," he explained.

"That's very nice." She stroked some strands of hair from her forehead and smiled. Could he read the signal?

Hard to say.

Mr. Willis returned the smile but seemed reserved, like a schoolmaster should. Too bad, but well, you couldn't have everything, even if it would have been a nice game for in between.

She'd better go home and take care of Dad. Once she finally had him where she wanted him, she could look for

90

other "game partners." After all, you didn't have to over-do it right away. Uncontrolled carelessness had already become the fate of many.

"I'll go home now. Goodbye, Mr. Willis." She turned away and hurried out of the room without looking back.

"Bye, Selina. See you tomorrow!"

***

When Dan woke up, she was sitting by his bed. Silent and motionless. He flinched and straightened up faster than was good for him—his head didn't like it, and his stomach immediately started to protest. Only the burning in his pants had subsided. Maybe the chili slowly lost its hotness or his cock had developed a resistance, just like the taste buds did when you often ate hot food.

Instinctively, he moved away from his daughter, as if she were toxic or dangerous, which actually was the case.

"Are you feeling better, Daddy?" she asked before he could say a word.

His throat was like sandpaper, and he cleared it thoroughly before he could speak. "About last night ... that should never have happened, Selina. I'm so sorry."

"But it was nice," she replied and then drew her famous pout.

"It was wrong!" Dan yelled and immediately regretted getting so loud.

Selina flinched when he jumped out of bed.

"It's terrible! I never should've let that happen. You apparently don't know what you're talking about."

"Am I so awful?" Selina asked. She seemed offended, as if he'd insulted her. "I thought you loved me."

Dan closed his eyes and tried to keep his composure. He didn't want to hurt her. He wanted to protect her.

91

"Yes, that's what it is! I love you! And it's a shame what I did to you!"

Selina tilted her head, as she'd done very often as a child.

"I've been thinking about it all day, and now … I'm sure it's best for both of us if …"

Selina narrowed her eyes. "What?" She suddenly seemed so grown up.

His princess.

Dan hardly had the heart to tell her what he'd thought about. But it was for the best. "You'll be staying with Grandma for a while," he said without looking at her. "Until we're all back to our senses."

Selina walked toward him. "I certainly won't, Dad."

"It's… it's for your own sake, Selina, believe me. I won't discuss it with you. I'm your father, and you'll do what I tell you!"

Selina shook her head. A strange smile played on her lips. "I think it's going to be the other way around from now on, Daddy. You certainly won't send me away."

"Oh, yes! My decision has been made! Tonight I'm going to talk to Grandma on the phone."

"Look what my daddy did to me," Selina suddenly screamed. Her voice sounded shrill and extremely theatrical.

Dan could only stare in astonishment.

Selina took off her pants at lightning speed. Then she waved her girlish panties and showed him the inside where his sperm was still stuck.

Dan froze.

The burning in his penis was there again.

"He shoved it very deep inside me! And that hurt so badly! Look here!" Selina spread her legs so Dan could see the bruises on the insides of her thighs.

92

Had that really been him?

Good God!

His mouth opened, but nothing came out.

"He's said he knows his daughter has sex with other men—and that it was time to enjoy it himself. I wanted to run away, but he held me down and tore my clothes off. He hurt me. It was like he was out of his mind. He has—"

"Stop it!" He found his voice again, but it didn't sound resolute enough by far. Bewildered, Dan stared at his princess, whom he hardly recognized.

"He pressed me to the ground and lay on top of me. I fought back, but he was stronger. And again and again he said it would be fun for me. I shouldn't act like I'm still a virgin. After all, it wouldn't be my first time. In fact, he's been fucking me since I was twelve. He always wanted me to sleep in his bed. Every weekend! It was so terrible …"

"Selina, please stop! Please!" Suddenly all his strength left him, and he sank helplessly to his knees.

Selina held her panties right in front of his face. The penetrating smell of his fluids crept into his nose and suppressed the coffee haze.

"That's a piece of evidence." Selina explained. "But they'll believe me anyway. Because it's exactly like you said: I'm the daughter, and you're the father. I'm not to blame. You abused me as a child. It took me a long time to find the courage to talk about it. But this last rape was one too many, and for that, you'll go to jail, Daddy. For quite a long time, if I embellish my story a bit."

"And that's what you want?" He thought of snatching her panties so he could destroy them later, but she was right. They would believe her anyway.

He watched with tear-soaked eyes as she dressed again. He couldn't believe this was Selina, his little girl, his princess.

What had happened?

It couldn't be true!

But even if he no longer understood the world and didn't know much at the moment, he knew he didn't want to go back to prison. Especially not as a rapist of his own daughter!

They would tear him to pieces!

After all, he'd been there long enough to witness how those guys dealt with rapists in general and pedophiles in particular. A little ass fuck was the nicest thing that awaited him.

When Selina wore her pants again, she came to him and stroked his head. "Of course I don't want that, Daddy. I want us to be together. Forever. But if you give me no other choice, then …"

He pushed her hand away. "So you're blackmailing me?"

Selina put her hand back on his head. "I wouldn't call it that. I love you. Maybe a little more and a little different than a normal daughter. But you liked it too, didn't you?"

Dan shook his head, but more desperate than fierce. No question: she'd won! There was nothing he could do. Or …?

"So I'm gonna stay here with you, right?" Her fingers dug into his hair until it hurt.

Dan nodded while tears ran down his cheeks. He couldn't and didn't want to understand what was happening here.

It was only Selina!

His beloved daughter, whom he always wanted to protect! How could she suddenly turn into this cold, calculating bitch? It was as if he'd never really known her. Pictures from the past came to his mind. Pictures of a funny little girl who perhaps wanted to cuddle up with her dad too much.

Had he ever intended anything?

Selina in his arms and on his lap.

Selina, who snuggled up to his chest and fell asleep in his arms.

Selina with the beguiling look and the irresistible smile.

A little Lolita.

Hadn't he enjoyed her long legs on his body? Her knee in his crotch? He should never have let all that happen! Instead, he'd felt lonely and alone when she started to go out and sleep in her own or even in a strange bed. He'd missed the little wet kisses with the tip of the tongue and her hands on his belly, sometimes a bit too far down, but never far enough.

Or …?

Nobody knew if he was Selina's biological father. The only sure thing was that he'd taken on this role from the very beginning and that it would be damn pathetic to get out of the affair with the help of this flimsy excuse. It was still an abuse of a ward—no matter whose sperm had conceived her. None of this changed the facts.

He'd believed that everything would be all right when Kate stepped into his life. Selina seemed to accept her. She also led her own life. She was a young woman with friends and sexual partners; she went out and had fun.

Or had she tricked them?

The fact was that all this would never have happened if Leila hadn't died.

Leila.

Was it still a coincidence now? "Did you do something to Leila?" he yelled that unbelievable thought.

Selina kneeled down to him, put two fingers under his chin and smiled. "No, Daddy, of course not. I just want to be with you, that's all. I love you so much." She bent over and kissed him.

Dan stiffened and pressed his lips defiantly together.

Selina paused and looked at him in disappointment. "I just want to be with you, Daddy. And I want your love. If I get your love, you'll never have to go to prison. But if you let me down"—she shrugged—"I can't promise anything."

This time he returned her kiss as the thought rolled over in his head.

Was it really that easy?

Did she really have him in her hand?

Was there any chance to trick her? He couldn't possibly let himself be made a slave by his own daughter! And the most important question of all: What had she done with Leila?

No, no, no! screamed a panicked voice in Dan's head. *That can't be true! She would never have done that!*

He still thought so while Selina was fumbling with his pants and kissing him with a passion that felt so wrong and yet so good.

***

When she discovered the chili in his pants and saw how badly it had hurt his penis, she gave him a loving look. "You don't have to hate yourself," she said gently. "I'll wait for you while you take a shower."

"Please don't make me do this, Selina."

"I just want you to wash this crap off and put on something clean," Selina said without any emotion.

Finally, Dan gave in. What should he have done?

He took fresh clothes and left. After taking a shower, he reluctantly and helplessly went back to the bedroom.

In the meantime, Selina had made her bed. Now she lay there, naked, with spread legs, playing with a strand of her long hair. In this position, her breasts were as flat as a child's.

When she saw her father, she reached out to him. "Just come here. Don't be shy. You kiss better than anyone else."

This time she didn't want him to undress. She felt sorry for his dick and promised to wait for the wounds to heal. Instead, he should spoil her with his hands and tongue. Selina knew how well he could do that. Kate had always looked very satisfied.

She relaxed and closed her eyes as her father's head sank between her legs. She felt the wetness of his tears, but that didn't stop her from enjoying it.

KATE

She sat on the couch staring at the steaming cup of tea that her mother, Stefanie, had just placed on the small table.

Kate didn't want to drink it. She didn't want anything at all.

"It'll do you good, hon," Stephanie said.

Kate shook her head. Her mother was wrong. There would never again be anything that did her good. Her little girl was rotting in her cold grave! Again and again she thought of the little snub nose and those sweet, pudgy little fingers. She couldn't believe this no longer existed. Maybe it would have been better to cremate Leila's body. Then she wouldn't have to think about what was happening. Like ugly moss growing on the cute cherub cheeks, or black beetles cavorting in the fine hair that had always smelled so sweet.

She wondered if all this really happened.

Kate only knew that Leila's body would no longer be beautiful. Whether it was beetles, maggots, or worms eating their way through the empty eye sockets—it was only of minor importance.

Whoever had the idea of burying dead people in the ground?

In Kate's opinion, there was something deeply humiliating about it.

Ashes to ashes.

Dust to dust.

Damn shit!

In the end, there was nothing but stench and decay and a child's small lips, which first started to mold and in the end simply disappeared, as if they had never existed. Like the rest of her.

Dear God, that's not fair!

How could this happen to such a sweet, innocent child? And why didn't anyone understand that the hottest tea and the nicest words wouldn't fucking change that?

Kate ignored the cup.

Her mother sighed and looked at her with compassion. "I know how badly it hurts, Kate."

Anger rose in Kate. She couldn't stand the sweet talk for another minute. "And how do you know that, Mom? Who have you ever lost?"

Stefanie looked at her daughter sadly. "Darling, I only want to help you."

"You're not helping! My baby is dead, and you have no idea what that feels like! None of you!"

"You're right." Stefanie tried to appease her. "Nevertheless, we want to be there for you. We won't leave you alone in your pain. After all, we've also lost our grandchild. Do you think I don't love Leila?"

Now she cried, and Kate felt guilty. This was her mother, who only wanted the best for her and to share her pain. She should be glad that she at least had this consolation. But it was so hard to appreciate anything. It was so hard to lead a life when you lost your beloved one.

Kate looked out the window with an empty gaze. There wasn't much left of her former beauty. Her face was red and swollen from all the crying. Sore eyes and nose ran almost continuously. She ate just enough to fight the nausea caused by the gnawing hunger and only sipped on the beverages her mother brought her.

Most of the time, anyway.

She had to mind her health. She mustn't become too weak.

But why?

For what?

Who cared whether she was healthy?

Why did she deserve to be healthy if her little girl wasn't allowed to live?

Stefanie took the cup and handed it to her daughter. "Drink a bit, muffin. Do it for me."

Kate sighed. Then she drank. The tea was hot and sweet and actually felt good in her cold stomach.

"Thanks, Mom," she forced herself to say. "I know you only mean well."

Stefanie nodded with a sad smile. "It's okay. I understand you, my darling."

Kate took another sip and put the cup back on the coffee table. "I wonder if I should call Dan."

Stefanie's gaze darkened. "I think you have your reasons not to call him."

"I don't know, Mom. At first I thought that because I was so mad at him …"

"He should have been there for you, but he let you down."

"What if he couldn't help it? He lost his child too."

"That's true, but he's your husband, and it was his duty to stand by you."

"Oh, that's just some old-fashioned crap," Kate shouted. "Men are not always stronger than women. I could have reacted in a different way. It was a mistake to leave him alone with Selina."

"Did he try to stop you?" Stefanie asked skeptically. "Or did he contact you only once in the meantime?"

"We don't know how he's doing. What if he's not able to get in touch?"

Stefanie raised her eyebrows. This argument didn't seem to convince her.

Kate stood up. Suddenly she was determined to take matters in her own hands. It hadn't been right to be angry with Dan and to blame him. It hadn't been right to just let him down like that either. He suffered just like her, and like her, he had no strength to comfort another person. It was wrong to leave him. They should be there for each other. They were going through exactly the same thing, had both lost their beloved child and had almost gone mad with the shock and grief. It wasn't his fault just because he'd thought Leila could sleep in her own room. He'd only meant well, and Leila didn't seem to mind. She always slept through the night. Nobody knew whether she'd still be alive today if she'd stayed in her parents' bedroom.

Kate even thought that was unlikely. In the last few days, she'd read a lot about SIDS, and in the end, most theories were based on assumptions. Certain points seemed plausible, but others were nothing but speculation. The children always died quietly in their sleep, because their breathing stopped. You wouldn't notice that even if you were lying next to them. You'd have to be on guard all night, which was impossible.

Nobody could completely rely on the various monitoring devices that allegedly gave alarm as soon as there was no breathing activity for a few seconds. In most cases, there were only a series of false alarms that regularly caused parents to become very worried. But no life had yet been saved by these devices.

The sudden crib death was simply a vicious twist of fate, which mankind has faced more or less helplessly to this day—even though the number of cases had decreased noticeably since it was known that one should not smoke in the presence of children and that it was better to not pile on warm blankets. However, it was impossible to know for sure what the right thing was. It was absolutely grueling to rack your brains about it. Above all, it would be fatal to hate your own husband for this.

"I'll call him now," Kate said and went to use the phone in the kitchen.

She tried it first on the landline and then on the cell phone. Dan didn't answer. Finally, she texted him a message: *Hi, honey, trying to reach you. Please call me back.*

She noticed that he'd been online a week ago for the last time. Probably not unusual. She hadn't had a phone in her hand for ages. Then she remembered Selina. She hadn't been online for three days, which surprised Kate. After all, most teenagers had become fused to their smartphones. Selina was no exception. Kate also wrote to her, asking her to tell Dan to contact her.

For the next few hours, she checked the two chat sessions again and again, without any result. Although Selina had to be at home from school long ago, she hadn't read her message yet. Just like Dan.

"That's kind of weird," she said when her father, Bill, came into the kitchen. "I hope they're all right."

"Sure," Bill replied and patted her hand. He'd turned gray, especially during the last few days. "They probably just don't feel like checking their cell phones right now."

Kate tried again on the landline.

Without success.

"I'll call Nora," she told her parents. "It makes me nervous." She searched her cell phone for Nora's number, who fortunately didn't seem to suffer from any telephone phobia and answered immediately.

"Hi, Nora. This is Kate."

"Oh, Kate, thank God! Have you heard anything from Dan?"

Kate froze. Her parents gave her questioning looks, but she just shrugged. "I wanted to ask you the same thing," she replied. "I can't reach him or Selina."

Nora sighed. "Same here. How long have you been trying?"

"Only since today," Kate admitted hesitantly.

"I've been trying to reach them for days. I hope everything's okay there."

Kate's heart pounded in her chest. It felt as if it wanted to break through the thin skin.

"That's weird," she finally said. "But don't worry too much, Nora. I'll drive over as soon as possible and will get back to you right away."

She felt the disapproving looks of her parents. Of course they didn't want her to go to Virginia alone. But that was exactly what Kate had in mind.

And that would do her good now!

"Can you do it?" Nora wanted to know. "I'd drive myself, but I have to work the next few days, otherwise I'll lose my job."

"No problem. I'll be fine. It's about time to get out of the house anyway. I'll let you know as soon as I get there. Talk to you soon."

Stefanie's lips twitched and Bill nervously rubbed his chin. Rarely had anyone seen the strict naval officer so distraught.

Kate hadn't even put down the phone when her mother said, "You're not going to Virginia alone!"

"Mom, I have to see them. Who knows what's going on there."

"Yeah, exactly," her father commented. "Who knows what's going on there? That is exactly the problem. And anyway ... such a long journey in your condition. That's irresponsible."

"We'll come with you," Stefanie added.

"I have to do this alone," Kate said. For the first time in weeks, she had some strength in her voice. "You can come later."

"It's too dangerous! You're in an emotional state of mind. And then this long journey, and the chaos that might be waiting for you ..." Bill said. His wife nodded in agreement.

"I'm an adult, and I know what I'm doing," Kate replied. "This is my family. It's bad enough that I've ignored it for so long. They need me. And the long trip might even do me good. I have to be on my own now to clear my head. Don't you understand that?"

Apparently they didn't understand at all.

"Kate, please think about it," Stefanie begged. "I can come with you."

Kate vehemently shook her head. "I have to do this alone, Mom. Please understand me! I also need the time with Dan. That's important now. I should have done this much earlier."

"But what if—"

"Mom, I can do this. I finally have something to do again and don't just have to sit here and drown in self-pity."

"But—" Stefanie started.

Bill put a hand on Stefanie's arm and looked at her firmly. "Let her go. It's her decision. Like she said, she's an adult and has her own family. I'm worried too, but I'm glad she has the strength."

He gave his daughter a timid smile. "Promise to take care of yourself, muffin."

Kate nodded. "I definitely will, Dad. Thank you."

Later she'd remember her father's request and become desperate about her inability to keep that promise.

***

She left the next morning. She'd called Virginia several times, but every time no one answered. Maybe they were worse off than Kate imagined.

She shouldn't have just walked away. After all, Selina was almost like a daughter to her, and Dan was the man she loved and with whom she wanted to spend the rest of her life. Nothing had changed. Leila's death had caused a deep wound that would probably never heal again, but it didn't change the love she felt for Dan and Selina. She'd only been so hurt and angry about Dan's apparent indifference. In the meantime, however, it had become clear to her that he'd only behaved exactly like her: unable to make decisions and respond to other people because the shock and grief had him firmly in its icy grip.

And who could blame him?

He'd lost the sweetest baby in the world.

They all had.

That's why they had to stick together now. Because nobody could understand it better than they could. Kate only hoped it wasn't too late.

What if desperation had driven Dan to madness?

What if he pushed Selina away in his pain instead of letting her in? How would the girl deal with this double burden?

Kate forced herself not to think about it. She'd see how they were doing and then take necessary action. She gradually regained self-control and the ability to think clearly. That was the most important thing. She was able to support her family. Everything would be fine if only they were together again.

However, according to the GPS, it would still take almost seven hours to get home. Nearly 450 miles lay ahead of her, and she'd be stuck in rush hour traffic to Nashville for at least the first fifty.

She turned on the radio and tried to distract herself with music. For a while Kate let herself be washed over by it. As soon as she was on Interstate 40 eastbound to Knoxville, and Nashville gradually disappeared in the haze behind her, the traffic decreased noticeably. She reached the exit to I-81 northbound without any further obstructions in pleasantly flowing traffic.

Kate started to relax. She used to like driving. She often had the funniest ideas on the road. But now she was happy when she didn't think too often about Leila and managed not to imagine one gloomy scenario after another waiting for her at home.

It was a sunny autumn day and the music was loud and country-style. After four hours, Kate actually caught herself humming quietly to Johnny Cash. At first she was scared and didn't know what to think of it. After all, her child was dead, and it could hardly be right to face this pain with meaningless humming. On the other hand, Johnny was also dead and was still allowed to sing and spread a good mood. Kate thought about it and decided to keep humming.

Despite a guilty conscience, it felt good not to cry. Even if it was only for a few hours.

***

During the last third of the trip, Kate stopped at a rest area to eat a snack and use the toilet. She was happy to have had a little break and to be able to start the last two hours of driving refreshed. The sandwich and Diet Coke filled her surprisingly starving stomach, and for the first time since Leila's death, Kate didn't feel the need to vomit after eating.

The guilty conscience was still there.

How dare she feel hunger and satisfy it when her little daughter would never eat again? How was it possible that she drank something she liked while the thirst of her little one would never again be quenched?

On the other hand, at least she had a choice. She could live or die. It was her decision. If she chose life, she had to eat and drink. Maybe she'd at least help other people, even if she couldn't do anything for Leila anymore. And maybe then it would be okay to have positive feelings from time to time because they were part of life—just like the negative ones. Unfortunately, you couldn't choose which one you preferred. If you suddenly felt more alive than you had for a long time when biting into a cheese sandwich, you had to accept it. Guilty conscience or not. Even a starving mother couldn't bring a dead child back to life.

Before driving again, Kate looked at herself in the rearview mirror. She'd put on some makeup this morning for the first time since Leila's death. Just a thin layer of powder and some mascara. Now she looked consciously into a mirror for the first time since Leila's death. Her skin was pale and looked dried out. Dark rings were visible under the eyes. Kate decided to take more care of herself from now on. She no longer wanted to walk around like a zombie. Sighing, she started the engine.

***

By late afternoon, Kate reached the small suburb of Roanoke, the city of the star. Despite her short stopover, she'd made good time.

The driveway to the house seemed quiet. In contrast to the busy city on this sunny afternoon, everything seemed silent and rigid here. Kate felt pressure on her chest as she got out of the car. The windows seemed to stare at her. The garage door was closed. Kate parked on the street.

She wondered if anybody was home.

Kate climbed the front steps as she rummaged in her pocket for the key. She'd grab her luggage from the car later. She wanted to make sure someone was home.

There was an overgrowth of weeds on the steps and in front of the door. She would have swept it away long ago. The sun was on her back as she unlocked the door. She left the gleaming light of a golden October afternoon and entered the cool darkness of the hallway, which had never felt less homey.

She noticed the mess: shoes and jackets lay all over the floor, Selina's open backpack in between, which had spat out notebooks and pens. Kate pushed the things aside with her foot. Her heart stopped a beat when she saw Leila's tiny white jacket, still hanging near the closet along with a few other garments.

Couldn't Dan have put it away?

Kate realized the house was full of things that had to be cleared away. She didn't even want to think about Leila's room. When was the right time to do something like that? Dan should have started long ago.

The playpen sat in the living room. Kate forced herself not to look. Instead, she went to the kitchen, which smelled strange. She put her handbag on a chair and started collecting plates dirty with leftovers and empty glasses from the table.

Two bottles of wine were on the sideboard.

Empty.

Kate frowned. She took a bottle in her hand and looked at it in disbelief.

Dan was drinking again.

That probably explained everything.

Kate put the bottle back on the sideboard and held a hand to her mouth to hold back the sobbing. God, she never should have left! She should have known something like this would happen.

Once an alcoholic, always an alcoholic.

That's what they say, right?

And if there was a certain time to relapse, it was now. His child had died, and his wife had left him. Who wouldn't reach for a bottle?

Kate shook her head. The guilt burned like acid in her entrails. How could she have been so selfish? She knew he was completely exhausted. And Selina was almost still a child. The two should never have been alone after everything that had happened.

She opened the door to the larder and saw more bottles of wine and an open six pack. At least nothing high-proof. Perhaps there was still hope.

But hope was destroyed a few seconds later when Kate turned around because she noticed a movement behind her back.

Dan stood there in boxers that had seen better times and a crumpled T-shirt, his hair disheveled, his eyes bloodshot. In his hand was a bottle of gin. The little daylight that fell through the half-closed blinds was enough to see that he was a wreck.

Kate felt tears in her eyes. She walked up to him. "Dan, I'm so sorry!"

Dan didn't move. He just blinked as if chasing away a mirage.

Standing right in front of him, Kate noticed how badly he smelled of alcohol, sweat, and vomit. She reached for the half-empty bottle in his hand and expected resistance, but he let go and watched silently as Kate poured the contents down the drain.

"That's not good for you, Dan." She left the bottle in the sink and turned to him.

Dan still hadn't moved or said a word. Kate pulled herself together and embraced him. At first he remained stiff, but then he slowly relaxed and returned the hug. Kate breathed as shallowly as possible because he smelled unpleasant.

"It'll be all right, honey. We'll go see the doctor. You can quit drinking again, I know that."

Dan, who had truly more serious problems, didn't answer. He only held on to his wife as if she were his lifeline on the high seas.

So they stood there for quite a while. And if Selina hadn't come, it probably would have been longer.

***

"Kate! You're back?"

Kate let go of the trembling wreck of her husband and turned to her stepdaughter. Selina's clothes made a good impression; she was styled and wore a touch of makeup that she didn't need.

With her arms stretched out, she ran toward Kate. "I'm so happy that you're here again!" She sounded as relieved as she was desperate.

Kate held her as she'd held Dan, but Selina smelled much better and didn't tremble.

After she'd hugged and stroked the girl extensively, Kate looked around for her husband again. He'd retreated to the wall and watched with a face that was hard to read.

"When did you start drinking again?"

Dan didn't answer. His gaze was glassy.

Kate looked at Selina, who shrugged. "A few days ago I came home from school, and he was sitting on the couch with a bottle of wine in his hand. I … at first I didn't know how bad that was, but now …" She sighed and reached for Kate's hand. "Thank God you're here!"

Kate lovingly stroked her cheek. "It's all right, sweetie. I know it was wrong to leave, but now I'm staying with you, I promise."

Selina nodded. "We're happy to hear that. Right, Dad?"

Dan's mouth twitched, but he didn't say anything. When Kate tried to make eye contact with him, he looked down. Good God, he was completely devastated! How could she have left the poor girl alone with him? It was unthinkable what could have happened.

"Okay," Kate finally said. "We'll fix this. I'll get my luggage out of the car right away and then call my parents so they won't worry. By the way, Nora is also quite distraught because she hasn't been able to reach anyone for days."

"I'll call her later," Selina replied quickly. "Now I can tell her everything's okay because you're back."

Kate nodded. "That's a good idea, Selina. Later we can cook together."

"I don't think we have anything left," Selina said.

Kate smiled. "That doesn't matter. We can buy something." Her gaze wandered to Dan. "And in the meantime, you can shower and get dressed, honey. Okay?"

Dan didn't react. Kate went to him and put a hand on his arm. "Can you do that?"

Finally, he barely nodded.

Kate breathed a kiss on his stubbly cheek and tried hard to ignore the unpleasant smell. "Now everything will be all right. We just have to stick together."

Selina approached her father from the other side and put her hand on his arm. He flinched reflexively. Or was Kate just imagining it?

"I already told him that," Selina explained with a broad smile. "Isn't that right, Daddy?"

This time he didn't nod.

***

After the calls to the grandparents were done, Selina helped Kate get her things out of the car. Meanwhile, Dan was upstairs and (hopefully) showered.

"Why didn't you call somebody when he started drinking?" Kate asked, standing in front of the open trunk.

"He didn't want that," Selina said and grabbed a travel bag.

Kate took a suitcase and closed the trunk. They went back to the house and left the luggage in the hallway.

Kate put both hands on the girl's shoulders and looked deep into her eyes. "How bad is it, Selina?" she asked in a muffled voice because she didn't want Dan to hear.

Selina's eyes glistened as she struggled with tears. "Pretty bad," she whispered.

"Did he do something to you?" The thought frightened Kate deeply, but she'd never seen Dan like that before and had no idea how to judge his behavior. She hadn't known him when he was drinking, but she knew that during those times, he'd been anything but a good father.

Selina avoided her gaze.

"Selina!" Kate shook her slightly. "Look at me, please!"

But Selina didn't manage to lift her eyes. She was very pale. "He can't help it," she whispered. "He drinks so much ..."

"But what ...?"

Selina's body suddenly stiffened. She looked nervously toward the stairs.

Kate turned around and saw Dan coming down the stairs with his shoulders hanging. He wore jeans and a clean shirt, his hair was still wet, and he hadn't shaved.

"What did she tell you?" His first words since Kate was here. His voice sounded different; there was no life left in it.

"Why? What could she tell me?" Kate wanted to know.

She looked at him, but Dan could only handle her gaze for a few seconds. Shaking his head, he went to the couch and dropped on to the upholstery like a wet sack. Dented beer cans lined the table next to an empty pizza box. Beside it lay a small yellow baby rattle.

Kate's heart contracted painfully. "This house is one big pigsty!" she growled. "Your daughter is completely distraught, and you're not talking to me! What is it, Dan?"

Dan shook his head and laughed hollowly. "Yes, what is it, Kate? I don't know either. But if you can wake me up from this nightmare, please do it."

"What do you mean?"

"Let's do some shopping first," Selina intervened. "I'm hungry."

Dan hid his face in his hands. Nothing could be expected from him for the time being.

Kate sighed and made one last attempt. "Okay, Selina, let's do that. Maybe you could at least tidy up a bit, Dan."

Dan ignored her. Again Kate looked at the rattle and then at the orphaned playpen and suddenly just wanted to leave. Without thinking, she grabbed her handbag and ran to the front door.

Selina followed her.

Only Dan remained alone in the nightmare his life had turned into, surrounded by the silence that had become his only retreat.

***

There was beer in the bedroom closet. Dan opened a can to help him think better. What should he do to make Kate believe him? He could never tell her the truth; she already looked at him like he was a felon. She probably thought he'd treated Selina badly since he drank again. But how could he explain that the truth was the other way around?

No one would ever believe him. Fathers were not seduced by their own daughters. When something like this happened, it was always the parent's fault.

He would also have seen it that way until recently.

Dan shuffled back into the living room and sat on the couch. He stared at Leila's rattle and wondered for the first time why all this stuff was still lying around. He should have taken care of it instead of feeling sorry for himself because his daughter had mutated into a femme fatale.

But there had to be a solution!

It was impossible that Selina had him in her hand like that.

Although Dan couldn't believe it, and it completely contradicted his perception of the world, he still couldn't find a solution. Nobody would believe him, and there was nothing he could do. Selina, on the other hand, would appear extremely credible with her innocent face and the desperate flickering in her eyes. And she had the panties with his sperm. Even if he succeeded in stealing it from her, it would hardly harm her credibility.

Dan pondered while he was drinking. That was also her fault!

The only chance he had was Kate. Maybe Selina would stop if Kate stayed. Maybe then everything would be the same as before. Except for Leila being dead, of course.

What if Selina had something to do with it? He considered the strong possibility.

I need to talk to Kate! No matter what else happens, and no matter what Selina accuses me of, I have to tell Kate!

And what then? Selina would deny everything. And she'd claim he'd raped her. Which was only partly a lie.

All he could do was play along or kill himself. Until he decided to do the latter, he clung to the hope that Selina would sooner or later lose interest. She was young. Teenagers were volatile. Everybody knew they were constantly changing their minds. And they all fell immortally in love with another one all the time. Maybe it was just a matter of keeping his feet still and waiting until this daddy-phase was over and she fell in love with the next one—in the best-case scenario, a boy her age. She was young and pretty. All doors stood open for her. How long would her old man be interesting?

Until then, he had to put a good face on the matter. That was perhaps not a real solution, but it was the only thing he could think of. It would pass. Perhaps even faster than expected now that Kate was finally back. Selina would sleep in her room again, and he'd no longer be alone with her all the time. Even the mere thought made him feel better.

Dan emptied the can and put it on the table.

Sighing, Dan bent over and took the rattle in his hand. He looked at it from all sides before pressing it against his chest and his heart. The tears came in a hot flood, and this time they felt good.

***

When they came back, there were no more baby clothes in the closet. The rattle had disappeared from the coffee table. Dan kneeled on the carpet and was about to dismantle the playpen. Kate went to him and put one hand on his shoulder, while Selina brought the groceries to the kitchen.

Dan looked up at Kate. "I should have done this much sooner."

Kate took off her jacket, threw it over the couch, and sat down. Dan continued to work, and it felt good to have her watch him.

"I'm so glad you're back," he said.

"I'm sorry I left." Kate sighed. "I shouldn't have left you alone."

"It's not your fault. I promise I'll stop drinking. I just need a little time."

She nodded.

"And I didn't do anything to Selina," he added. "You must believe me."

Kate got up. She had tears in her eyes. Dan also stood up. He wanted to feel her, put his arms around her, and breathe in the smell of her hair. When he went to her, she let him.

"I love you so much," he whispered as he pulled her tightly against him.

"I love you too," Kate finally replied. Her voice was nothing but a warm breath on his ear. "Together we can do it."

Dan would have loved to believe her, but when he slowly released from the embrace, he saw Selina standing silently in the kitchen door.

His hope burst like a soap bubble.

Selina grinned wickedly, and then her lips formed a kissing mouth. But when Kate turned to her, she'd already put on her innocent face again.

"Will you help me now, Kate?" she asked without letting Dan out of her sight.

"Of course, sweetie. I'm already there." Kate hurried into the kitchen.

"Oh, and Daddy ..." Selina started.

Dan stiffened. She approached him quickly, held on to his arm, and kissed him on the cheek. Then she whispered, "Be careful. Don't try to pull her to your side, or you'll regret it."

She kissed him again and touched his crotch. Dan flinched like from an electric shock. "You belong to me, Daddy. There's no room for her here. You have exactly until tomorrow to tell her that."

"But she can stay." Dan looked at her pleadingly.

"No, she can't. The clock is ticking. She'll be gone by tomorrow evening or I'll tell her everything the big bad Dan did to the cute little Selina. Details included."

She bared her teeth in a wolfish grin. "You certainly don't want to experience that. It would be very bad for you and very humiliating. These men who abuse their own daughters are so disgusting!"

She shook her head regretfully and stroked his stubbly cheek. "And you will shave. You've already scratched me all over down there."

Dan would have loved to grab her and shake her, yell at her and beat her, but what if Kate saw that?

He gathered his last bit of self-control and kept quiet while Selina marched back into the kitchen with a grin to help Kate cook.

At that moment he became painfully aware that he hated his daughter.

***

The dinner together demanded all the self-control Dan still had. It almost caused him physical pain. For Kate's sake he drank only water, but he couldn't eat. Although Kate's lasagna had once been one of his favorite dishes, he now barely got a bite down.

Kate also poked around her food without appetite. Only Selina gobbled as if she hadn't eaten anything for days.

"I don't feel well. I need to lie down," Dan said when he finally couldn't take it anymore. Selina gave him a meaningful look.

Kate took his hand and squeezed it. "You should do that, Dan. We two girls will do the dishes." She winked at Selina, who smiled with her lips but not her eyes.

Dan hurried to the bedroom, where a few cans of beer waited for him. They would help him stop the panicked noise of his thoughts. Today he didn't want to remember that tomorrow he had to dump Kate under some pretext just to satisfy his wicked daughter, who had been the dearest girl in the world only a few weeks ago.

118

***

An hour later Dan was half asleep when Kate crawled into bed. She snuggled up to him, and Dan noticed she wore nothing but panties. Her skin was soft and warm. That felt so right and made everything he'd experienced with Selina lately seem all the more absurd. Never before had he felt so helpless and desperate. The more comfortable he felt with Kate, the more he wanted to cry.

"It's all right," Kate whispered, pressing herself harder against him. "Everything will be fine." She stroked him with both hands and finally slipped into his crotch but stopped when she noticed his tension. "It's okay, honey. We don't have to do this. Let's just cuddle."

Dan pulled her arm around his shoulder and held it there. "Thank you."

He stroked Kate's arm until she fell asleep.

He lay awake for a long time.

***

His full bladder finally forced Dan out of bed. Yawning, he trudged into the bathroom and closed the door. In the past, he'd always left it open when he had to pee at night, but not now. But he didn't think about locking it.

Dan had just relieved himself when someone opened the door. He turned around. Selina stood behind him. Her long blonde hair hung far over her bare shoulders. Her face was without makeup. Dan thought for a tiny moment that she was beautiful, breathtakingly beautiful. But then his former princess came up to him with a nasty grin, and all he saw was her ugliness.

"Hi, Daddy. You can get your cock right back out."

119

Dan stared at her. In the glaring light of the neon tubes her hair looked almost white. She puckered up her lips as she came closer and closer.

"Did you fuck her?" she wanted to know.

Dan shook his head. His tongue was just a thick, useless lump.

"That's good. You saved yourself for me."

Dan wanted to say something. Maybe he wanted to yell at her, maybe he just wanted to beg her to leave him alone. At least for this one last night. But nothing came out.

Selina was with him now. He smelled her, and she smelled good, no different from the girl from before. Dan wanted to move backward, but he didn't get far because the back of his knees hit the toilet.

He closed his eyes. Selina pulled down his boxer shorts. Her hands felt warm and soft. She knew exactly how to touch him. Dan kept his eyes closed. A soft moan came out of his mouth. How could something you didn't want feel so terribly good? He imagined she was someone else.

Kate.

When he finally felt her warm wet lips closing around his glans and sucking hard on it, it was as if he saw Kate right in front of him. He had to lean with one hand against the tiled wall to avoid landing on the toilet seat.

Selina massaged his testicles, which felt so unbelievably horny that it literally took his breath away. Waves of arousal shot through Dan's body. His hips twitched uncontrollably.

And then Selina did something Kate had never done. She drilled a finger into his anus, pushing hard enough to penetrate to the limit, stimulating his prostate.

Dan gasped.

He couldn't help himself.

He closed his eyelids so tightly that his eyes watered.

Just don't open your eyes, then everything will be fine.

Meanwhile, he was approaching an historic orgasm. When the time finally came, he gave a suppressed scream as he unloaded himself with a jerk into his daughter's expectantly open mouth.

At that moment, the door opened.

Dan opened his eyes. He saw Kate pressing both hands in front of her mouth. Her eyes bulged like marbles.

He knew the image she saw was a man with his pants down, standing over the open toilet, his daughter kneeling in front of him with her finger in his ass, and his own half-erect cock in his hand, while his freshly sprayed juice ran over the chin of the girl who was breathing heavily.

Within a split second, this image destroyed everything.

Dan roughly pushed Selina away. She fell backward, landed on her back, and stared at Kate with her sperm-smeared face. She began to cry.

"Kate, it's not what it looks like," Dan shouted. He wanted to walk up to her and almost stumbled over his shorts. By the time he pulled his pants up, Selina had picked herself up and ran sobbing into Kate's arms.

Kate held the trembling girl and pointed her finger at him. "Stop," she screamed. "Don't you dare come closer!"

Dan stopped. "It's not what it looks like, Kate. She forces me to do it!"

The punishing look she gave him was worse than a punch in the stomach.

She didn't believe him.

Of course not!

"She set it all up, Kate. Please, you have to believe me! Tomorrow I have to break up with you so that she has me all to herself!"

"You son of a bitch!" Kate yelled as she rocked the crying girl in her arms.

"No, Kate! It's not like that! I had no choice! She's been blackmailing me all the time. The only reason I did it was because otherwise she'd out me as a rapist."

"You piece of scum! How could you do that? You ... you're an animal!" Kate was crying now too. And she was angry. God, she was furious!

"Maybe she even killed Leila," Dan yelled and knew at the same moment that it was a mistake.

Kate backed away with Selina. "You're sick, Dan," she said as she walked backward through the door. "I don't know since when, and I don't know why, but I know that I have to take Selina away from here ..."

"Yes!" screamed Dan. "Yes, you have to! She has to leave here, and then everything will be fine!"

Kate turned away. She hurried into the bedroom with Selina. Dan followed on stiff legs.

"Selina has to get out of here, Kate. She's the one who's sick. She needs help!"

Was Kate listening to him at all? She frantically threw on pants and a sweatshirt.

Selina held clothes that Kate had given her.

"Put these on, baby, and we'll get out of here."

Selina nodded with a sob. She played her role really well. Dan would have believed her if he hadn't known better. He stood helplessly in the doorway with his sperm-stained boxer shorts and felt like the biggest loser of all time. "Kate, at least give me a chance to explain everything."

"I don't need any explanation," Kate said harshly. She was packing her suitcase. She stuffed pants, sweaters, and underwear for her and Selina.

"We'll get your things some other time," she said to her stepdaughter, and then she took the suitcase in one hand and the girl in the other.

"Let us pass," she commanded, and Dan stepped back as if controlled by remote. He followed them down the stairs.

In the hallway, the women put on shoes and jackets, and Kate grabbed their handbags. They were only five feet from the front door when Dan stepped in their way.

Selina screamed pitifully and theatrically held her hands in front of her face, as if he was going to hit her.

That goddamn bitch!

"Get out of my way," Kate demanded breathlessly.

Dan shook his head. "First you listen to me."

But Kate didn't even think about it. She pushed her way past him with Selina. Dan held her by the shoulders.

Kate dropped her suitcase and punched him in the face. "Leave us alone, you bastard!"

"Please, Kate, believe me! I didn't do anything to her. She started it all, she got me drunk and then—"

"You're disgusting, Dan! To do something like that to the girl and then make her the guilty one, that's really miserable! We're going to the police now while the evidence is still fresh."

"Don't do this to me, Kate! I beg you! We're a family, aren't we?"

"That's history," Kate said tonelessly, trying to push him away from the door.

Suddenly Dan saw red. He grabbed his wife by her slender shoulders and shook her like a doll. "You're not going anywhere, you understand? Nowhere!"

Kate tried to reach his face with her hands, but this time Dan was faster and he took advantage of his physical superiority for the first time by hurling Kate brutally against the wall. He smashed his fist into her face several times.

She didn't raise her hands anymore. Blood ran out of her nose. She'd stopped defending herself, just stared at him in fear, and this would have been the best moment to stop, but Dan was too furious. He struck until Kate only whimpered and could barely stand on her feet anymore. She'd had enough, but that didn't interest him.

He pressed her against the wall and swapped his hands around her neck. He started to choke her, and she perked up again and wiggled her feet. The tighter he pressed, the more her face swelled. Her eyes filled with blood, and several veins burst. Her resistance grew weaker.

Little Leila came into Dan's delusional thoughts. Suddenly he remembered that his daughter had died in a similar way. He abruptly let go, and Kate lay motionlessly on the floor. She'd lost a shoe.

"Bravo, Dad. Now you're really fucked." Selina stood behind him and smiled. She slowly raised her hands and started to applaud.

FUCKED

It was only a second that determined the rest of his life. Dan stood with hanging shoulders over his wife's writhing body. He clenched his fists.

There were two options. Either he overpowered Selina, took Kate to a hospital, and lived with all the consequences—or he made sure Kate didn't leave this house anymore, which meant he was finally in the hands of his psychotic daughter. And live with those consequences.

But it's not quite true. There is another option. The last resort, so to speak.

Right.

He could choose suicide.

This option was available to him at any time.

Or at least as long as he wasn't in prison. In jail it would probably be more difficult or he wouldn't have too many ways to die to choose from.

So much for that.

It was up to him.

He had to decide.

He was fucked either way.

While Selina watched him with interest, as if he were the actor in some daily soap, Dan squatted next to Kate. She breathed shallowly, and blood still trickled out of her nose. It was probably broken. He carefully touched Kate's shoulder, but she didn't respond. He pressed one hand to her mouth. This was the woman he loved, and he'd lost her.

There was no turning back.

Filled with hatred, he looked up at his daughter. She remained silent so that he could make his own decision. At least he thought he could read that in her eyes.

Had he ever seen anything so evil?

***

The dice would fall now. Selina knew this moment was crucial. Her father had to decide. He could help Kate and spend the next few years in prison, or he'd keep his wife silent and spend his life with Selina, his princess.

She couldn't understand why he still had to think about it, but she decided to give him time to choose. He'd lost two people he loved. Selina was convinced that with her help, he'd quickly get over the loss. After all, she was his first and greatest love.

At the moment he didn't see it, and perhaps he even thought he hated her, but over time he'd understand, and his true feelings would return.

She knew how much he liked their sleeping together. He'd never had an erection problem when she lay her hand on him. She couldn't be that wrong then, right?

He only had to learn to deal with the fact that she was his daughter. He had to let go of everything and everyone else. It was that simple.

But first they had to think about what to do with Kate. Having her here was an incalculable risk. It would be best to make her disappear forever.

But what did Dan think about it?

Selina decided not to talk him into it for now. She'd wait and see whether he came up with the same idea on his own. He first had to cope with the shock. Somehow she even understood his dilemma, even though it was great fun to have him in her hand. But on the whole, she only wanted his best. She loved him with all her heart. As much as only a princess could love her daddy.

He sat helplessly next to the unconscious Kate. If this continued, Selina would soon have to give him a leg up. After all, it was only a matter of time before Kate regained consciousness.

She was about to say something when he looked up. His face was a mask of pain. "You win," he whispered. "Get the duct tape from the kitchen."

Selina's heart opened up. She'd been waiting for it. Soon he'd understand that her victory didn't automatically mean his defeat, but it was still too early. The main thing was that he had given up. She dared not wish for more.

"I will," she replied with satisfaction.

***

Together they took off the jacket and the remaining shoe of the unconscious Kate. Selina handed him the roll of duct tape, and he wrapped it around Kate's wrists and ankles. To tie her hands behind her back, he turned her on her stomach, which made her moan softly.

She'd wake up soon.

Dan turned her on her back again and looked into her swollen, bloodstained face. He seemed to hesitate for a moment, but then he tore off more tape and placed it over her mouth.

Selina was proud of him. "Where are we taking her?" she asked when they were halfway up the stairs.

Dan went backward and held Kate under his armpits. Selina held her feet. A weak trail of blood marked the path.

"The bedroom," Dan replied tonelessly.

"But we sleep there," Selina said, though she liked the idea.

"I want to keep an eye on her," Dan said, panting.

So they carried Kate into the bedroom and lay her on the floor at the foot of the bed. Her blood would ruin the carpet, but that couldn't be avoided now.

Dan turned her head to the side so the blood could drain away. Selina thought it would have been better to put something underneath. Towels at least, but it was too late.

"And now let's fuck!" she shouted cheerfully.

Dan looked at her in bewilderment.

"Somehow it gets me in the mood," Selina added, shrugging.

"I can't do it now," he said with the nagging undertone of a toddler.

Selina came to him and grabbed his penis through the thin fabric of the shorts. "You can do something." She pulled him by the cock over to the bed.

While her dad took her from behind (in the end he'd been able to do much more than expected), Selina positioned herself in a way that Kate had to look her right in the eye when she finally regained consciousness.

***

After he'd shot his load into his daughter's soft pussy, Dan lay breathless on his back for a moment. His cock hurt because she wasn't one of the most tender lovers. His body felt uncomfortably wet and sticky. Other body fluids had mixed with Kate's blood. He urgently needed to take a shower. He also had to clean the hallway and the stairs.

128

"We should get some sleep." Selina bent over him to kiss him. Her naked breasts touched his belly.

Groaning, he straightened up. "You can sleep. I have to clean."

"That can wait until tomorrow." Now she stroked his back. Her touches had been pleasant before, and they still were, even though Dan would have liked to talk himself into the opposite. He tried to catch a glimpse of Kate lying on the floor, but Selina pushed herself in between.

"You stay here now, Dad. You can do everything else tomorrow when I'm in school."

"And that's an order now, or what?" he barked at her.

Selina stroked him again. "That's a request, Daddy." She looked at him with big eyes.

Dan sighed. Actually, he was dead tired and just wanted to rest. He lay down again without having seen more of Kate than the blonde head of hair. Selina snuggled up to him. He'd have liked to push her away but felt too weak for that. His muscles were filled with lead.

The whole world seemed to be made of lead—rigid and cold!

He closed his eyes and ignored Selina's fingers playing with his chest hair. He just wanted to sleep and forget. And he did that for the next six hours.

***

At seven o'clock Selina woke up. Her inner clockwork was reliable. The first rays of sunlight were already shining through the blinds. She sat up and yawned heartily. The daylight was as brilliant as it was merciless. In its glow, Selina saw bloodstained sheets and a bloodstained Dan lying on his side, snoring quietly. She looked at her arms and thighs and realized she didn't look any better.

In her crotch she felt the familiar feeling of sticky sperm. When she had sex with guys she didn't like very much, she always peed afterward to get rid of the spunk as soon as possible. With Daddy it was different. She would have loved to preserve every drop of him for eternity.

Smiling, Selina watched him sleep for a moment. Without all the blood it would have been a perfect picture. He was so beautiful. She drove her index finger along the line of his spine. His back was covered with freckles and small moles. She would have loved to kiss each one of them now.

You can do that later, maybe even tonight.

Right.

Because there wasn't any time now. Besides, she didn't want to wake him. He needed his beauty sleep. At that thought Selina almost giggled, but then a muffled moan came to her ear.

Shit, there's still Kate!

Selina crawled on her belly to the foot of the bed and looked over the edge. Kate was almost lying there like yesterday, maybe she'd moved around a bit, but she wouldn't get far. With big tear-stained eyes she stared at Selina, who silently stared back. Probably the strange moaning meant that Kate wanted to say something. She seemed to struggle hard; her face was all red. Or was it because Dan had almost strangled her yesterday? No, not really, you could only see that now in the bluish marks on her neck.

Kate lifted her head and went on with her pathetic moaning. She tried so hard that fresh blood ran out of her nose.

Selina emotionlessly watched her efforts. Kate probably still believed she was the victim here and that she'd probably help her. She assumed Dan had gone crazy and

130

was now doing everything he could to continue abusing his daughter. She probably wanted to believe that because it was still easier to cope with than reality.

Selina got up and climbed over the helpless woman without giving her another look. She went straight into the bathroom, once again refraining from intimate washing so she could smell her father for as long as possible. Last night he'd taken her harder than ever before. She was sore and had a few new bruises. Selina smiled as she put on a fresh pair of underwear. She liked it when her body carried his stamp. His cock would certainly remember her all day, and tonight she might use her fingernails. She wanted to mark her father as a lover, just like a dog did with his favorite tree. But in that case a little piss wouldn't be enough.

When she was fully dressed, Selina took a last look into the bedroom. Dan was still lying on his side sleeping. He didn't seem to have moved—unlike Kate, who threw her head back and forth and moaned even louder. The lower half of her face was rust-red from all the blood, the upper half soaking wet from tears, snot, or sweat, perhaps a mixture of everything.

Selina knew that today would be a test for her father. There was still a risk that he'd try to work against her. Then she'd come home this afternoon and Kate would no longer be there because he'd taken her to the hospital. For Selina, that would mean losing her dad. For him, it would mean losing his life. Because while she would end up living with her grandmother (or maybe even Kate) again and would have to get used to fucking other guys, he'd end up in jail to "enjoy" sexual encounters of a special kind. Selina knew her dad wasn't stupid, and she knew there was nothing worse for him than jail. He'd talked about it often enough. Would he take it all on his account just to save Kate?

What if he kills himself?

It wasn't the first time Selina asked herself that question. She didn't really believe he'd go that far. Of course, there was some residual risk, but that was always there, right?

She had no other choice but to continue going to school and to lead the more or less normal life of a teenager on the outside. She had to leave Dad alone with his demons, whether she wanted it or not.

The decision was up to him.

Just like the guilt.

What he'd done to Kate was no longer a trivial offence but the most serious bodily injury in concomitance with deprivation of liberty—as they called it in *Law & Order*. In addition there was the fact that he'd been abusing his own daughter, for which there was now even a witness. He was totally screwed and had no other choice but to surrender to Selina as long as he didn't want to die or go to jail.

No, she didn't think he was suicidal. A suicidal man wouldn't fuck his own daughter sore while his wife watched. There was something in him that Selina was convinced had never wanted it any other way. What he did to her in bed didn't feel like the desperate act of a victim of blackmail. And anyway, what man let himself be forced to have sex with his own daughter?

Selina remembered the nights in her grandmother's house. He'd never had any objections against lying in bed with his teenage daughter. Not even as she grew older and more feminine, and her touches became more targeted and demanding. If she'd done it to the extreme at that time, he would probably have gone for it too. She was pretty sure that he hadn't said no.

Because he was weak? Or perverse?

Or because he just loved her too much?

Nobody would be interested if it ever came to light. He'd always be the bad guy and she the innocent victim.

And he knew that.

Selina smiled.

He wouldn't have any other choice. He had to get rid of Kate. She was the only witness. Selina hoped he would have found a solution by this afternoon. She would prefer not to have anything else to do with it; after all, she already had enough on her plate.

She was startled to realize the school bus would leave in less than five minutes. She had to hurry. Swearing, Selina hurried into her room to pack up her school supplies. Since she had no idea which subjects she had today, she randomly stuffed notebooks and textbooks into her backpack.

The bus was already there and she barely made it. Selina didn't notice the curious gazes that followed her as she retreated into the back row of seats, completely exhausted. She thought only of her dad and hoped he'd do the right thing today. She didn't want to lose him, even though she suspected she could cope if it happened. Again and again she reminded herself that he was the one who would face a life of shame and pain if he made the wrong decision.

The idea that a life with her could mean exactly the same thing didn't occur to her.

***

When Dan woke that morning, he had the familiar disgusting taste in his mouth. It had been back since he began drinking again. He had to wash it away every morning. Unfortunately, water didn't work. Groaning, he sat up and rubbed his penis, which was still hurting. Images of a naked and hot young woman shot through his head. How she'd sucked on his balls as if they were damn lollipops ...

He quickly dispelled all further thoughts of his daughter by pinching his testicles so tightly that he cried out loud.

Someone whimpered under the bed.

Kate!

How could he have forgotten her?

He jumped out of bed and saw stars dancing before his eyes. He stood over his tied-up wife and stared into her bloodshot eyes. She looked terrible, her swollen face covered in blood. The tape on her hands and feet seemed too tight, but the piece over her mouth had slipped off a bit, so she could make those pathetic noises. Dan was terribly thirsty and wondered if she was as well. She didn't look good and she smelled unpleasant.

Dan's eyes wandered over Kate's cramped body. She must have been struggling with her ties for some time while he'd been sleeping peacefully. There was a dark spot in her crotch. Had she wet herself? That explained the foul smell.

Dan was torn between pity and fear. This was the woman he loved, but she'd also be the person who finally caused his fall if he let her go. Selina wasn't here, so everything was up to him. He had the chance to do the right thing. The chance to make up for it. The only question was what there was left to make up for.

134

There was pure hatred in Kate's eyes. He'd beaten her up, choked her, tied her up, and all that after letting his own daughter give him a blowjob. He'd fucked Selina while Kate was lying next to them.

So what exactly did he expect from her now?

The burden of evidence was damning.

He could never talk his way out of it. He could read that on her face like an open book.

"I'm sorry," he whispered, and at the same moment he realized that in Kate's eyes, this was a confession of guilt.

She stared at him.

She wasn't able to do more.

Dan tore the tape off her lips. Kate flinched. Her lips were chapped and bleeding. She licked her tongue over them and swallowed heavily. Her throat had to hurt like hell. The strangulation marks looked terrible.

"Let me go!" Kate's voice sounded hoarse and strangely pressed, as if she had a seriously sore throat.

"I can't."

Kate licked her lips again as her eyes wandered fearfully across his naked body, which was still covered with her blood. She was probably afraid of being raped.

"I need water," she said breathily. Her eyes shined wet. "Please!" Her whispering turned into a dry cough that hurt as soon as you listened.

Of course she was thirsty. And that would get much worse. He could bring her a glass of water. There wouldn't be much to it. She could drink it with the help of a straw without him having to move her even a millimeter. Then she'd feel better.

Also her throat.

But did he want that?

Did he want her to be better so she could regain her strength and continue to fight against her shackles? What if he ignored her request and gave her nothing to drink? How long would she last?

"Please, Dan," Kate repeated with a croaking voice after the cough had subsided. She licked her dry lips obsessively, but it didn't look like she had much saliva left.

"I'm sorry, Kate, but there's nothing I can do for you."

Her eyes widened.

"I can't because you don't believe me. It's Selina. She did all that."

He remembered how he'd beaten his wife last night. punched his fist right in her face until she was unconscious. And now he played the innocent one? That was ridiculous.

Kate seemed to be pondering her chances by now. She wanted water, and she wanted to go. How long before she said and did everything he wanted just to achieve those goals?

"I didn't believe you, that's true," she panted. "But we can talk about anything. I can help you, Dan."

He shook his head and gave a resigned laugh.

"You're still in shock," Kate continued. "Just like all of us. But there is help for that. You just have to allow it. Please ... please, bring me water, Dan. You don't have to untie me if you don't want to. Just bring me something to drink, and then we can talk."

"We're already talking," Dan replied. "But it doesn't matter. You'll report me, and then I'll go to jail. And don't say you won't, because I'm not stupid."

"No," Kate complained. "I know." Her tongue shot out like a dervish and desperately tried to moisten her lips. "I'd report you, I admit that. But not because of me, but only to protect Selina. You want that too, don't you?"

Dan shook his head. "You can't protect Selina. She doesn't deserve it."

"I ... I don't know why you think that way about her, Dan, but you have to stop hurting her. She's your daughter!"

Dan didn't know whether to laugh or cry. He grabbed his penis, a gesture Kate could only misunderstand, but he didn't care.

"It doesn't feel like she's my daughter. And maybe she's not my child at all. What do you say to that? Quite a few men come into question there, you know? Many guys from the trailer park. I always treated her like my daughter, but she doesn't have to be. That changes everything, doesn't it? After all, she's an adult and can decide for herself who she wants to have sex with. I can't help it. I'm just a man, too."

Did that sound like some pathetic excuse?

Of course!

But it was the best he could come up with.

Kate stared in horror at his hand and the genital that was still covered with the secretions of his daughter (biological or not).

"What she does to me is really cruel, even if you'll never believe it," he said slowly. "It's all the crueler because sometimes it feels so damn good."

A lack of understanding now lay in Kate's eyes. It simply had no purpose. Dan went to the closet and took out a pair of socks. He stuffed one of them into her mouth, ignoring the sobbing and whining. Now she could no longer speak or lick her lips. She only twitched spastically and groaned deeply from her throat. Dan squatted and stroked her hair. Kate turned her head to the side and tried to escape his touch. On her forehead a small blue vein pulsed like a crooked worm.

"I'm so sorry," Dan said and continued stroking through his wife's sweaty hair.

That he loved her like no other … that they'd had and lost the sweetest baby in the world … the day at the supermarket parking lot … all that was now far away and almost forgotten. It was as if it had never happened. Just a dream in a life that was dominated by Selina. If he wanted to go on living somehow, he had to let go of her. That hurt terribly, but he'd learn to numb the pain. Without giving Kate another look, Dan went to the door.

He was terribly thirsty. It was unthinkable what a terrible feeling it would be not to be able to satisfy that thirst.

***

Kate was still too shocked to understand what was happening to her and what had happened to Selina. Despite her pain and the burning sensation of thirst, she'd been thinking about what was going on here for the past few hours. Had anything been wrong with Dan for a long time, or had Leila's death made him lose his mind?

He claimed Selina is responsible for the baby's death.

Yeah, Dan said a lot of things. Even now, when he stood in front of her, naked and bloody, he still claimed it was all his daughter's fault, who might not be his daughter at all, which seemed to excuse everything for him somehow. But in Kate's eyes, it didn't play the slightest role.

Hadn't he always idolized Selina? The two had been as thick as thieves. How could this relationship have changed so quickly and dramatically?

I never should have left. Maybe I could have stopped it then.

Maybe, or maybe not.

Maybe the whole thing had started long before Leila's death, and she'd simply ignored the signs. She'd never wondered about their relationship. It had been intimate, but never lewd. Kate had never thought Dan saw more in his daughter. Shouldn't Nora have noticed that otherwise, too? She knew her son and her granddaughter inside and out after all these years. She should have been the first to notice if something was wrong.

It's probably just been a little while. Selina's no longer a child, but a young woman, and Dan suddenly saw something in her that hadn't been there before. The shock of Leila's death has now brought it to the surface. For whatever reason.

Yeah, for whatever reason.

There was no satisfactory explanation. The fact was, he ruthlessly abused the girl. Kate had finally seen this in the bathroom when the poor girl just got a load of sperm while her finger ... at first Kate had thought she was wrong, but it had been like this. Selina's finger had actually been up his ass—for Kate, the epitome of all perversion. He'd forced the poor girl to do this, which Kate could hardly believe because he'd never asked her to do anything like this.

Why now?

And why Selina?

Later he'd attacked the girl like an animal and had raped her mercilessly, while Kate was lying next to the bed and had to witness everything, which didn't seem to bother him.

Quite the opposite! Probably it even turned him on. Kate hadn't been able to see much, but the noises had been enough to get her imagination going.

Exhaustion paralyzed her body. She could only breathe jerkily through her shattered nose, and her throat felt like it was tied up. Kate noticed the damp spot between her legs and whimpered with shame and hopelessness.

How could she help poor Selina?

She had to do something!

139

She couldn't imagine what the poor girl was going through. And then in the morning she got out of her father's bed right in front of his gagged wife and just went to school as if nothing had happened. Kate could only guess what irreparable damage this had already done to her young soul.

Selina needed help.

Now!

Kate knew she was her only chance. That she loved Dan and still couldn't believe what he'd done to her and his daughter played only a minor role now. It was important that she managed to free herself and Selina from his claws. She had to try to appease him as soon as she got the first opportunity. Even if she had to tell the biggest lies, the main thing was that she somehow got him to release her.

How's that gonna work? You couldn't even get a glass of water from him. You could die of thirst here!

No, that was nonsense, of course. It would never happen.

Right?

How long could she actually survive without water? She read somewhere that a person could survive without food for quite a long time, sometimes even up to a month, depending on their physical constitution. But with liquid it was different. Maybe a few days? Kate already had the feeling that she was drying up inside. Her throat burned like fire, and she could hardly swallow because her saliva became thick. The sock Dan had stuffed into her mouth triggered a feeling of panic, which she tried to suppress with all her might.

She wasn't allowed to suffocate now.

She wasn't allowed to die of thirst either.

Selina needed her help!

140

Without hesitation, she would have sold her soul for a sip of water.

But nobody came to buy her soul.

BREAKING THE CHAINS

School... who invented this shit?

Selina sat bored over her biology book. The anatomy of a frog was just about the last thing of interest. She leaned her head in her hand while chewing on her pencil. Instead of a sketch of an amphibian, she saw her father's cock in front of her and dreamed of taking it into her mouth with relish ... so deep that she choked. Because only then it was really good. She wanted him to fill her up, wanted to feel, taste, and smell him with every pore on her body.

Smiling, Selina sucked on her pen, which was Daddy's erect member in her mind. She hardly had to do anything to taste it. Now she even felt his big warm hands on her ass as they spread her buttocks to quickly reach this sweet, expectantly throbbing crevice that was wetter than the Amazon during rainy season.

Why the Amazon?

"In the Amazon?" Mrs. Pauls just asked.

Selina took the pencil out of her mouth and looked at her teacher in astonishment. "Hm?"

"I just asked you how many species of frogs are estimated to live in the Amazon, Selina," repeated Mrs. Pauls, who was old and quite ugly, with yellow horsy teeth and strangely dry skin. Sometimes small flakes of dandruff lay on her collar.

I wonder if anyone still wants to fuck her?

Selina shuddered at the idea.

"I don't know," she replied honestly.

Mrs. Pauls nodded slowly—as if she'd guessed what was already obvious. Every teacher and the entire class knew by now that Selina Meller couldn't answer any questions in class because she was no longer able to follow them. They also knew, of course, that these difficulties were related to the death of her little sister. Before that, Selina had been very popular with her classmates and with the teachers, so they accepted her strange behavior of the last weeks. Nobody laughed at her or said bad things. Nevertheless, Selina's classmates dissociated more and more from her. They simply didn't know how to deal with her.

That was absolutely fine with her. She had enough to do and couldn't care about the sensitivities of these ignorant teenagers. At the moment, she didn't need any of them, so she ignored them. It was similar with the teachers—although Mr. Willis was still worth a look or two, and she couldn't stop imagining tearing his glasses off his face before she sat on his cock …

"I'm sorry, Mrs. Pauls. I haven't studied," she said sheepishly, because then Mrs. Pauls would have pity. They always had pity. Probably they assumed that at Selina's home everything had gone haywire since Leila's death.

Which they weren't all wrong about.

"Then please read both pages again this afternoon," Mrs. Pauls relented. She wouldn't give her a bad grade, although Selina wouldn't have given a shit.

She nodded nicely and lowered her eyes back to her book, which was open on the wrong page. Mrs. Pauls, meanwhile, turned to the overweight Peter Smith, who also had no idea of the biodiversity of the Amazon, even though nobody in his family had died.

Selina smiled when Peter accepted his F. He wasn't given a second chance. Strictly speaking, that was a blatant injustice. But why would Selina care as long as she was the beneficiary?

A few minutes later the alarm sounded. Peter snuck out of the classroom with hanging shoulders and looked as if he was about to cry. Mrs. Pauls hectically gathered her stuff because she had to go to the next class. Selina stared at her book while her classmates giggled and talked loudly. Selina was quite content with minding her thoughts. She still saw her father in front of her, could feel him, smell him, and taste him if she concentrated enough on it.

Suddenly someone put a hand on her shoulder, and Selina turned around in shock. She felt caught, as if you could look inside her head, which would have been a disaster. But it was just Stacy, a friend.

"Hey, are you okay?" Stacy had huge blue eyes and brown hair, which she usually wore in a thick ponytail.

Selina nodded. She didn't feel like talking. On the other hand, she was also aware that she had to slowly pull herself together and behave like a halfway normal teenager again. At least for a few hours a day. She'd done that before, despite the chaos in her head.

"Would you like to go to town this afternoon? Just us girls?"

Selina shrugged. That was definitely not possible. She had to go home immediately after school to see what was going on with Kate.

"I'd like to, but I can't. I have to go home to my dad right away."

"Oh," Stacy said. "I understand."

Of course Stacy didn't understand anything. She just thought Selina had to take care of her dad because he was still suffering from the death of little Leila. She should think that. Selina didn't care.

"Then maybe some other time? We miss you."

Stacy was talking about herself and three other girls from the class: Mona, Naomi, and Tiffany. Selina had been out with them regularly before her father's seduction took too much of her attention to think of anything else.

She forced herself to smile and was only too aware of the looks from the other girls.

"I miss you too, sweetheart, but right now it's really difficult. I always feel guilty when I'm not home."

Stacy nodded understandingly. "Must be hard on your parents."

"Yes," Selina sighed. "They're far from over it, and I'm trying to help them as much as I can."

"That's great of you. But don't forget that your girl-friends are always there for you. You can call us any time."

Selina gave Stacy and the other girls a fake smile. "This is totally sweet of you. Thanks."

Before Stacy could answer, the door opened and Mr. Willis came in. The students returned, grumbling, to their places, and cheerful chatter turned into suppressed murmurs.

Selina took the pen in her mouth again and looked into her book. Mr. Willis's voice was pleasantly lulling. For the first time that day, she didn't think about Kate or her father; instead, she imagined herself sucking Mr. Willis's cock.

***

She seemed so terribly lonely and lost that it tore his heart apart. While Mark Willis tried to sensitize his students for the monstrosities of Nazi crimes, Selina's deeply hanging blonde head caught his eye again and again. She stared silently at her biology book, although history was now on the timetable, and she chewed on a pen while she was lost in thought.

What was going on in that pretty little head?

It wasn't the first time Mark asked himself that question. He'd immediately noticed Selina when she sat in his class for the first time a few months ago. She was very pretty, had delicate features, and an incredible charisma. Of course, Mark was aware that these were not necessarily the thoughts one should have when looking at his student, but there was nothing he could do about it. Selina was not the first girl who had caught his attention so much. Two years ago, he'd fallen head over heels in love with a seventeen-year-old girl from senior classes. The whole thing had never gone beyond his fantasies, but Mark had suffered a lot from the situation and in the end had even considered quitting his job just to avoid seeing the girl. It had become so bad that he could hardly teach anymore. He regularly had panic attacks and stomach cramps and had often hurried to the toilet in front of the astonished eyes of his students.

Fortunately, nobody knew these afflictions were by no means of a physical nature. Pupils and colleagues assumed at that time that it was a health problem. Mark had been to the doctor and had described the symptoms (but without talking about the girl), so that he was diagnosed with burnout. At the age of thirty-one this was relatively early, but it was possible. The doctor had prescribed an antidepressant and gave him sick leave for several months.

When he came back, the girl in question (Melissa) was about to graduate, and somehow his feelings had diminished—or he could handle them better now. Mark gradually found his way back to the school routine. All in all, he was a good teacher and the kids liked him, which was why he recently had taken on the position of guidance counselor. He liked the job and never wanted to do anything else. To be on the safe side, he continued to take the pills his doctor had prescribed because he imagined that they would still help him. After all, something like this had never happened to him before. Of course, he once found one or two girls attractive and liked to risk a second glance when they walked around in their short skirts in summer. After all, he was just a man, and some of these girls acted like adult whores, so that was no surprise, right?

Mark had only ever had very short, superficial relationships, but to prove to himself that he was normal, he jumped head over heels into a relationship with a woman two years his senior. It hadn't worked out for long, but it had been his confirmation that everything was okay with him.

For half a year now, he was single.

And then came Selina Meller.

She was eighteen and therefore no longer a minor like Melissa, but it could still cost him his job. Teachers were not allowed to do anything with their students. That was absolutely out of the question. One of the most important basics of the job was that you had to have a damn grip on yourself and didn't jump at your protégés like a wild animal.

No matter how old or sexy they were.

Mark tried to ignore his body's signals when he was near Selina. Despite his pills, the pains in his stomach started again. Sometimes he vomited on the way to school. On other days he managed to get home, only to puke into the toilet for half the evening. He really fought against it and was determined not to give in to those feelings. Especially now, when Selina clearly needed serious help. Since her little sister had died, she didn't seem to be the same. One could only guess what was going on at home. The cheerful, open-minded girl had become mopey. Despite all concerns, Mark had already offered her a conversation in his position as a guidance counselor, but she'd declined—which was probably better.

He just couldn't stop thinking about her.

Was he already getting lost in something again?

That wasn't allowed to happen.

Especially not with Selina. After all, she'd lost her sister and was obviously severely traumatized. She'd completely withdrawn from her classmates. Mark had noticed this because he regularly kept an eye on her during lunch break. Selina sat alone most of the time, and it didn't seem like she ate much of anything.

Without a doubt, she needed help.

Whether she should get it from the guy who already got wet hands and an upset stomach when just looking at her was rather questionable. If he really wanted to help the girl, he had to inform and, if necessary, entrust an outsider. He himself would only make things worse.

Still, he couldn't help but approach her after school. As usual, the other students rushed noisily out of the classroom into the hallway. Selina stayed behind and slowly packed her books, as if taking her time to avoid any contact with the others. Or did she do it because she wanted to be alone with him? That was crazy, of course, but …

"Do you have a minute, Selina?"

She looked at him with eyes as beautiful and as deep as the ocean. Mark was now so close to her that he could smell her. A scent of vanilla lay in the air, making his knees go weak. With a trembling hand he pushed his glasses back.

"I'd like to talk to you for a moment," he explained, concentrating on breathing calmly.

Selina still didn't answer. She just looked at him.

Mark licked his dry lips. Her gaze drove him crazy. He wondered how this long blonde hair would feel if he stroked it from her face with both hands before he pressed his mouth on her full lips …

"It's nice of you to worry so much, Mr. Willis," she finally said. "But that's not necessary." She took her backpack and looked at him firmly.

Mark was paralyzed. Then Selina did the incredible. She reached out and stroked his cheek.

The touch was nothing more than a breath, but it triggered an earthquake. He felt his cock getting hard. His balls tingled.

Selina took her hand away and smiled. "Everything's fine, Mr. Willis," she whispered, "but now I have to go, unfortunately!" And she was gone.

What remained was a lost man in a scent of vanilla.

***

Another lost man sat on his bed and looked at the motionless woman at his feet. He'd spent the morning cleaning the house. The last room on his list was the bedroom. The sheets had to be changed again. Before he'd started to clean, he'd been in the shower and had washed away his wife's blood, his daughter's juices, and his own sweat. To his surprise he hadn't felt any better afterward. He'd gone back to the bedroom to get dressed. Kate had whined and twitched. She managed to move a few inches on the floor, but she wouldn't get far.

So Dan didn't pay much attention to her. It was important that he ignored her. Otherwise he might become weak. After all, she was his wife, and he loved her. It wasn't her fault that she now thought so badly of him. That was just the damn game of a vicious girl they had underestimated all these years. Unfortunately, that couldn't be reversed now. The circumstances demanded a sacrifice, and he wasn't ready to make himself available as such.

Now he sat here and watched his wife breathe, which was audibly difficult for her because of her broken nose. Dan could have made it easier by removing the gag, but he preferred to make things easier for himself by forcing her to keep quiet. She would die one way or another, for he had no intention of removing the gag again. Not today and not in a week, if it took that long. She urgently needed water to survive. But she wouldn't get any. It was ridiculously easy. And could you even talk about murder? Perhaps denial of assistance, but that was all, right?

Dan watched her ribcage rise and fall under the bloody sweatshirt, although he knew he shouldn't do that. Was she asleep or unconscious? She'd fought like a tiger and in the end had actually crawled to the door that Dan had left open. Before she could reach the hallway, however, he pulled her back into the bedroom by her legs. She was completely out of breath from the hours of effort. The worm-like vein on her forehead throbbed every second. If you struggled so hard, you got thirsty above all. Dan didn't want to know how badly it was burning inside her by now. She should have kept calm, then maybe she'd live a little longer. But she'd fallen asleep or fainted after a

150

short time and some angry glances. Since then she hadn't made a sound.

That was okay with Dan.

It was easier that way.

Nevertheless, he squatted here and stared at her.

That wasn't good, because it brought back memories.

Memories of supermarket parking lots, of kisses and touches. Memories of whispered words and delicate laughter. Memories of a round pregnant belly and invisible feet bulging against it from the inside. Dan had kissed this belly so many times. He still knew exactly how plump and warm it had felt. Sometimes he'd stuck his tongue in the belly button, and Kate had giggled because it tickled. Selina had painted hearts and a sun on that belly with watercolors. When Leila was born, Dan held his little girl in his arms …

Sometimes love was so overwhelming that you wanted to push it away before it went too deep because you knew you would lose it sooner or later. It could be a mistake to let feelings have an all-too-unfiltered effect on you. But what was worth a life that you couldn't even enjoy when it was really enjoyable?

Dan sighed and got on his feet. It was better not to look at Kate any longer. He also had something to do. His mother would be on pins and needles because he hadn't called for so long. Kate had called her parents last night and given the first all-clear. But had Nora received it too? Of course she worried about everything, and it was important that he calmed her down before she got the stupid idea to show up here, which she was quite capable of doing. She would have done so long ago if she hadn't been so stuck in her job. When he'd moved in at her house with Selina, Dan had built an intimate relationship with his mother, even though it had been different during his teenage years. He knew she had a hard time because of their move, especially because of Selina, who was like a daughter to her. If she hadn't heard from them for so long, she would quickly become nervous.

And she'd know something was wrong.

Of course, even in her worst dreams, she wouldn't know what it really was, but the restlessness she felt could be enough to make her come here as soon as she had the chance. And how would she react if she knew what Selina had done? What he'd done!

Who would she believe?

Dan knew the answer without having to think much, and it was definitely not in his favor. Nora had always been against Selina sleeping in his bed. Even though at that time she probably only cared about the girl's independence.

Never mind.

Now he had to calm the waves the best he could. To inform Nora or even hope for her help would have been pointless. That was clear. All he could do was keep her from coming here in the near future. For she'd find more than just a disturbed father-daughter relationship as soon as she set her foot over that threshold.

Dan went to the living room, which had seen better times, grabbed a half-empty can of beer (he had to get supplies urgently, or it would be unbearable), emptied it in one go, and took his cell phone from the coffee table, where it had been plugged into the charger for days. He wasn't sure if he'd reach his mother or if she was working, but either way she'd see that he'd called, and that was better than nothing.

Nora answered on the second ring. She sounded exhausted.

"Hello, Mom."

"Dan! How are you?"

"I … everything's fine so far … Did you … am I disturbing you?"

"No, not at all," Nora said quickly. "I'm on my break."

"Ah, okay. Well, what I wanted to say—"

"Kate's back with you now, right? Her parents told me last night."

Actually, that had to be expected. Dan sighed and rubbed his unshaven cheeks. "Yes, exactly. Kate's here and … I'm happy about that … it helps me a lot …"

"How's Selina?"

Dan had to swallow a lump in his throat before he could speak again. "Oh, she's okay."

"But that doesn't sound very convincing," his mother objected.

She knew him and noticed everything.

"Well, what do you want to hear, Mom? We're still all pretty messed up, but we're getting along. It's good that Kate is back," Dan said lamely.

"Is she going to school?"

"Who?"

"Selina, of course."

"Oh … yeah, sure, she's been going to school all the time."

"And you?"

"What do you mean?"

"When are you going back to work?"

Dan sighed. Work? Since Leila was dead and Selina had turned into a sex-addicted vamp, he didn't care about his job.

"I … I haven't thought about it yet, Mom."

"Don't they want to know when you'll be back?" she asked.

Dan tried to think. In fact, the two weeks that his boss had given him were long gone. Since then, his cwll phone had rung several times, and surely some mail had arrived. However, he rarely picked up phones, and Selina had taken care of the mail (if at all).

"I'm still on sick leave," he lied.

"Does that mean you've been to the doctor?"

"Uh, yes."

"And what did he say?"

"Not much, Mom. He just put me on sick leave because he thinks I still can't work."

"But I see it differently," Nora replied.

Of course you do, Dan thought grumpily.

"I think it would be good for you to go back to work. You have to go outside again, Dan."

"Right now I don't feel ready, and the doctor agrees with me."

"Oh, what do you expect from a doctor? They all have no idea." Nora played down the issue.

Sure, here comes the same old story again.

"Listen, Mom, I don't have time, I ... I have to go shopping. Now you know that we're fine ..."

"Can I talk to Kate for a second?"

"No, not right now."

"Why not?"

"Because she ... she's sleeping ... she needs to recover from the journey."

"And that's all?" Nora asked suspiciously.

"Yes," Dan said. "What else do you want to hear, Mom? Life isn't a party right now. We try to deal with it somehow. I'll get back to you, okay?"

"I would have loved to come visit, but I only get two days off in a row in the next few weeks, and that time's too short."

Yeah, thank God, Dan thought and inwardly gave a sigh of relief. "That's okay, Mom."

"Are you sure everything's all right so far?"

The woman just wouldn't let go!

"You sound so strange, Dan."

"I … I put some stuff of Leila's away earlier …" This time the lump couldn't be swallowed. Dan burst into tears.

Nora did the same. "I'm so terribly sorry for all this."

Yeah, so am I, Dan thought. "I love you, Mom," he finally whispered. "I'll get back to you."

"I love you too, Dan. Say hello to Selina and Kate."

"I will."

He hung up, stared at dozens of empty beer cans, and cried until he thought he had no more tears.

***

When Selina came home two hours later, he was still sitting there. She put the backpack in the closet and the key on the dresser. Then she came into the living room and looked pitilessly at her father. Dan looked back at her with red eyes. Fucking was probably not an option today. He'd never get a hard-on.

"What about Kate?" Selina asked.

Dan shrugged.

Selina kicked his shinbone. Dan flinched and looked at her in horror. She'd never done anything like this before, but she'd never had such power over him before.

"Answer me!" she hissed.

"Why don't you go check it out yourself? I didn't touch her."

Selina couldn't believe it. What a damn pussy!

"And what now? What will you do with her?"

155

"Did you really think I'd kill her?" Dan shook his head and laughed sadly.

"If you let her go, you'll end up in jail!"

Dan nodded tiredly. "I guess you're right."

"And that's what you want?"

Dan shook his head. He looked terrible. Only a shadow of the once attractive man.

Selina slowly lost her patience. "What the fuck is that all about?"

"I didn't say I'd let her go. I only said I won't touch her."

It slowly dawned on Selina. He just wanted to leave Kate lying there and wait. She'd die on her own. He didn't want to get his hands dirty. Not that they weren't already completely dirty.

What a wanker!

"And I'm supposed to sleep in a room with her all night long until she finally bites the dust—or what do you think?"

Dan shrugged again. "You can sleep in your own room."

"No, that wasn't the plan. I certainly won't sleep in my room while you're with Kate. What if I finish it?"

He looked at her as if she were a stranger. "You should think twice about that, Princess. It might stain your white dress when the truth comes out. They're pretty good these days. They always find out who killed who."

"I can say you forced me," Selina countered.

"Sure you can," Dan agreed.

Selina stared at him. She seemed to think for a moment, then kicked his shin again and turned away in rage.

Dan's leg hurt, but he smiled anyway. He smiled because this pain was good compared to all the others and because this was his first little victory since this nightmare had begun.

That night, Selina slept in her own bed.

Alone.

***

The third night after Kate's arrival, Dan couldn't stand being in the bedroom anymore. The sharp smell of urine emanating from her body became more and more penetrating. She breathed shallowly, and her skin had taken on a brownish tone that looked like parchment. She didn't move anymore, and since yesterday, she didn't whine, either. Dan didn't know what happened to her, but he'd Googled a little and found out the urine smell had something to do with kidney failure. The disgusting dark yellow piss that occasionally seeped out of her matched this diagnosis.

The carpet was completely ruined.

Dan hadn't thought it would get so bad. He should have Googled earlier. Now it was too late. It wouldn't take much longer. From time to time Dan came to the conclusion that his wife was dying. It felt like a fist punch.

But then he could suppress it again.

He finally was okay with the hard-on he got every time his daughter snuggled up to him on the couch (where he slept now).

***

Some people died after three days without water. Others made it almost a week. This depended on the individual's physical condition, but it also depended on where you were. In the Sahara (where it would happen very quickly), somewhere in the mountains, in a crevasse, or in the bedroom of a house on the outskirts of Roanoke, Virginia.

Kate had no idea how good or bad her chances were. But she knew her broken nose and the other injuries Dan had inflicted on her didn't make it any better. She'd fought to free herself but hadn't succeeded.

Dan had tied her up like a damned package!

And then there was this disgusting gag. What was that anyway? A sock? The thing hindered Kate's breathing and made her physical efforts more difficult. If she'd had enough time (and as long as he left the door open, which he usually did), she might still have made it to the stairs or even down to the kitchen where there were many sharp objects. But Kate didn't have the time because Dan was always here.

Almost always.

Once he'd left the house for about an hour (probably to buy booze), but he'd closed the bedroom door—he even locked it.

At night he left the door open, but he no longer slept in the bedroom, but probably on the couch in the living room, where he'd have seen Kate struggling down the stairs like a caterpillar in a cocoon.

Why didn't he sleep in his bed anymore?

Kate had a hunch. He probably couldn't bear to watch her die. Maybe she didn't smell too good either. It hadn't happened deliberately, but she'd noticed that from time to time urine ran out of her bladder. It surely stank miserably, even though Kate couldn't smell it due to her broken nose.

Whatever. She had other problems.

Escape seemed more unrealistic with every passing hour. She'd thought about the window. It was only about

158

four feet away. She could have opened it to scream for help. But not only would she have had to make it to the window and into a standing position, she'd need her hands, which were tied behind her back.

So she had to give up the idea. It was impossible. The duct tape didn't loosen a single inch, no matter how hard she tried. Without a knife or something like that, it would never come loose. Here in the bedroom there were no sharp objects, not even a nail file.

So what else?

The more time passed, the harder it was for her to think about it. Her brain gradually stopped working. In the beginning, she still had gnawing headaches like from a thousand hammer blows. Again and again she tried to spit out the gag, but the more she tried, the deeper it slipped into her throat. Until she gave up because she feared suffocating. Her nose was tight. If she didn't die of dehydration, it would probably be from lack of oxygen.

Just like Leila.

She forced herself not to think about her little daughter or her death. The headaches gradually subsided, but now she seemed to be in a crazy merry-go-round, spinning at breathtaking speed. Kate got nauseous and once again panicked and realized she was going to die.

Right now, when she suffocated on her vomit. She gagged dryly and sucked air through her tense lips—left and right past this cursed gag. Luckily, her stomach was long-since empty and there was nothing to puke. Kate closed her eyes and continued to breathe spasmodically. Behind her eyelids twitched wild flashes. She felt like the two or three times in her life when she'd drunk too much. The dizziness and nausea were similar. Only now also the broken nose and the fact that she was dried up inside.

Kate whimpered desperately. She wanted it to stop. She wanted her mom to wake her up from this nightmare and place a cup of tea in front of her intact nose.

She should have drunk more of that tea.

Now it was too late.

In despair, she tugged on her shackles and tried to turn around. She only got worse. The world tilted from one side to the other. Kate felt like a drunk on a ship in rough seas. She stopped moving and instead tried to concentrate on her breathing. She kept her eyes tightly closed, hoping it would ease the dizziness. It worked.

At some point.

But Kate lost consciousness.

***

On the fourth evening since Kate's return, Selina cooked spaghetti while Dan sat apathetically on the couch, drinking one beer after the other. He'd decided that the booze was only half as bad as long as he stayed with beer. But in the meantime he needed a lot of it to achieve the desired effect. He'd just opened the seventh can. It was a good thing that he'd stocked up yesterday. Selina had asked for a dinner together.

Yes, she'd asked for it.

She could still be nice and sweet. The looks she gave him were unique. When she'd looked at him like that earlier, she'd been his princess again for a moment. Dan would have loved to take her in his arms and beg her to stop. He also would have begged like a dog that she was just his sweet little princess with the charming smile again.

But then she grabbed his crotch and winked at him lasciviously. She was still the calculating, cold-blooded bitch he hated so much. Maybe she'd been that all the time. A bitch, disguised as a princess. But his cock didn't seem to care. Even the slightest touch of those skillful fingers made Dan hard, and his balls tingled expectantly. At the same time, everything inside him cramped and his heart crawled up his throat and got stuck there as a thick lump.

Dan made a whimpering sound that wasn't unlike his wife's death sounds. Tears shot into his eyes.

Selina smiled as she noticed the wetness on his cheeks. She stood on her toes and licked his stubbly skin. "I know that you want it too," she said breathily into his face. "Let it go, Daddy. Stop resisting."

Dan shook his head. He wanted to say something, wanted to contradict, but there was only that whimpering again. Selina closed a hand around his testicles and squeezed them gently. Dan's abdomen twitched uncontrollably. His penis pressed painfully against his pants.

"We both know you want it," Selina whispered in his ear.

She took her hand away, and Dan didn't know whether he should feel relieved or disappointed. Was she right? Was that what he wanted?

No, never! something screamed in Dan's mind.

Suddenly he had to think of Leila, how small, sweet, and innocent she'd been. Selina had taken her away from him, he was sure of that by now. She'd stoop to anything to have him to herself. And now she'd not only made him commit fornication with his (possibly) own flesh and blood, she'd managed to get him to attack his beloved wife, who had perhaps just taken her last breath. Selina had left him no choice.

But wasn't there always a choice?

Dan covered his mouth to muffle the pitiful sounds that made their way out of his throat. He was weak and scared. He was still trying to save his own pathetic ass. If he hadn't been so cowardly, he'd have faced his demons long ago and stopped Selina. She should never have gained so much power over him.

How did she even do that?

Because you're weak!

Would it be better to go to jail if he could save Kate? Maybe it wasn't too late!

"What are you thinking about, Daddy?" Selina wanted to know. "Are you weighing your options?"

Dan didn't answer.

"You're right. It's your decision. I can't stop you when the going gets tough."

Right! Had he ever thought about it?

"Exactly! You can't stop me!" He left Selina and hurried up the stairs.

Hopefully it wasn't too late!

***

The stench of urine was so intense that it made Dan's eyes water. Kate was still tied up and motionless on the floor. It didn't look as if she'd moved since yesterday. A wide, dark patch had spread under her pelvis. Her jeans were soaked. The biting smell almost robbed Dan of his senses. He coughed and choked.

Kate's face had sunken and had taken on an unhealthy yellow-brown complexion. The skin showed wrinkles in places where none had been before. She looked like a corpse in the early stages of decay.

Dan squatted beside her. With a trembling hand he touched one of those flabby cheeks. It felt strangely coarse and dry. And ice cold. Shocked, Dan pulled his hand back.

Was she still breathing?

Horrified, he stared at this withered body, which no longer looked like Kate.

Could it really be?

After only four days?

The horror crept slowly through his body. With a sob he retreated.

Kate was dead.

Just like Leila.

He'd lost one half of his family and the other half was a walking nightmare!

Dan turned around.

There she stood and smiled. The stench didn't seem to bother her.

"See?" she said calmly. "It can't be changed anymore. You have to come to terms with it now. Or you will go to jail for life."

Dan stared at his daughter. He wanted to shout at her, grab her and shake her, bang her head against the wall until she was quiet. Until she was finally silent.

Instead, he just pushed past her, weeping.

He thought of calling his mother. And the police. He didn't care if they believed him, he just wanted to tell the truth so that it was over.

He wanted to beat up his daughter until she eventually came to her senses. Instead, he ran into the bathroom, locked the door, and squeezed himself into the small area between the toilet and the window, slung his arms around his knees, and cried like a child.

***

After Dan locked himself in the bathroom, Selina went into the bedroom and checked if Kate was really dead.

Her once-pretty face had turned into an ugly grimace. And the stench was really bad. Selina wouldn't have believed that dying of thirst could be so ugly. There probably wasn't any lovely way to die … in the end, we became a shadow of ourselves and stank like shit, and that's the way it was.

Too bad about the carpet.

Selina looked at the dead woman and waited to feel something.

Anything.

Her father's suffocated sobbing came through the bathroom door. But he cried more for himself than for his wife. She was sure of that. He'd hate himself for not having stood up to Selina when it was still possible. This hate was just perfect for Selina because it would cost him his last strength. All the sooner, he'd belong to her. He'd give up and see that he had no choice. So his last resistance would break.

Because he was weak.

Just as weak as Selina had suspected. She was proud of her judgment. She'd assumed that she knew her father inside out, and she'd been right. After all, it could have been a complete flop. Then she might already be sitting in some institution and Kate would be in the best of health. Dan alone had that in his hand. But he hadn't seen his chance. And now there was a dead person who had his fluids on her body. Now it wasn't just abuse anymore. Dan would be charged with murder. He knew that as well as she did. And it wouldn't be easy to save him from such a sentence. After all, it was only a matter of time before someone would miss Kate. And everyone knew she was here. They didn't have too much time to make the body disappear and come up with a plausible story.

Selina decided to leave her father alone for that one night. But by tomorrow at the latest a plan had to be drawn up. She'd use the weekend to get things in line here. Somebody had to do it.

She probably couldn't hope for Daddy.

And now I've cooked for nothing, Selina thought grumpily. She left the bedroom and closed the door without looking around. He could clean up the dirt on his own. She had no intention of getting her fingers dirty. Well, maybe she'd give him a hand if he asked her to. Selina smiled at the idea. She liked it when her father begged. She liked to see him desperate and helpless. Not because she hated him and wished him bad things (quite the opposite), but simply because she liked to have him on his knees in front of her—and not just figuratively.

So tonight she'd eat alone in front of the TV. Tomorrow Dan would join her again. She'd make sure.

***

After four days without water, Kate Meller died of acute organ failure. Her last thoughts, before she lost consciousness, were of her mother and her little daughter Leila, who had walked this path before her. That was good, because therefore she carried no hatred but only love into the eternal light. She'd had no time and no strength to continue thinking about the motives of her husband, who had apparently lost his mind from one day to the next. She died without ever knowing what had really happened between Dan and Selina.

Maybe it was better that way.

Maybe not.

Who could know?

Kate Meller was twenty-nine years old. She died on a sunny Friday in October. She'd been a beautiful and kind young woman, but her death was ugly and smelled of shit.

That was one of the truths you had to live with.

***

Dan spent the night on the bathmat. On Saturday morning he awoke with stabbing back pain from a sleep full of confused dreams. He sat up moaning and stretched his stiff limbs. There was no part of his body that didn't hurt. Slowly he got on his feet and shuffled to the sink. He drank from the tap and splashed cold water in his face. The look in the mirror revealed the ugly truth. He was as white as a sheet, with swollen eyes and chapped lips. The dark stubble looked like ugly marks on his pale skin. Dan sighed and turned away from the mirror. He wanted to cry, but his burning eyes didn't have a drop left. That made him think of poor Kate.

Was she still in the bedroom?

Of course.

Selina certainly hadn't taken her away. When he thought about what was still ahead of him today, Dan would have loved to scream loudly. But only a hoarse cawing came out of his throat.

It wouldn't have helped anyway.

His watch told him it was eight o'clock in the morning. Maybe he was lucky and Selina was still asleep. In former times (until a few weeks ago) she'd always been a late riser. But back then she'd also been a normal girl who was interested in boys her age and went shopping with her friends.

Or was that just the Selina he wanted to see?

How much of it had been her and how much only a guise? She'd probably known exactly how she needed to behave so everyone would see in her what they wanted. She'd known it was important to mime the perfect daughter on the outside before she finally revealed her true face to her father.

So no one would believe him.

Even his own wife had died believing he was a sick son of a bitch.

So far Selina had probably achieved everything she'd intended. And if he wanted to take that away from her, he'd first have to rat himself out.

Dan didn't want to think about it now.

He would have liked to stay here in the bathroom, just to avoid his daughter, but a thirst was burning in his throat that had to be quenched as quickly as possible.

So Dan went downstairs to drink the first beer of the day. On the way, he passed the bedroom door without even paying attention to it.

***

An hour later Dan was sitting at the kitchen table sipping his third beer.

"We have to talk," Selina said. She stood in her bathrobe and slippers at the counter and made coffee.

The smell was as bad in reality as it was in Dan's head. He couldn't remember Selina having drank coffee or making it before. Did she do this on purpose? Did she know how much the smell disgusted him?

"About what?" he asked.

"About Kate. What we'll do with her. Her parents will soon wonder why they won't hear from her again. And then they'll come here."

Dan shrugged in resignation. He wanted to go back to the bathroom and lock out this crazy reality.

"This is about your ass, Dad. Don't forget that!"

He laughed miserably. "How could I?"

"I was thinking that I could write her parents a message from her cell phone, telling them that everything is okay, but we just need a lot of time for ourselves. Later we can say there was a dispute and Kate went away. We can say we thought she was going back to Tennessee. Something might have happened to her on the way there. Do you understand?"

Dan nodded. There were many things he didn't understand, and he didn't want to understand them. Only one insight made its way into his alcohol dazed brain. His daughter was a psychopath, hardened like a serial killer.

"But it's your decision," Selina reminded him. "We can leave her up there until somebody comes and finds her. But you know who owns your ass then."

Dan sighed. He still couldn't believe it was his girl who bawled him out. But she was right; it was his decision. That was the worst part of it.

"That seems to have already been decided," he said quietly.

Selina nodded. The coffee was ready. She poured some into the cup that she placed in front of him.

"No, thanks," said Dan.

"You'll need it," Selina replied. "I know what we have to do, but you'll have to do most of it. So you can't afford being totally drunk."

"I'm the drinker you wanted," Dan sneered. Yes, he was a drinker. A goddamn loser!

So what?

Selina shoved the cup toward him. The steaming black brew looked like death, and it smelled the same … and it would taste like that.

"You need your brain, Dad. At least for today."

Dan put the beer away and grabbed the cup. His stomach contracted.

"Do you want milk or sugar?" Selina asked. She sounded satisfied.

Dan shook his head. Then he closed his eyes and took the first sip. The warmth in his stomach felt surprisingly good. Maybe it wasn't always wrong to listen to his daughter.

**

This morning, Stefanie Krueger received the first message from her dead daughter.

Hi, Mom! I just wanted to let you know that everything's okay. Now we pick up the broken pieces together, and of course it takes time. I'll get back to you. Love also to Dad.

She pondered over this for a while and frowned. It wasn't like her daughter to just send a message when she could call. On the other hand, this wasn't a normal situation, so she decided to leave it at that. It was important that the little reunited family somehow managed to cope with this tragedy together. She didn't want to get in the way again, like she'd done too often in the past. Stefanie knew exactly how much Kate hated it. She was now an adult and a mother herself. It was important for Stefanie to accept that. Bill would say the same to her.

So she clenched her teeth and held her feet still, as hard as it was for her, and wrote back, *All right, my dear. I wish you much strength and look forward to hearing from you again soon.*

Greetings also to Dan and Selina. See you soon! PS: You can contact me at any time. Love, Mom.

The blue checkmark indicating that the message had been read appeared instantly, but there was no further response.

Stefanie hadn't expected one anyway.

***

"Best regards from Kate's mom," Selina said.

Dan turned to her. He was naked from the waist up, and on his skin shimmered a mixture of sweat and blood. The hand in which he held the bloody butcher knife pounded painfully. Tomorrow he'd hardly be able to move his fingers.

"You think that's funny?" he asked and gulped. His throat was burning from the stomach acid that had come up along with the beer and coffee when he'd started working on Kate's corpse with the ax. The worst thing was when the blade hit a bone and the vibration shot through his body. He was done with her arms by now; her legs were next, and he didn't want to think about her head.

***

Selina looked at Dan's muscular torso with fascination. He was sexy—so sweaty and full of blood. She would have liked to make love to him right here and now on the bloody tile floor, but that had to wait. The mess had to be cleaned first. Kate's cut off arms, which Dan had placed next to the bathtub, looked disgusting. Later he'd wrap them in plastic and put them in garbage bags. The metallic smell of blood was in the air, mixed with the sour aroma of the stomach contents that Dan had puked on the bathroom floor.

He was a wimp, but that's why she loved him.

Cutting up the corpse had been Selina's idea, and it made her mighty proud to watch him do it. Blood dripped from the blade of the knife to the floor. Selina noticed flaps of skin sticking to it. She was curious to see what it would look like when her head was cut off.

This is biology class to my taste, Mrs. Pauls!

"Go ahead. I'll watch a while."

Dan looked as if he'd rather tear off her head than Kate's, but after a short hesitation he turned wordlessly back to the corpse he'd previously heaved into the bathtub without Selina's help.

Now for the legs.

Selina watched with interest as her father struggled to cut up the body. Of course he wasn't a butcher and had never learned how to handle a big piece of meat. He cut, chopped, and tugged until the bathroom looked like a charnel house. She wanted to help him clean it. Anything else would have been unfair. Besides, he shouldn't ruin himself completely—she still needed him. Kate had had long legs, which Dan now had to cut through at the knee joint so they would fit in the garbage bag. The sound of breaking bones sent a shiver down Selina's spine.

Kate was now just a torso with a head. She didn't look like Kate anymore, and not like a woman, certainly not a human being. Dan had undressed her before he'd started to cut her up, and her naked breasts looked strangely intact and perfect, as if they didn't belong to her at all. They were beautiful breasts. A bit small, but very well shaped. When Dan briefly turned away to catch his breath, Selina curiously touched one of the nipples.

It was hard and cold as ice.

"What are you doing?" Dan shouted at her.

"I just wanted to know what that feels like."

"You're welcome to go on if you're so interested," he said and offered her the bloody hatchet in his trembling hand.

Selina shook her head. "No, that's your job."

"Then get out of the way." He lifted the ax and let it crash down on Kate's neck. Selina stepped back in disgust as she got a few splashes of dead Kate in her face.

"Are you crazy?" she complained, but Dan didn't listen. He'd struck a deep notch in Kate's slender neck, which he now worked on until it cracked because he'd reached the spine.

Selina sat on the closed toilet lid and wiped her face with toilet paper. They could have avoided the mess if that stupid bitch hadn't come back here. Selina's rage mixed with nausea. She'd definitely imagined the weekend differently.

When Dan finally lifted Kate's head by the hair out of the tub, Selina stared at it with a mixture of fascination and disgust. Torn tendons hung from the open neck, resembling bloody tentacles. Fortunately, the eyes were closed. Dan put the head with the other body parts. He seemed emotionless. Probably he was in shock. As long as he was still functioning, Selina didn't care. Now all that was left was a bloody torso with shredded stumps. Selina took a look at Kate's hairless vagina, which could also have belonged to a child.

"Who would you rather fuck tonight?" she asked dreamily.

Dan's face awakened to new life. He looked at her aghast. "What?"

"If you had to decide, would you fuck your daughter or the dead pussy of your wife?"

172

"Why are you asking me that?"

Selina stood up and came to him. She touched his stiff member, which was clearly visible under the fabric of his pants. "Because you have a boner, Daddy," she said with a smile. "All the time."

***

A day that stank of copper and coffee slowly continued. For Dan it felt like he was wading through thick jelly. The things he'd done were so cruel that he couldn't put them into words. It was important to turn off all thoughts and feelings. The numbness in his mind, which was now gradually taking possession of his body, was a welcome gift. The initial nausea caused by the stench of blood and the sound of shattering bones eventually subsided. Dan now saw no more Kate in front of him. He didn't see a human, not even a corpse. What he saw was nothing more than a pile of meat, bones, and bits of tissue that had to be packed and disposed of. The smells and the splashing blood didn't matter, and the cracking of the bones grew quieter with time. It was just a job to concentrate on to get done as quickly as possible.

When Selina made him aware of his erection, it didn't matter to Dan. He hadn't noticed that he was hard. Had he thought about it, it would probably have scared him, but he didn't have time to think.

He didn't care.

It didn't change anything about the facts.

Perhaps it came from the superhuman effort and the panic to make some mistake. Sometimes the body just went crazy.

Just like the mind.

It was no big deal as long as it didn't keep him from his "work." He ignored Selina's allusion with a shrug and just went on.

She left the bathroom but returned a short time later with rubber gloves, which Kate had worn for cleaning, and helped Dan packing up the dismembered body.

Head and limbs were soon stowed away and hopefully packed somewhat airtight.

The torso still remained.

Dan and Selina looked at it silently for a while and probably both thought the same thing.

Finally Dan said quietly, "I don't want to hack this up." And he thought, *There's guts in there. Feet of intestines and her heart. I can't do that.*

Selina nodded slowly. This time she seemed to have sympathy. "But we won't get it in the freezer like this."

Dan hmmed and ran his hand over his face, leaving a slimy trail of blood.

They had decided to store the body parts in the freezer in the cellar for the time being, only to drop them off somewhere later on the route from here to Tennessee. Dan also wanted to park Kate's car with her luggage somewhere there. If parts of her body were found, it would look as if she'd been assaulted and murdered on the way home. Maybe from a mentally ill hitchhiker. There were so many possibilities. The world was bad, and terrible things happened every day, committed by evil people.

But how exactly they wanted to do all this was still not clear. After all, Selina couldn't even drive a car to help him get rid of the vehicle. And even if Dan taught her, it would still be much too risky. If the cops stopped her and she couldn't show a license, they'd be fucked. No, wrong. He alone would be fucked. Because Selina was only a victim, young and innocent, helpless at the mercy of her crazy father.

But Dan had to think of something very soon, because Kate's car was outside the house. Clear proof that she was here. It screamed of his guilt.

Since Kate's torso was too big for the freezer, they decided to put it in garbage bags as well and then put it in an old suitcase where it just fit. Dan then wanted to put it in the car with the rest of the luggage.

When he lifted the blood-soaked rest of the human remains, a stinking gush of feces fell into the tub. Selina screamed in shock and pressed one hand over her mouth. The stench was overwhelming. Dan didn't even twitch. He'd long since gone beyond that point. The fact that he was now not only covered with blood, but also with shit, didn't bother him.

Not anymore.

He just went on.

His daughter had shown him how.

***

Despite Selina's help, the cleaning continued until late in the evening. At least the bathroom was easy to clean.

The bedroom turned out to be more difficult. The carpet couldn't be saved. Dan would have to tear it out and replace it. In order to be able to use the room until then, he treated the urine and bloodstains with bleach. That didn't make the carpet more beautiful, but it helped with the stench. Dan then spread out newspapers and finally laid the large fur carpet from Selina's room over it. The result was impressive, as long as nobody thought of lifting the rug. But who would do that? Nobody was here but them. A house search by the police would of course be an absolute disaster. That's why the car had to be removed.

As quickly as possible!

After having stowed Kate's things (as well as her torso) in the car and the rest of her body in the freezer, Dan took a shower. Selina cooked in the meantime. And although Dan never thought it possible, he ate two huge portions of pasta and drank a whole bottle of wine. Rarely had he been so hungry. Selina only ate a small portion and drank a glass of milk, but she watched happily as her dad shoved one bite after the other into his mouth and washed it down with plenty of wine.

He'd finally broken his chains.

FAMILY TIES

Two days after her daughter's last message, Stefanie couldn't bear it any longer. No matter what her husband said and no matter if Kate would be annoyed, she had a bad feeling and just had to know how she was doing. She called her daughter but only reached voice mail. So she tried the Mellers at home.

No one answered.

At last she dialed Dan's cell phone number.

Without success.

It was Monday morning, and Selina would be at school, so Stefanie didn't call her. Finally, she wrote a message to her daughter asking her to call back soon. This time the checkmarks didn't turn blue to indicate that Kate had read the message. According to WhatsApp, the last time she was online was Saturday, when she'd written the last message.

Stefanie found that strange, even though it was probably normal under these circumstances that Kate wasn't on her cell phone all the time. She now needed time for herself and her family. Stefanie understood that. Nevertheless, she was worried. She was used to talking to her daughter regularly, especially after her terrible tragedy. They had to stick together and give each other strength.

Why did Kate want to go through this on her own with Dan and Selina when it also concerned them as grandparents? Stefanie missed the little girl so much! And she couldn't talk to Bill. He tried to downplay the whole thing and tried to suppress it as much as possible. Most men were probably like that.

And Dan? Did he also suppress it?

Wouldn't it be important for Kate to talk to her mother in this situation?

What if all this overstrained her? What if Dan had something against Kate involving her parents, but she lacked the strength to assert herself?

Stefanie waited the whole day for an answer, which unfortunately didn't come. When Bill came home that evening, she confronted him. He couldn't even take off his uniform jacket.

"Give her time, honey," he said, trying to soothe her.

"I would if I knew everything was all right. But she doesn't answer at all, and that's just not like her."

"Didn't she answer on Saturday?"

"It's Monday now," Stefanie replied. "She knows I'm worried."

"Maybe she just has too much on her mind right now."

"If she doesn't answer by tomorrow, we have to do something."

Bill sighed and slipped out of his jacket. "Okay, we will. Is there anything to eat?" He took a doubtful look at the empty dining table. The kitchen behind it was dark.

"How can you think of eating now?" Stefanie demanded.

Yes, how could Bill?

***

On Tuesday evening Selina went back to her room after dinner. It was time to do something for school again. Slowly moving up was in danger. So she tried to get French vocabulary into her head for an hour, which worked out quite well. Only the grammar was a problem. Kate had helped her sometimes, but Kate didn't exist anymore. She'd dissolved into her components, so to speak. The thought didn't do much with Selina, only the memory of the feces splashing around caused a tiny shiver in her body.

So far she hadn't known how disgusting a dead person could be. It had been relatively harmless with little Leila. Of course nobody had hacked her to pieces, and she'd worn diapers that discreetly absorbed her last bowel movements.

Whatever.

Anyway, in the future, she'd have to deal with French alone, because her father couldn't tell a baguette from a croissant.

After she'd finished—or her head was about to burst—Selina went downstairs to get a Coke. Dan sat on the couch holding Kate's cell phone. It should have been in her car by now.

"Kate's mother is getting nervous," he said, hearing her enter the room. "We have to get rid of the car."

"Do you have an idea?"

Dan sighed. "I'll do it tonight."

"Alone?"

He nodded.

"How will you come back?"

"Hitchhike." He didn't sound convinced.

"What if someone remembers you?"

"I guess I'll have to take that risk. Or do you have a better idea?"

She didn't. Everything would have been so easy if she'd gotten her damn driver's license early on. She wanted to wait until she saved enough money to buy a car. Now she regretted her decision.

"I'll send Stefanie another message that Kate's leaving tonight. She can't stand it here in the house any longer. Too many memories."

Selina smiled. "That's good, Daddy."

"You know I don't like doing that. I just have no other choice."

Selina was still smiling. "Sure."

***

Stefanie shot up when her cell phone beeped. She grabbed it, and Bill, sitting next to her on the couch, looked at her with big eyes.

"It's her," she said as she opened the message with trembling fingers.

Hey, Mom. I tried, but I'm afraid I can't make it. I can't stay here. It hurts too much. That's why I'm coming back. I'm leaving tonight. See you soon.

Stefanie turned to her husband. "I have to call her! That's far too dangerous!"

Kate was still online. That was the chance! Stefanie pressed the call symbol and waited with a beating heart.

Nothing happened.

Kate didn't answer.

"Why does she do that?" With resignation, she let the phone sink.

Bill sighed. "Maybe she just doesn't feel like talking."

At that moment the phone beeped again.

I have to pack now. We'll talk when I'm home. Don't worry.

Stefanie read the message aloud and immediately tried to call Kate again, but she didn't answer this time either.

"Damn!"

"Then let her," he said. "At least she's coming home."

180

"But in the middle of the night? That's not normal! Sounds like a rash decision."

"What do you want to do, Stef? If she doesn't want to talk on the phone, she just doesn't want to."

"It seems strange." Stefanie was close to tears. "Don't you think?"

"Yes." He put his arm around her shoulder. "But she's going through a lot right now, honey. That can change a person. The main thing is that she's coming home. Then we can take care of her again."

"I'm just so afraid for her," Stefanie sobbed.

"I know. But nothing will happen to her, honey, I promise. And by this time tomorrow she'll be sitting with us again."

Stefanie nodded, but in her head an ugly voice told her she wouldn't see her daughter again.

***

It was just before midnight when Dan closed the trunk of the VW Golf while he took one last look around the dark neighborhood. If anyone saw him now, it could destroy him later.

But that couldn't be changed.

He finally had to take action!

He hadn't had a choice for a long time. His wife and everything she'd had with her were now in the small car. Dan was glad he'd packed the body parts so well. This made it easier for him to imagine that there was something other than a dead person in the parcels.

A dead person.

Kate!

Only the torso had caused him trouble. The suitcase, which had become a coffin, didn't fit in the trunk, so Dan was forced to place it on the back seat. A circumstance that caused a certain uneasiness in him. He would have preferred to have everything in the trunk.

Out of sight, out of mind.

Furthermore, he would have had a better feeling in case of a police check. At least he hadn't drank alcohol since this afternoon, which had anything but a positive effect on his condition. But no matter, he finally had to go. Every second this car stood in the driveway was one too many.

Dan went back inside one more time. Everything was quiet. Selina was probably sleeping. He didn't want to wake her. He stuffed his wallet into his back pocket and grabbed his cell phone and a jacket. The car was already in the ignition. Dan wanted to hurry out of the house when something came to his mind. He ran back into the living room and put Kate's cell phone in his jacket. As soon as she was missing, she'd be tracked on this device.

When he finally sat in the car and adjusted the seat, he breathed deeply and closed his eyes for a moment. Dan breathed out, shivering. It smelled of the living Kate, not of the dead one, even if he'd have preferred the latter at the moment. With a sigh he switched on the radio and drove off.

***

According to the GPS, Dan first had to drive toward the city to get to I81 south. At this time of night this wasn't a big problem. There was hardly any traffic. His plan was to drive on the 81 toward Knoxville until the opportunity seemed favorable to leave the interstate and continue on a quieter country road. Later, when the GPS data was analyzed, one would wonder why she'd left the highway in the middle of the night, and no one would know. But Dan thought there might still be some explanations. Maybe Kate was afraid that the monotonous ride on the interstate might make her too tired. Maybe she wanted to stretch her legs and didn't feel like having a rest. Maybe (and this version would probably be the most plausible) there was already a stranger in the car at that time, who had either persuaded her or forced her to leave the interstate. This stranger could have been picked up by Kate at one of the rest stops Dan had already passed—he'd also driven into two of them so that everything seemed as realistic as possible.

Would Kate have picked up a hitchhiker?

The answer was definitely no. Her parents would see it that way, and so would he. But what if she'd been so desperate that both her caution and her knowledge of human nature had let her down? Perhaps that hitchhiker had also made a particularly likeable impression and Kate was hoping for some company. After all, it was a long ride. Maybe it had been a woman who seemed reasonably trustworthy. Or a woman had been there to make the perpetrator seem more harmless to his potential victims.

Whatever Kate's motives were, and whoever was with her, after a little more than three hours of driving, she left the interstate near Johnson City, Tennessee, and from there moved southeast on a low-traffic country road.

Into the woods.

***

Of course it wasn't Kate but Dan driving the car. Nevertheless, she was there. The biggest part of her was very close to him and was shaken up on the back seat when he finally left the paved road.

183

Dan had no idea where he was. He only saw darkness and trees. He couldn't leave the car here, even if he wanted to, because he couldn't walk around in this godforsaken area. He'd get lost and either die or get caught. Although he had his cell phone for orientation, the GPS signal wasn't the best out here, and at some point the battery would fail.

However, Dan stopped and got out of the car. It was time to get rid of unnecessary ballast. He wiped Kate's cell phone with a cloth he'd found in the car and dropped it onto the hard asphalt. Those things were pretty solid these days, and there wasn't even a crack in the display. But that changed when Dan stomped on it. The crunching of splintering plastic was satisfying. In the beam of the headlights Dan continued until there wasn't much left. Then he picked up the remains with the cloth and buried them at the foot of a large fir tree. Maybe they would find the device, but that wasn't important anymore.

Dan went back to the car. What about the GPS? Should he also destroy it? They'd be able to track Kate's tracks on the smartphone up to here anyway, so fuck it.

Dan wiped off the GPS and then took it out of the holder. This time he didn't bother to smash it before burying it somewhere else in the ground.

When he was done, he looked up at the stars flashing in the usual cold and unemotional manner. They didn't care what the people did down here. They watched everything without batting an eyelid.

Dan wiped cold sweat off his forehead and got into the car.

He found his way back to the interstate without a GPS. There he drove south for another twenty minutes before taking the next exit. There were lots of woods and small roads out here, but it was almost four o'clock in the morning. Soon dawn would set in. There wasn't much time left.

Again he drove into the forest on a dirt road, and when he stopped this time, there was much more to unload. Fortunately, Selina had reminded him to take rubber gloves, a shovel, and a flashlight.

Dan pulled the heavy garbage bags out of the trunk and walked as far into the undergrowth as he dared. After all, it would be a blatant irony of fate if he didn't find his way back to the car in the end or was attacked by an evil person.

He didn't dig too deep. After all, nothing better could happen than to make some animals happy with Kate's remains.

Finally, only the luggage and the suitcase with the torso were still in the car.

For another twenty minutes he drove on the dirt road. Meanwhile he regretted that he'd not brought anything to drink. His throat burned like fire, but there was no time for a break.

He stopped a third time and dragged the suitcase into the forest. When he'd finished burying it, the sun rose.

Dan trudged back to the car. Every muscle in his body hurt, and his throat was like filled with sawdust. He could hardly swallow. In the inside mirror he stared at his sweaty face. His cheeks and forehead were covered with dirt, which he wiped away with the back of his hand.

And now?

It was almost daylight, he was in the middle of nowhere, and he still hadn't gotten rid of the car. Had he overestimated himself? He remembered seeing a small lake just before he'd turned onto the dirt road. The interstate wasn't far from there.

So, let's go!

He sighed. He was completely overtired and could hardly think clearly. The noises from the radio got on his nerves so much that he turned it off.

He drove back the road until he had the lake in front of him, which was basically nothing more than an oversized pond overgrown with reeds. By now it was almost six. But who without a skeleton in the closet would be hanging around at this time of day in this wasteland?

Dan made sure that he had his cell phone and wallet with him, then set the automatic gear to drive and got out of the car. With the driver's door open, it rolled into the water by itself.

Dan watched the rear lights slowly sink into the mud. Thin wafts of mist hung over the surface of the water. It only took a few minutes for the car to disappear. A few last bubbles came up, and then it was as if nothing had ever happened.

As if there had never been Kate and him.

No Leila.

No happiness.

He rubbed his frozen hands. It had been stupid to go on this trip with only a light jacket. Even more stupid was the fact that he was at least 250 miles from home. How was he supposed to get away from here?

You wanted to be extra smart, but maybe in the end you were just extra stupid.

Desperate, he looked around. There was nothing here but trees, fog, and swamp. The road was empty, and in the gray twilight it seemed more desolate than death itself. Dan's body hurt. After all the exertion, he just wanted to go to bed and longed for something to drink.

A cup of tea would be great now.

Dan didn't really like tea. Today he'd drink it down his dry throat without batting an eye. Hopefully the sun would soon come out and warm his frozen limbs.

How he'd have liked to sit down, right here and now, just to rest a little. But the wet grass seemed uninviting. With sagging shoulders he dragged himself back to the road. The asphalt was wet and cold as well, but he sat anyway and thought about calling the cops. Then all the effort would have been in vain, but it would finally be over.

Yeah, he just wanted it to be over.

He didn't want to have to worry anymore and didn't want to be afraid anymore. What awaited him at home? A psychotic daughter who wanted to swallow his life like a vicious shark. She'd already swallowed most of it and kept the rest for later. There were only two ways to escape: death or jail.

Dan didn't feel able to weigh these options. He wanted to just lie down on the road and let fate take its course. Instead, he forced himself to pull his cell phone out of his pocket. He had seven new messages, all from Selina. The first had been sent two hours ago. He was probably not the only one with a sleepless night. Selina wanted to know where he was. Whether everything had gone well. Whether it was already done. When he'd be back.

With stiff fingers he typed, *I'm still on my way. Could take a while. Please go to school. See you later.*

He placed the phone on the road and pondered. He could walk back to the interstate and hope somebody took pity on him. Maybe a lonely trucker. He had to hope for a little bit of luck. Or inspiration, a divine coincidence! Something. The devil couldn't always shit on the same spot, damn it!

His plan wasn't well-developed. There was a state of emergency in his brain. Dan wouldn't dare stand on the road with his thumb out. He certainly looked frightening. And even if he'd gotten rid of all the dirt somehow, there would still be his guilt, which certainly stood out on his face like hazard lights.

But what else?

Kate's parents would eagerly await her arrival. How long would it take for them to call the police if Kate didn't show up and they didn't reach anyone? The police would want to question him first. Maybe in the next few hours. What if he wasn't home, his car sitting in the garage?

How would he explain that?

Dan sighed. This damn cold crept through his body like a bad omen.

What could he do? If he wasn't back in Roanoke in the next few hours, it meant his end.

Finally, Dan grabbed his cell and did what probably everyone did when the shit hit the fan: he called his mother.

***

Nora answered on the second ring. She'd probably already been awake.

"Danny? What …?"

Dan didn't make anything up. This was his mother, and he just let himself fall. "Mom? I need your help." He swallowed the tears. "Urgently."

"What's the matter?"

"I screwed up … but you can't ask any questions now, please."

There was silence on the other end of the line.

Dan gasped, trembling for air. "You have to pick me up, Mom. Please."

"Pick you up? Where?"

"I'm near the interstate. I'll send the data to your cell phone."

"Dan, I … I don't understand. I have to go to work in a minute."

"It's life and death," Dan cried out. Saliva sprayed from his lips. "I'm really fucking deep in shit, Mom. And I can't get away from here."

Again this silence. It drove him crazy.

"Mom?"

"Dan, I … I can't go to Virginia now … why doesn't Kate pick you up?"

"I'm not in Virginia, I'm in Tennessee. And Kate can't pick me up."

"What? But—"

"Mom, if you ever loved me, you'll stop asking questions. Call in sick and pick me up. Please! I'll explain everything during the ride. Okay?"

Silence. She seemed to struggle for composure. And then: "How far is it?"

"About 125 miles from you."

He thought he heard a sigh. "I'll send you the data and then walk to the off-ramp, okay? Mom? *Okay?*"

"You don't sound good, Dan. What happened?"

"Just pick me up, okay? Then I'll feel better."

"Okay," she finally said. "I'm hanging up now. I'll get back to you when I'm on the road. But it will take some time. This drive isn't a stone's throw."

Dan sighed with relief. "It doesn't matter, Mom. Just drive carefully. The main thing is that you come. Thank you."

She'd already hung up.

After Dan gave her his approximate location, he stayed there for a while. It was miserably cold, and he thought he'd be screwed as soon as the cops suspected him. They certainly had ways and means to analyze this conversation and the GPS data. Then they would find Kate's car and shortly afterward her body parts. He'd then be fucked and would have dragged his mother into it.

***

Nora hardly recognized the picture of misery that she picked up two and a half hours later at a gas station in the no-man's-land east of I-81. Dan wore a jacket that was far too light. He was completely frozen and as white as a sheet. Nora was glad that she'd taken the time to bring coffee in a thermos. She'd also added a good portion of milk and sugar.

With trembling hands, Dan reached for the steaming cup. Nora feared that at any moment he'd pour the hot brew over his pants, which were terribly dirty. But somehow he managed to get the stuff into his mouth instead.

Nora turned the heater up all the way and watched him silently. She had lots of questions but didn't want to overwhelm him. He seemed on the verge of exhaustion, had probably been out all night, for whatever reason.

But she had to know one thing right away. "What about Selina? Is she all right?"

Dan nodded. "She's probably already at school."

"Good. How did you get here?"

Dan looked at her with swollen eyes. The skin underneath was bluish. She knew such rings under his eyes, although not with such intensity. Suddenly a thought came to her mind, and it took her breath away.

"Have you been drinking, Dan? Or drugs …?" It all fit together: the shock and the grief, and now he'd lost his orientation—wherever his car was.

He'd relapsed! Why hadn't she thought of it earlier?

But Dan shook his head.

"Have you been drinking, Dan?" He didn't smell like alcohol, but Nora knew that wasn't necessarily the case. Some alcoholics, for example, only drank vodka because you couldn't smell it. Others prepared themselves so well with mouth spray, chewing gum, and various sweets that nobody noticed anything. But Dan didn't smell like peppermint.

"I've had a few drinks lately, but not last night. I swear it."

She looked him in the eye and believed him. She knew that the smallest drop could trigger a massive relapse, but she didn't want to give him a sermon now.

Instead, she asked, "What happened?"

"I'll tell you, but please let's go now. I need to get home as soon as possible."

"Good," Nora relented. "We'll talk on the way."

***

Stefanie waited until nine in the morning before she called the police. She hadn't been able to reach Kate for hours. Either her battery had run out or her cell phone had been intentionally switched off. Dan seemed to receive Stefanie's messages but didn't respond. When Bill wanted to drive to the military base at seven, she almost went crazy.

"She'll be arriving soon," he said.

But Stefanie felt there was more trouble here than a dead battery. She was convinced her daughter was in danger. So Bill called his superior and explained that he'd be late. A family matter.

Waiting was nerve-racking. If Kate had really set off as she'd written, she should have been here long ago, heavy traffic or not. Bill suggested she might have changed her mind at short notice, but Stefanie couldn't imagine that.

Finally, he could no longer keep her from calling the local police station. The result, however, was extremely sobering. Although Stefanie described the facts in detail, she was referred to this stupid forty-eight-hour rule. Before the expiration of this period, they wouldn't search for missing adults unless there was direct evidence of a crime.

"I understand you, Mrs. Krueger," the idiotic officer on the other end of the line said, "but your daughter's probably just taking a nap somewhere before she goes on, which is very reasonable."

"But she would have contacted me," Stefanie objected again.

"Try to stay calm, please. If your daughter hasn't shown up in forty-eight hours, you can report her missing. But I'm sure everything will be fine by then. Have a nice day."

Click.

You can shove that nice day up your ass, Stefanie thought. She couldn't believe it. Of course, she knew about the forty-eight hours because she often watched crime series, but she never thought it would apply to Kate's case. The whole thing screamed crime!

With a trembling voice she turned to her husband. "They won't do anything for now."

Bill didn't seem particularly surprised.

Stefanie hated him for it!

"And neither should we," he said quietly. "We just have to have a little patience. I don't think she's been driving all night. I'm sure she took a room somewhere."

"And what if not? What if something happened to her?"

"Stef, that—"

"I don't know what you're up to, but I'm going to Virginia."

"What? Are you crazy?" Bill stared at her in bewilderment.

"I need to see what's going on."

"But she's probably long gone, and you'll just miss her," Bill said.

"Maybe. But maybe not. Something happened—after all, she was so strange the whole time. And Dan doesn't answer the phone either. He'll know more."

"None of this makes any sense," Bill complained. "We should stay here in case she comes—"

"You can do that. I can't stand it any longer!"

"I'm not going to let you drive alone—"

"Then come with me. I don't care."

Bill finally gave in. "We need to leave a message in case she comes home in the meantime."

A soft smile flashed over Stefanie's-fear distorted face. "That's a good idea. She knows where the spare key is."

***

Dan had never been good at making up stories, but this time he surprised himself. He knew he had to at least give his mother an explanation so she'd continue to support him. This time his lie was enormous and frighteningly detailed. It was definitely the lie of his life, and he served it up to his mother without batting an eyelid.

Kate had returned, he said, but didn't manage to feel at home again, although Dan and Selina had done everything in their power to make it as easy as possible for her.

He'd removed Leila's things, and Selina tried to distract her from her grief. All without success. Kate withdrew and developed a hatred for the house and everything and everyone. Last night the situation had escalated completely. After a heavy argument, Kate packed her things because she wanted to go back to Tennessee. Dan tried to stop her. He didn't want to let her drive through the night alone. But Kate had been unreachable. Dan saw no other way than to get into the car with her. He assumed she wouldn't leave or at least would return after a short time, but Kate had pretended that he wasn't there and took him to the Tennessee border, where the dispute finally escalated. In the end things got so bad that she started beating him, completely hysterical, until he had no choice but to get out of the car.

Dan told his mother that at first he'd thought Kate would turn around at any moment and come back so he could get back in, but that didn't happen. He didn't see her again and had no idea where she was now, but probably at home with her parents.

"Shall we call them?" Nora asked after he'd finished his story.

Dan shook his head. "I also have to ask you to keep that to yourself. It's better if Kate's parents don't know that I went with her in the first place."

"And why not?"

"I'm afraid it will unnecessarily complicate the whole thing," Dan replied weakly. He had no idea if his mother bought his story. All this certainly didn't seem quite kosher to her, but he'd no other choice.

"I don't understand this," Nora said just as he'd expected. "That doesn't make sense."

Dan nodded. "I know. Not for me either, but Kate was … she hasn't been herself since Leila. I thought it would get better with time, but it's gotten worse."

"Why did you sit in the car with her when you knew Selina would be alone?"

"At that moment Selina was a minor concern, Mom. She's not a child anymore, and she gets along very well on her own."

In the truest sense of the word.

"Do you think so?"

Oh yes, definitely! "I'm completely exhausted. Do you think I can sleep a little?"

Nora smiled weakly. "Yes, of course. Get some rest."

Dan returned the smile with pale lips. "Thank you. I owe you one."

But it wouldn't be good.

***

Dan had only intended to doze a little, but then he fell into a deep and fortunately dreamless sleep. When he woke up, Nora had just driven into his driveway.

They'd really made it!

Groaning, he straightened up in the seat and stretched his back. He had pains, but at least he was warm again and wasn't thirsty anymore. The house looked like always. On the steps to the front door lay old foliage. It hadn't been swept here for a long time, as Kate had already noticed.

"Everything okay?" his mother asked.

He licked his lips and nodded. "Thanks, Mom."

"And what now?"

"We can go inside and eat something," Dan said.

Together they walked to the door. Dan picked the key out of a flower pot. He thanked God that he'd cleaned the house properly before he'd left. Nora would find nothing unusual. Except maybe in the bedroom, but he wasn't planning to take her there. It was okay if she stayed for a few hours or maybe overnight. He owed it to her. She could sleep on the couch. Selina probably wouldn't like that, but he didn't give a shit. It would steal the little bitch's thunder. That only served her right. She'd caused enough damage and it was time to take her down a peg or two before she completely lost touch with reality.

Nora looked around the living room before she sat on the couch. Of course she saw the empty beer bottles, but she remained silent.

"Do you want something to drink?"

"Water, please."

He went into the kitchen. Selina had cleaned up and you could almost think a normal family lived here.

"When will Selina be home from school?" Nora asked when he handed her the glass.

"Around four."

"Then I'll cook us something nice for dinner," Nora said. "Do you have anything here, or do we still have to go to the grocery store first?"

Dan shrugged. "You can check. I'm gonna take a shower, okay?"

It was time to get rid of all that dirt. Once upstairs, Dan locked up the bedroom and took the key to the bathroom. He didn't know whether his mother would come in here, but he wanted to be on the safe side. The room was clean on the surface, but somehow it still stank of piss. And Selina's pink carpet in front of the bed looked pretty out of place. It was literally begging to be lifted. And anyone who saw the stain underneath would know that not only a small mishap had happened here, but a real disaster.

***

Meanwhile, Selina had to suffer the worst school day of her life. As soon as the bus stopped in front of the flat brick building, she regretted that she'd come here today. She should have called in sick and stayed at home. Of course, as a pupil you were not allowed to do this yourself, but she suspected that they would have made an exception for her. She was the walking exception. In any case, it would have been better to stay at home. Here she had to switch off her cell phone and wasn't even allowed to use it during the breaks.

How could she endure that?

She needed to know how Dad was doing.

She needed to know if everything had worked out.

Whether anyone had seen him.

Whether he'd arrived home safe and sound.

Now she regretted that she hadn't stopped him from taking the body parts with him. It would have been safer to leave them in the house and just remove the car. The cops wouldn't get permission to search the house so soon. First there had to be well-founded suspicion. She knew that from television shows. Probably he'd driven much too far.

How would he come back?

Without being seen?

It was almost impossible.

And if the whole thing leaked out … if Dad was arrested … if they could prove the murder of Kate to him … what would become of her?

Her life would go on, but it would only be half as much fun. Sooner or later she'd probably find someone to play with again, but nobody was like Dad.

He was everything to her.

She was a part of him.

His princess!

Nothing would ever be the same without him. Of course she didn't let it show in front of him and pretended she didn't care if he went to jail. But she only did that to control him. Actually she didn't want him to go to prison.

Of course not!

That would be totally counterproductive.

The first two classes were sports. Gymnastics, in which Selina was actually quite good. Only not this morning. She fucked up the first leapfrog and hit her knee, so she spent the rest of the time with a cooling pouch on the bench. When one of the other girls approached her worriedly, Selina snarled at her in such a way that she flinched in shock and from then on observed her only from a distance, while she whispered with the others. Selina didn't care. The time when friends interested her was over.

As soon as the bell sounded, she hobbled to the toilet with her cell phone.

Dad hadn't written and hadn't been online for hours.

The silence drove her crazy!

What if he was sitting in a police station?

Would he tell the truth and take all the blame? Selina didn't believe he'd give her away. Not only because nobody would believe him, but because she was his little girl. Even if at the moment he thought he hated her. Selina was sure that he only hated himself. After all, she was the helpless little child he'd once rescued from the hell of drugs. The little innocent child who couldn't help the junkie mother and the alcoholic father. Deep in his heart, this guilt lay buried forever. He'd never turn against this child. Because she was his flesh and blood, his little princess, and because he knew inside that none of it was her fault. She believed that very strongly.

Nevertheless, the next few hours were like a particularly realistic nightmare. She went to the toilet three times to check her messages, but Dan still hadn't called.

Selina spent her lunch break almost entirely in the girls' room. She wasn't hungry anyway and could drink from the tap. Of course the other girls looked at her skeptically. Who cared? They knew by now that something was wrong with her. She had a free ride, so to speak. So nobody would wonder about her so quickly.

The break was almost over, and Selina was standing in front of one of the sinks to wash her hands for the hundredth time when the vibration of her cell phone made her flinch. With a beating heart she pulled it out of her pants' pocket.

It was him!

"I'm home now. Everything went well. Grandma Nora is here too."

Selina stared at these words as if they were a revelation.

Granny Nora?

Why granny Nora?

Where did she suddenly come from?

Selina put the cell phone and put it away. Although she didn't like the news very much, she suddenly felt better and her heart was beating in time again.

She still had to find out why Nora was there, but it was important that he'd arrived at home seemingly without any problems. The first step in the right direction.

During the remaining three hours Selina almost enjoyed her lessons. She could even give a correct answer and managed to return the smile of a classmate. However, she was the first to jump up and storm out of the classroom this time when the bell sounded at the end of the school day. She even forgot her bruised knee.

***

Stefanie was looking at every oncoming car. It could have been Kate. Each of these cars could be hers. She could be sitting behind any of those steering wheels. Desperate and with weeping eyes, but alive and safe.

That was all that mattered.

But in the end, none of these cars was Kate's little Golf, and no blonde woman was Kate, no matter how much she reminded Stefanie of her in the first moment. Just people. Strangers with whom she had nothing to do and who couldn't give her any comfort. At some point, fear came over Stefanie like an ice-cold avalanche and she began to cry. Bill sat next to her and doggedly grasped the steering wheel. He hadn't expected to see Kate here on the street, but he'd have wished it to come to an end so that his wife could calm down.

But the chances were very bad, because his wife had never been further from normal behavior. She tore her hair and stared at him with shiny eyes.

"What if we never find her, Bill?"

"We'll find her." He started a new attempt to calm her down. "Or she'll find us. But it's been unlikely from the start that we'll meet her here on the road. I'm sure she'll come home while we're away …"

"And how much do you really believe that?" Stefanie asked in a cold voice.

Bill was silent. He didn't know what she wanted to hear. There seemed to be nothing to soothe her. For the felt thousandth time she reached for her smartphone, only not to reach Kate. She also tried Dan and Selina again.

Without success.

"Isn't it strange that none of them is available?" Stefanie wanted to know.

Bill stared at the road. He just thought it was a coincidence. Or they all didn't feel like it, which he could understand somehow.

"We'll definitely know better once we get to Roanoke," Bill finally said. "Maybe Kate's there because she changed her mind in the end."

"But she would have told us," Stefanie objected.

"I don't know. It would be normal for her, but nothing is really normal here at the moment. We have to come to terms with that. And now try to relax a little and stop staring at every car."

Stefanie actually leaned back, but continued to focus on oncoming traffic because her daughter could be sitting in one of these cars …

And because hope died last.

***

When Selina came home, Dan and Nora sat on the couch together and it smelled like food. Selina let her grandmother hug her while she fixed her gaze on Dan.

"It's so good to see you, my darling," Nora said and patted her cheek. "Are you all right? That must have been a shock for you yesterday, too."

Selina gave her father a questioning look. The prick could have at least informed her by WhatsApp. She had no idea what Dan had told his mother. That seemed clear to him as well, since he quickly took the floor.

"Kate actually threw me out of the car, Selina. Would you have thought that? She was completely out of control. Then I had Grandma pick me up. Unfortunately, I don't know where Kate is."

Selina nodded slowly. "Oh … well … then she … just drove on alone?"

What the fuck did you make up, Dad?

Dan nodded. "At first I thought she'd come back, but …" He shook his head.

"Then she probably drove to her parents, didn't she?" Selina suspected. She seemed calm on the outside, but a hurricane raged inside her.

That fucking idiot! What kind of stupid story is this?

Nora agreed. "We suspect so. Dan didn't want to call yet. He's worried that they might somehow blame him."

"But it's not his fault. Kate couldn't be stopped," Selina forced herself to say. The hurricane tore everything down.

How could you call Grandma, Daddy? You shouldn't have done that! Anything but that!

Nora took her in her arms. "Yes, I believe you, muffin. It's a hard time … for all of us."

Again Selina stared at her father while she was lying in her grandmother's embrace. Her gaze spoke volumes, but Dan simply turned away.

***

Shortly after dinner, Nora left them alone. She wanted to take a bath and then go to bed. Selina lent her a pair of sweatpants and a T-shirt. Dan forced herself not to think

202

about what had happened recently in the bathtub. They had cleaned it thoroughly, so everything was fine.

Selina had offered to do the dishes, and Dan, for whom dinner lay like a rock in his stomach, helped her anyway.

As soon as Nora was out of sight, he grabbed a beer and drank it in one go. That was good and helped his stomach.

"Are you a complete moron to let your mother pick you up?"

"I had no choice. It was already daylight. I never would've gotten away unseen."

"Now we have a witness, do you understand?"

"She knows nothing. If necessary, I can also tell the police the story I told her."

"Are you crazy?!" Selina snapped at him. "They won't believe a word you say! This story is so stupid that only your mother can believe it. As soon as it's clear that Kate has disappeared, Nora won't believe it either."

"What should I have done? What—"

At that moment the doorbell rang.

Selina dropped a plate, and it broke at her feet.

"Who can that be?" she whispered, showing an honest feeling since a long time.

Fear!

"No idea," Dan replied, but in his mind's eye he already saw two policemen standing on the doorstep. They would have a lot of questions he couldn't answer, and he'd spend the night in a cell with a horde of stinking petty criminals.

Because it was over.

Because he was fucked.

With or without an alibi.

"Go look," Selina urged.

"You go," Dan wanted to say, but he was already on the move. On legs like rubber, he skulked to the door.

IT CAN ALWAYS GET WORSE

Stefanie and Bill were outside. She wore a gray coat and was unkempt and red-cheeked. He wore his uniform and was narrow-lipped and as pale as a corpse, but he was as formidable as ever.

Dan should have expected it. Stefanie had been trying to reach him all day. Somehow he'd suppressed it in order not to burden himself.

And now the fat was in the fire.

It could always get worse.

He opened his mouth to say something, but Stefanie beat him to it.

"Where is she?"

Dan felt his rubber legs suddenly turn to pudding.

Would he collapse?

With one hand he held on to the door frame, and he would have preferred to slap himself in the face with the other to somehow keep his senses.

"Where's our daughter, Dan?" Bill asked.

"I don't know." He managed to shake his head. That was all. He wasn't prepared for this, and the lie was probably written on his face. Where was Selina? Why didn't she come to clear this shit up herself?

After all, it was her fault!

Everything!

Her damn guilt alone!

"I don't know," Dan repeated lamely. "She left here late last night. I haven't heard from her since. I thought she was with you long ago."

"And why don't you answer the phone?" Stefanie wanted to know.

Dan cleared his throat. "I didn't see you called."

Stefanie looked at her husband. "I don't believe a single word he says."

Bill took one step forward, and Dan instinctively backed away. "You tell us what really happened or we call the police."

"But that's the truth! She left because she didn't want to be here anymore."

"Do you know this house belongs to Kate? Not you," Stefanie snapped.

Dan lowered his gaze. "I know, but she wanted to leave nonetheless. If I have to move out, she has to tell me that herself."

"You wanna get cocky now?" Bill stood threateningly in front of him. He was broad-shouldered and about as tall as Dan. Not the youngest anymore, but in better shape.

Dan wouldn't have liked to mess with him. He'd never attached much importance to fighting. He tried to avoid conflicts or solve them with words (or drown them in alcohol).

But how could he do that now?

"Listen, I don't want to argue." He tried to give in. "You drove here all the way from Tennessee, so come in first. Then we can talk in peace."

"All right." Bill grabbed him by the arm and pushed him back into the house, closely followed by the raging Stefanie.

"Would you please let me go?" Dan wanted to pull his arm out of Bill's grip, but it was too strong.

"I want to know what's going on here. What's really happened between you and Kate? Say it!"

Dan tried to free himself again. Bill actually let go, but at the same time he slapped Dan in the face.

Bill grabbed him by the shoulders and pushed him onto the couch. He bent over him, digging his fingers into his shoulders.

"Let's get things straight, boy!"

Dan stared at him with big eyes.

"What's going on here?" Selina asked.

Finally!

Bill and Stefanie looked in her direction, and Bill let Dan go. Dan used this moment of distraction to jump at his father-in-law and throw him to the ground.

Stefanie gave a throaty scream.

Dan didn't hesitate but punched Bill in the face. Stefanie jumped on his back like a wildcat and clawed at his shoulders. Dan threw himself back to get rid of the raging woman.

Bill's fist hit his temple and made him see stars. Dan landed on his back, breathing heavily. Stefanie sat on his stomach and scratched his face with her long nails.

"What did you do to her, you bastard? What did you do to my Kate?"

Dan could only stop her with a punch to the nose. Bull's-eye. Stefanie remained on her butt, trying with both hands to stop the blood that was splashing out like from a fully opened water pipe.

And the next carpet is ruined, Dan thought incoherently.

He was looking for Selina, but she wasn't there anymore.

Great!

First she got him into trouble and then she just fucked off. He was about to get up when he looked into a black hole. The muzzle of a pistol. Could that be true? This motherfucker actually had a gun with him! Dan lay down and nervously licked his lips. The situation had gotten out of control, and he had no idea how to change things now.

"You tell me right now where my daughter is," Bill gasped.

"I don't know," Dan whined, now close to tears.

"You bastard broke my wife's nose," Bill said and slammed the barrel in his face.

Dan felt his lip burst, and blood ran down his chin. It filled his mouth, which didn't necessarily make speaking any easier. "I only defended myself," he mumbled.

Bill nodded slowly, as if this explanation seemed plausible. Then he kicked Dan between the legs without warning. The pain hit him like a bomb. Dan screamed and curled up. This time it was his blood that defaced the carpet. It felt like his balls were squished. His guts were burning. A second later he felt the cold iron in his neck.

"Are you gonna shoot me now just because I had a dispute with your daughter?" he panted. "Do it! Then Kate loses one more person."

"I only want to know where she is."

"And I can't tell you."

"Get up," Bill commanded.

Dan tried, but he could only crawl across the floor like a toddler, because the pain in his loins was just too much.

"Get up, you damn pussy!"

Dan reached the couch and slowly pulled himself up. He'd just made it to his knees when a shrill scream made him freeze. He turned to Stefanie. She still squatted bleeding on the floor, but now Selina stood behind her and held a big kitchen knife to her throat.

Bill stared at the girl in confusion. "Selina, sweetie …"

"Drop it," Selina said coldly.

"The gun? Okay. But first you have to put the knife down before anyone gets hurt."

"You take the gun away or I'll cut her throat," Selina replied.

Bill shook his head. "I understand that you're excited, baby, but you don't really want to do that."

Stefanie whimpered quietly. She pressed her hands on her nose. Selina grabbed her by the hair and pulled her head back to free her throat. Then she cut into it until it bled.

Stefanie howled like a kicked dog.

"I'm serious," Selina said to Bill. Her voice sounded sinister. Did she now show her true face?

"I'll kill her if you don't put the gun down right now."

Bill spread his arms. "Okay, you win." He slowly squatted. "I put it down. See?" He put the gun on the floor."

Dan forgot his pain for a moment and grabbed the pistol. Stefanie howled as Dan pointed it at her husband.

"Kate's dead," Selina suddenly said.

Stefanie howled even louder. Bill was completely frozen, his face distorted.

"It was inevitable, unfortunately," Selina continued. Calmly and objectively, as if she was giving a lecture on physics. "Just like this."

With all her strength she pulled the blade across Stefanie's unprotected throat. Blood splashed from the gaping wound and speckled Selina's face. Gurgling, Kate's mother tilted forward.

Bill still didn't move.

A Marine in shock.

Who would have thought that?

The blood quickly spread under Stefanie. Her body twitched a few more times, and then she was motionless.

"Oh my God," Bill finally panted. He staggered in Stefanie's direction and fell to his knees in front of her. His pants were soon soaked with blood.

Selina looked at her father, but this time there was no need for any further request. Dan lifted his pistol and aimed at the hairless back of Bill's head. He hadn't fired a gun since his youth. Back then he'd shot squirrels from time to time, but most of the time at empty beer cans and whisky bottles. But shooting was like drinking or cycling. You never unlearned it.

He felt a slight recoil when Bill's skull exploded in a shower of blood and bone. Parts of his brain that reminded him of vomit landed on his dead wife's back.

Selina stared in fascination. Dan lowered the pistol.

He thought of his mother the same moment he noticed her on the stairs. Soaking wet and dressed only in a towel.

When their eyes met, he burst into tears.

***

Nora had been standing at the top of the stairs for quite a while, watching with widened eyes as her son and granddaughter murdered the Kruegers. She hadn't understood it. When the blood splashed from Stefanie's slit throat, she'd only thought again and again, *Selina? It couldn't have been Selina. Not Selina. Not Selina … my Selina …*

And then Dan shot his father-in-law in the back of his head.

Just like that.

Why had they done that?

And how did it happen that the two of them behaved like a finely attuned team, as if they had done something like this a hundred times before?

What had happened here?

A little girl had died, and that was bad enough, but now her family had suddenly lost their minds! That couldn't have anything to do with Leila's death.

Something else was going on here.

Something nobody would have expected.

Nobody but Kate?

And now she'd disappeared. What had Dan really done to her out there in the wilderness? And what did Selina know? Probably everything. The girl hadn't hesitated to cut the helpless woman's throat. Normal girls didn't do that.

Damn it! In a normal world such things didn't happen!

A few minutes ago, everything had been fine. Not really great, no; after all, sweet little Leila was dead, but everything else was fine.

Or not?

They had eaten together, talked, even laughed a bit. Selina had been cheerful and charming, as always. Dan had seemed downcast, which was understandable. Only a few weeks ago he'd buried his daughter and now his wife had left. He had every right to mope. Nora even found that he handled himself quite well given the facts.

And now?

Now he was pointing a weapon at her, his own mother, who would have given her life for him without hesitation. The world hadn't only started to tremble at the edges, it had gone completely fucking off the rails!

Nora still couldn't believe it, but the man with the gun was real. He was the child she'd given birth to forty-one years ago on a hot August evening.

Her baby.

Her little darling.

She'd lost him once before, but then she'd gotten him back. Back then she'd won. But today the battle seemed to be lost before it had even begun.

And why Selina?

This great bright girl, into whom she'd put all her hopes? How had he managed to manipulate his daughter in such a way that she became a murderer for him?

"Dan ..." she said at last.

He walked up to her, the gun at the ready. Tears mixed with sweat on his face. Nora saw small drops of sweat in his curly hair. She remembered how soft those hairs felt. She'd always been proud of her boy, who had grown into such an attractive man. She'd always believed he could and should have made more of himself. The time in the trailer park with this drug-addicted Clara had been really bad, and Nora had almost given up praying. But then he'd returned to her and given her this little angel to make up for everything.

At least that's what she'd thought back then. How could she have guessed that the worst was yet to come? Dan and Selina had always had a great relationship. A bit too close perhaps. Nora hadn't thought much of Selina sleeping in her father's bed until she was a teenager. That hadn't seemed right. But then Selina had grown older and had ended it herself. She had friends and was a good student. Everything seemed to be in perfect order. But what had Dan done? He found a new, lousy paying job to be at home more often.

Why?

Hadn't he granted his daughter independence? Did he want to have her all to himself? What had happened? What had Dan done to the girl? Nora had been absolutely sure that he'd never harm his daughter.

But what did it look like now?

212

He'd made a murderer out of her.

"I'm sorry, Mom," he said and started to climb the stairs.

What was he up to?

Was he gonna shoot her right here and now?

In the living room, Selina was still standing between the bodies, holding the bloody knife in her hand. Her face was expressionless.

Nora decided she didn't want to wait for whatever he was up to. She turned around and ran back toward the bathroom. She lost the towel but didn't stop for a second; she continued to run naked.

Dan followed but didn't shoot. Nora reached the bathroom door with a sufficient lead. God was merciful. She hurried in, slammed the door, and locked it. For a short moment she leaned her back against it, but then she remembered that bullets went through doors.

Where was the hope she'd always preached? She'd always tried to encourage Dan when he felt bad.

Now she was doing badly, and it was his fault.

Nora moved as far away from the door as possible. She huddled against the wall next to the toilet.

Dan didn't shoot; instead, he knocked on the door and said, "I wish I could explain all this to you, Mom. But it's probably too late already."

"Kate's dead too, right?"

Selina had claimed that, and now Nora wanted to hear it from him.

"Yes," he replied tonelessly.

"But why, Dan? I don't understand."

He laughed dully. "I didn't understand it either. But Selina convinced me. She's pretty good at that."

"What does all this have to do with Selina?"

He laughed again. "Quite a lot, Mom."

"Why don't you put the gun down and we'll talk in peace? Just the two of us. What do you think?"

"I'd love to, but I can't. It would be better if you came out voluntarily."

Nora pressed a fist against her mouth so that he wouldn't hear her sobbing. "Why all this? What are you going to do with me? Do you want to shoot me like some dog? Your own mother!"

Silence from the other side of the door.

Nora suddenly realized she was still stark naked. She'd have liked to put on something because she might have felt less vulnerable, but her clothes were on the laundry basket next to the sink. She would have had to cross the room to get there, which she didn't think was a very good idea now.

A thought shot through her head like lightning. *My cell! Do I have it here? Is it in my pants?*

Nora straightened up. Her heart pounded against her breast. To get her cell, she'd risk a little sprint and then kill two birds with one stone: she'd get dressed and dial the emergency number. At lightning speed (hopefully) help would come and (perhaps) bring light into the darkness. Dan would probably spend the rest of his life in prison, but at the moment, Nora didn't give a fuck about that.

This had to end! Three people were dead. And if she did nothing, she'd die too.

Trembling, she got on her feet, jumped to her clothes, slipped into the borrowed T-shirt and Selina's sweatpants, fumbled for the cell …

Hope died last. Well, maybe that was a fairy tale. Nora remembered that she hadn't taken the cell phone with her to the bathroom. Instead, it was probably still in her handbag, which was downstairs. Was it on the coffee table? Never mind. It might as well have been buried on the beach in Miami.

Shit!

Nora huddled in front of the bathtub and wrapped her arms around her knees.

There was silence outside the door.

Was he there?

As long as he didn't talk to her, she probably wouldn't find out.

Nora closed her eyes and imagined she was somewhere else. Preferably far away. Far away from the people she loved more than anything and who gave her the nightmare of her life.

This life wasn't fair.

It was only a deep ocean, in which a few tiny fish floated as the only glimmer of hope. And every day the devil came with a big black fishing rod and caught one for lunch. The poor little guy who fidgeted so helplessly on the hook this time belonged to Nora, and she only had this one left.

***

Dan turned around when he felt movement behind him. He held Bill's pistol at the ready, and for a moment, as intense as it was short, he aimed it right between his daughter's eyes. It was only a second that he saw her skull explode before his mind's eye. He saw a hail of bone fragments, blood, and brain matter descending, as it had been with Bill. Only the hair stuck to the bloody remains of the burst skull was now blonde.

Dan lowered the gun. He had to blink several times to get rid of this horrible picture, which wasn't so horrible at all, and to recognize again only what was really there: a pretty young woman who had destroyed his life. Her face and parts of her clothes were splattered with blood that could have been red paint in a normal life.

But nothing was normal here.

Never again.

After Leila died, Dan thought it couldn't get any worse, but he'd been wrong.

It can always get worse.

How could he have been so wrong? He'd been living under one roof with the devil for years!

Selina still held the knife. She looked at him questioningly, and Dan knew what that meant. She wanted to know if Nora was still alive.

"I'm not doing that," he said and tried to sound determined. "She's my mother! Your grandmother!"

Selina nodded.

That surprised him.

"Then what are you going to do?" she asked soberly. "Do you want to give up?"

Give up? He'd done that long ago!

"I don't know. I only know that I won't kill my mother."

Selina looked at him expectantly, but he didn't go on. There was nothing to say. The living room was one big battlefield. It was impossible to cover up what had happened. Kate was his wife, Stefanie and Bill his parents-in-law. Sooner or later they would look for them. And the first place to search for them was here with him, of course. Maybe he could have denied the guilt for Kate's death. Even if she'd been found, the suspicion wouldn't necessarily have fallen on him immediately.

But what now?

There were two more bodies plus a witness, and both their cars were outside his house.

216

What else was there to cover up?

It was over.

Either way.

"You don't have to kill her," Selina finally said. "But we have to get away from here. You know that, don't you? We can't stay."

Dan looked at her, shaking his head. "Where will we go? Haven't you had enough yet?"

"I'll never have enough of you, Daddy." She threw him a kissing hand. "We still have a chance. We can go into hiding. Others did that too."

"Where did you get that? TV?"

She smiled. There it was again, the smile of a lunatic.

"I don't care," Dan said. "I don't care about anything now." He sat down on the floor with his back to the bathroom door. He put the gun beside him, then hid his face in his hands. He cried silently, only the twitching of his shoulders gave him away.

Selina went to him, kneeled down, and put one hand on his thigh. "Just do what I tell you," she whispered gently. "Then everything will be all right, I promise."

She put the knife next to the pistol and took his face in her hands to cover it with kisses. Dan closed his eyes and let it happen. He had no more strength to resist. Finally he felt Selina's tongue in his mouth. It tasted like his tears. When she started to massage his crotch, he flinched in pain. Bill had done a good job.

"I just want you to love me, Daddy," Selina whispered into his ear before caressing it with the wet tip of her tongue. "Kiss me and hold me tight."

And to his own surprise, it was exactly what Dan did.

***

They were talking in whispers outside the door. Nora recognized their voices but couldn't understand what they were saying. For this she'd have had to get closer to the door, which she still didn't feel comfortable with. She preferred to sit in her corner and wait. At some point they had to leave. That would be her chance. She only hoped that Dan wouldn't come up with the idea of monitoring her all night. Or even worse: to break open the door if she didn't come out voluntarily.

Would he be able to do that?

She had to reckon with everything.

And Selina?

That was an even bigger mystery. She'd killed Stefanie, so much was certain. Nora had seen it with her own eyes. What had happened to her before, to what extent Dan had influenced her and under what pressure she might have been ... all that was speculation. Nora had no idea what her son had done to the girl, but it must have been something terrible, something profound, if it drove her to such a deed. They never should have been alone after Leila's death. Dan was somehow insane and had dragged Selina into it. Maybe at some point Nora would find out what had actually happened.

Now it was important to keep calm and wait. She only had to survive long enough until help arrived. And how long could that take in the case of four missing persons? Of course they were all grown-ups and it would take a few hours (maybe even days) before they were seriously looked for, but Nora knew that her boss would react very quickly if she stayed away from work without an excuse—even if he did it out of anger alone. Probably he'd personally drive to her place. Also Bill would quickly be missed. He was a member of the Marines. That would get things rolling. Out there their cars were still parked, and apart from that, they would pay Dan as soon as they found out that most of his family had disappeared from the face of the earth.

There was silence outside the door now. At least nobody was talking. Instead, other noises came to Nora's ear: a scraping on the door, breathing noises, and then, a moaning that clearly came from Dan.

Nora held her breath. What were they doing?

She concentrated and listened with a tense facial expression. What she heard was actually unmistakable. She hadn't lived to be sixty-two without knowing what it sounded like when two people had sex. Only the people still alive in this house were her son and granddaughter. And that, great God, couldn't be true!

Nora feverishly considered whether it would be possible for a third person to have joined them without her knowing. Was there another woman? Was that perhaps the answer? Had Dan met another woman who misled him to all this?

Again she held her breath because her own breathing sounds disturbed her listening. On the other side of the door two people had sex or at least did something similar. One of them was definitely Dan, she could hear that very clearly. But who was the woman? Nora hadn't heard anyone else. A stranger? Could this be the explanation for Dan's and Selina's mysterious behavior?

Nora waited tensely. At some point they'd hopefully talk again and she'd finally be the wiser. Minutes went by. Then Dan gave a suppressed scream that sounded like pain. Nora flinched without knowing what was going on. Dan now moaned loudly and breathed hectically.

And then a voice, familiar and clear: "I love you, Daddy."

Nora held her breath. Her heart stopped for several beats. Tears ran down her face as she thought again and again: *Not Selina. Not Selina. Not Selina.*

But it was Selina. It had been her all along.

***

Dan was grateful for the pain that came with this climax. It distracted him from the horror of what he was doing here.

His daughter sat naked on his lap and moved to the rhythm of his breath while his cock was deep inside her. Dan gritted his teeth and moaned more out of pain than pleasure because his genitals still hadn't recovered from Bill's kick. There was no lust. It felt like punishment.

Could his mother hear them? Was she able to make sense of all this, or was she still in the dark? She wouldn't believe what was really going on anyway. At most she'd think her son had decided one fine day that it might be quite nice to stick his cock into his pretty daughter. Just a little treat.

She'd hate him for that.

To the grave and beyond.

Dan knew her well enough to know she'd never forgive him. No matter what he said to talk his way out of. How would it sound if he said something like, "Selina started it, it's her fault"?

That was ridiculous! Apart from the fact that he should never have been blackmailed by his daughter, there would also be the question of why his cock behaved like a roly-poly as soon as Selina even breathed on it. He'd persuaded himself that he had no choice and thus surrendered to a fate that he himself had chosen in the end.

What if Selina wasn't his daughter?

220

Nora wouldn't care. It didn't make his behavior more honorable.

Quite the opposite!

The orgasm rolled over Dan in a wave of pain and insane bliss. He screamed and squirted his juice deep into the dainty as well as shapely girl he once wanted to save from a life in the dirt, only to suffocate in it now himself. Her mother had been a drug-addicted slut with no good trait, but Dan had loved her anyway and done everything she wanted. He didn't understand why this had to happen again and why he was so damn weak. He only understood that basically the same thing like fifteen years ago happened to him now. As if Clara had returned from the dead to finally make him pay for that night in the trailer, when he'd not saved her from dying so miserably beside him.

Selina snuggled up to him with a sigh. Without thinking, Dan put his arms around her. Her soft skin smelled so good. Dan inhaled her scent as his slack penis slowly slipped out of her.

"I love you, Daddy," said Selina.

Dan didn't answer, but he pressed her tightly against him. Maybe it wasn't so bad. You just had to stop thinking about it.

***

They decided that at least one of them had to stay in front of the door overnight so that Nora couldn't escape. They agreed that this should not happen. First, Selina went downstairs to wash herself in the guest bathroom. She didn't give the bodies in the living room a second glance. As long as they didn't start to stink, she could handle it. And it wouldn't come to that, because they would leave here tomorrow, that was a fact for Selina. She'd expected to have to do some persuasive work, but this time she was wrong. It had been easier to talk Dad into it than she'd expected. Selina almost felt as if disposing of Kate's body and murdering her parents had broken something in him. As the saying goes, "You live freely if you don't have a reputation to lose."

Was that what had happened to Dad? He had to cross the line once to lose all his inhibitions? Selina had been sure that sooner or later, she'd have him where she wanted him, but she'd actually imagined it to be more difficult. Part of her was almost disappointed because it had gone so fast now. A few minutes ago he'd not only fucked her, he held her in his arm and that was a first. He hadn't done that since Leila died. Selina had often wondered if it had been the right decision to kill her little sister, but now she knew it couldn't have been better.

Dad needed to feel like he had nothing left to lose so he could finally let go.

She wanted to make sure Nora would be dead tomorrow, then they would leave this house together and never return. Dad would finally belong to her, because then he'd only have her.

It was so easy.

Selina got all jittery when she thought about it. They would then be on the run, which certainly wasn't a walk in the park and also damn dangerous, but they would also be together and could finally enjoy their love without any limits. Just like Bonnie and Clyde. She ignored the fact that they had both died in the end and hadn't been any particularly pretty corpses. She'd become accustomed to only pay attention to the pleasant aspects.

After she'd washed herself and drunk something (for Dan she took a bottle of wine with her; it would help him fall asleep), Selina went upstairs again. She handed the open bottle to her father, who accepted it without a word and started drinking. He leaned with his back against the door, pistol and knife next to him. Selina would soon take over, but she might bring him a second bottle first. Wait and see.

First, she scurried to her room. She had to put on something new. She chose a yellow sweater and black jeans. In the bottom compartment of her closet, she found a blue travel bag into which she put underwear and some comfortable clothes. She also had to remember her toiletry bag, but it was in the bathroom, so that was something for later. Suddenly she saw her school backpack, which she'd carelessly pushed under the desk. Two notebooks had slipped out: English and history. For a moment she had to think of Mr. Willis. This chapter was now closed, although it would have been fun to play a few games with her favorite teacher. Of course you couldn't have everything and she wouldn't shed a tear over school. All her so-called friends had only been a means to an end. Just like her friends in Tennessee. She was popular and had had a lot of them. But they didn't mean the least to her. They had only been necessary so that no one would get the impression that something could be wrong with her. Pretty, sporty girls at junior high had a lot of friends, everything else wouldn't fit into the picture. The weeks after Leila's death had been comparatively a pleasure, because she finally hadn't had to pretend being a normal girl anymore. Everyone had assumed that she was in shock and mourning and that everything was upside down at her home—the latter was even true. Selina smiled at the thought.

Upside down, yeah, that's what you might call it.

Smiling, she took the travel bag and left her room.

She'd never enter it again.

***

Dan still sat there drinking. He'd already half emptied the bottle. Selina knew he'd noticed the bag in her hand. But he said nothing.

"You'll have to pack later too," she said.

He looked at her with glassy eyes and drank.

"Dad?"

Finally he put down the bottle and nodded.

"I'll relieve you here now, so you can go outside and drive the cars into the garage. Ours can be standing outside overnight. That's more inconspicuous."

Dan placed the almost-empty bottle next to him but remained seated. "Yes, okay."

"Do it now, please, before you get too drunk."

Dan came to his feet with a painful expression. Selina sat on his pre-warmed place.

***

Reluctantly, Dan went downstairs. His mother's car key was in her handbag with her cell phone, on which the messages were piling up. Probably from her boss. He opened WhatsApp and read a message from a woman named Mary. Probably a colleague. The other six were from her boss, who wanted to know how long she would be out sick and told her that she needed a doctor's note after the second day of illness, otherwise he couldn't guarantee she still had a job.

Asshole! Dan didn't want her to lose her job. He knew how important it was for her. So he wrote back, *I have the flu, and I'm trying to get better. If I don't feel better tomorrow, I'll go to the doctor. I'll get back to you.*

Okay, done. Dan hoped Nora would appreciate his efforts. He put the phone back in her handbag and grabbed the car key.

Now all he needed was the key for Bill's Chevrolet. Hopefully the giant sedan would fit inside the garage.

On stiff legs he went into the living room, where a penetrating smell of blood hung in the air, competing with the coffee stench of his nightmares. Dan gasped for air and caught too much of the thick, blood-soaked aroma. He got nauseous. He forced himself to walk past Stefanie without looking at her. It was a good thing that he had shoes on, because the red juice of life soaked the carpet so that it made smacking noises with every step.

Bill lay on the remains of his face. Blood of all shades sullied his body. The problem was that Dan would have to turn him around to reach into his pockets.

Finally he managed to squat down and put his trembling hands on Bill's back. Turning him around was easier said than done. This motherfucker was really heavy! As he pushed him onto his back, Dan stared into the cruel mess that was left of his father-in-law's face. Bill's own mother wouldn't have recognized him. There was nothing but bloody mud. Dan forced himself to look away and concentrate on the pants' pockets instead. He fumbled until he came across something hard.

A cell. Fuck!

Second try. Dan inspected the jacket pockets and finally found what he was looking for. The car key was hanging on a thick wad together with other keys, probably for their house and garage. But there was something else.

Dan's blood rustled in his ears, and his heart pounded in his throat. Stunned, he stared at the small round key

225

ring with the photo. The picture showed Kate on a bench in her parents' garden. It was summer, and she wore a white dress that Dan remembered well. All he'd have to do was go upstairs and find it in the bedroom closet. Kate had died a few feet away.

Could that be?

Dan dug his teeth into his damaged lower lip until it bled. He wanted to feel the pain, but he barely could. The eyes of the smiling Kate on the photo were looking directly at him. On her lap sat a little girl in a pink dress. She had to hold on to the girl because she couldn't sit alone yet. She was still too small. Maybe four months, five at the most. Pink bows adorned the fine blonde hair. Kate had loved to make the little one pretty. Leila smiled too.

Was there anything more innocent than a baby's smile? Was there anything worse than a person who destroyed something like that?

Kate had been a proud mother and had loved her little girl with all her heart. She'd always been there for Selina as well. A good mother and the best woman a man could wish for.

Something burst in Dan's chest and stomach. A lump exploded, and its pieces poisoned his whole body.

He clenched his fingers around the bunch of keys until his knuckles turned white. Parts of this disgusting lump had slipped into his throat and he swallowed to get rid of it, which he failed to do. This pain couldn't be put into words. Dan rose and stumbled away from the body. Tears blocked his view.

She'd taken everything from him.

Everything he'd ever loved.

Now only his mother was left. But she'd hate him for the rest of her life. If he'd known all that, he'd have gone away and just left Selina in the stinking old trailer together with her disgusting junkie mother.

He should have left her there to die.

Alone and in her own filth.

But what should he do now?

Kill her?

No, he wouldn't be able to do that.

Never!

She was evil, but she loved him. And sometimes, when he looked at her or let her touch him, he loved her too.

Maybe he should have let her down when she was little and couldn't do much, but by now she'd crawled under his skin like a tick. She'd attached herself to him and hollowed him out. He could do nothing to her.

She was everything he had.

***

"Shall I relieve you?"

Startled, Selina opened her eyes. She'd actually nodded off. But surely only for a little moment. She blinked to get the tiredness out of the burning eyes. There was no time for sleep now.

"Did you manage everything?" she asked with a yawn.

He looked strange somehow. Exhausted. So weary.

"Did something happen?" she wanted to know.

Dan shook his head. Was he bleeding? There was something red on his chin and lip. He bent down for the wine bottle and Selina saw his hands tremble.

"Dad?"

"It's all good. The cars are in the garage." He swallowed hard.

"You don't have to relieve me," Selina explained. She had other plans. "You better freshen up. You look like shit. You also have to pack, and you're surely tired."

"Just like you," Dan replied.

"Yeah, but I can sleep here, it doesn't bother me." She grinned. "I sleep everywhere, you know me."

Dan nodded. He seemed anything but convinced but had no objections.

"Well then, see you tomorrow," Selina said cheerfully. "I'm looking forward to our little road trip."

She was planning on heading southwest.

Mexico.

Everyone with a skeleton in the closet went to Mexico.

And why not?

Every place was the right one, as long as they were together. She'd not yet informed her father about this plan. She suspected that he'd have other problems tomorrow morning. However, Selina was convinced that with her help, he'd swallow this last bitter pill, and she wanted to make it as easy as possible for him.

At least she owed him that.

***

Two hours later Selina heard his snoring from the bedroom. He'd also drunk the second bottle of wine, and she didn't think he'd be on his feet again so soon. It would have taken an earthquake or a bomb to wake him up. So she had enough time but just couldn't get too loud.

Selina hid the gun under her sweater. She took the knife in her hand. Then she stood up and put her ear to the smooth wood of the door.

"Grandma?" With her free hand she rubbed her face until it looked red and swollen. She blinked a few times and the first tears began to flow.

"Grandma, can you hear me?"

Still no answer. The old lady was a tough one. Or was she asleep?

"Grandma?" Selina knocked on the door.

"Please, say something!"

"What do you want?"

Nora sounded suspicious, which didn't surprise Selina. She'd watched her granddaughter slit the throat of her other grandmother.

She was almost a child after all. An innocent girl who had been used, abused, and manipulated by her own father.

What did that sound like? Quite good, right?

"He's sleeping now," Selina hissed in an attempt not to speak too loudly. She wasn't allowed to wake him up, and that made this little game even more exciting.

"So we can leave now," she added conspiratorially.

"Just call 911," Nora replied. It sounded as if she was a little closer to the door.

"First I want to get out of here," Selina whined. "He might wake up any moment. I'm scared!"

Silence. Then, "Wait. I have to get dressed."

Selina waited. She barely dared breathe.

It rustled and seemed to take an eternity. But then Nora spoke again and she seemed to be right behind the door. "I'm sorry, Selina, but I can't trust you. It could be a trap."

Fuck!

"But I'd never lie to you, Grandma!"

"I don't know. I don't even know what's happening here. What's going on with Dan and you …"

"I don't know either." Selina sobbed and tried to speak as dramatically as possible. "Dad suddenly started looking at me so strangely and saying such weird things. At first I didn't think anything of it, but then he touched me … and then …" She swallowed. Now she had to be careful with what she said.

"When did this start, Selina?"

When did it start? Good question.

"I can't remember exactly. It started when we were still living with you. But it got worse when we moved here. And … and really bad since Leila …"

Was that credible? Hopefully. Nora wasn't a psychologist and was anything but unbiased. She was currently in an extreme situation herself.

"He's sleeping with you," Nora stated in a muffled tone.

Selina laboriously cleared her throat. "He promised not to hurt me, but sometimes it hurts …"

"My God!" Nora whimpered. "How can he?"

"He said it was okay. That we belong together and everyone who wants to break us up is wrong. Like Kate and her parents. He said I had to help him cover the whole thing up because otherwise I'd regret it. If he wants to punish me, he won't sleep normally with me, Grandma. I have to do disgusting things then … I want to avoid that, so I helped him …"

"I can't believe this. That's not Dan!"

Yeah, that's how we all feel, Selina thought.

"And Kate found out?" Nora asked through the door. "So was that why she had to die?"

"Yes," sobbed Selina. "Dad said I had to help him if I loved him. And I love him, but … you have to get me out of here, Grandma. Otherwise he'll go on forever! I'm too weak to stop him."

Now Nora sobbed too. "I'm so sorry, Selina! If I had known …"

"Last night he tied me up and smeared my butt with cream. And then he … you know. It was terrible. He promised not to do it again if I was good …"

That was well played!

And it was enough.

Finally!

The door opened.

For a moment they stood face to face and stared at each other. Then Nora reached out her arms and Selina let herself fall in. Perhaps she didn't know what love was, but she'd always liked her grandmother very much—she'd been like a mother to her. Actually, it was a pity to lose her now.

Too bad, but inevitable.

Nora Meller hadn't realized yet that her granddaughter was holding a knife in her hand when the blade was already drilling into her stomach.

***

She felt the pressure as the knife pierced her entrails, but there was no pain. She froze and tried to move away from Selina. Their glances met, and Nora finally saw the truth in her granddaughter's eyes. She opened her mouth to say something, but at that moment the knife slit her stomach open.

Selina slid the blade through Nora's innards. Instead of speaking, Nora moaned. The center of her body filled with warmth. She pressed her hands on the wound after her granddaughter pulled out the knife. She felt something wet and slippery that she held so it wouldn't flop out of her. It was her intestines.

She staggered backward into the bathroom. Selina watched her. Blood dripped from the knife in her hand. Nora knew it was hers. She opened her mouth again but remained mute. The slippery stuff kept seeping out of her. Nora took one hand away to blindly grope for a hold that didn't exist. A piece of intestine slipped from her, hanging over her waistband like an ugly worm. Now Nora looked down on herself and finally lost her balance. What hung out of her looked like special effects in a cheap horror movie.

Nora gave a shrill scream. Instinctively, she threw her arms up to ward off the inevitable fall. Another piece of bowel fell out and stuck to her thigh. Groaning, she landed on her back. Without thinking, she grabbed the slimy mass and tried to stuff it back inside. She made sounds that were hardly human. At the edge of her consciousness Nora noticed Selina entering the room and closing the door. Her face was without expression when she sat on the edge of the bathtub. Nora reached out a bloody hand to her granddaughter, although she knew no help would be forthcoming. She should have screamed loud enough for Dan to hear, but she could only weakly groan.

As her spirit faded, she constantly looked into Selina's rigid face and tried to find an answer in those cold eyes.

In vain.

ON THE DEVIL'S FISHHOOK

It was a cool October morning. There had been frost in the night, and the remains of thick fog were still hanging in the lowlands when Mark set off for work early in the morning. He'd had a bad night's sleep and had rolled from one side to the other most of the night. He didn't want to admit it, but he couldn't get this girl out of his head. It had been pleasant to replace the warmth of his bedroom with the humid cold on the balcony. Dressed only in boxer shorts, he'd leaned against the icy railing and smoked one cigarette after another until he was finally frozen so stiff that he could hardly think clearly.

Goal achieved.

He took a hot shower and then a cold one. Then he dressed and looked at the clock: 6:30. Still much too early. Breakfast wasn't an option. His stomach rebelled at the mere thought of it. Sleep was also out of the question. Nevertheless, Mark sat on his rumpled bed. Selina's picture appeared in front of his mind's eye and his penis immediately began to twitch. One hand disappeared in his pants. He routinely pulled it down to his knees and then leaned back and closed his eyes. Selina's face appeared. She sat in her chair and everything was as usual. But then she came to his desk, sat on it, and spread her legs. She wore nothing under her skirt.

Mark grabbed his cock.

The Selina in his fantasy also had a hand between her thighs. In a moment he'd lick the sweet juice from her tender fingers …

Mark had been jerking off for weeks now to this fantasy, which ended with him pounding the schoolgirl from behind and discharging himself in her sweet ass. But what could a guilty conscience do against a hard-on?

After he "finished," he rubbed himself clean with toilet paper. That had to be enough. He didn't feel like taking another shower, although it was still much too early. Nevertheless, he decided to go to school. He could correct a few tests and save time for the afternoon. Maybe he could knock off early today—and then he'd have more time to wank.

Great prospects.

But what should he do?

He'd tried long enough, but it wasn't something you could fight so easily. Maybe it would have been better if he'd had a girlfriend again, but things were looking rather bad at the moment. He could have looked around on the internet, but before he took the trouble to chat for hours with some females he just wanted to fuck, he could take the cock into his own hand, let the Selina of his fantasies lift her skirt and experience the proverbial heaven on earth within minutes.

Why complicate things when you could do it easily?

Mark didn't give a shit. These fantasies about Selina didn't do him any good, but it wasn't any better without them. *With or without you* ...

Sometimes he thought it might have been advisable to seek help. After all, he couldn't work in a school on a permanent basis, constantly imagining how he was fucking his female students' brains out. Besides, he didn't do himself any favors. He could have found another job. One where he didn't run into dozens of attractive teenage girls every day.

But what else could he do?

234

He'd always only wanted to be a teacher. He regarded that as his great passion. He loved to teach and to be surrounded by children. Yes, but he loved it too much. That was a vicious circle, and Mark saw no escape from it. Perhaps it would have helped to talk to someone confidentially. Wasn't this what he used to preach to his students? If you had problems, you should look for someone to talk to about it! That was the be-all and end-all. And if there was no one in your own environment to whom you wanted to open up, then there were still the guidance counselors or therapists who always had an open ear.

Blah-blah-blah.

But what did Mark Willis actually do when he had problems? He hid in his shell, swallowed all this crap, and did the same as the children he wanted to lead on the right path. Crazy as he was, he'd even made Selina an offer to talk. As if that wasn't the most stupid thing he'd ever thought of. Sure, Selina actually seemed to need help, and as a guidance counselor that was basically his job. But it wasn't his job to keep imagining fucking her!

How naive could he be?

It was probably his luck that Selina had refused all offers of help so far, although she sometimes looked at him in a very special way. As if she saw more in him than just a teacher. Maybe he was just making it up. It was difficult to trust yourself when you thought with your dick most of the time. So he tried to somehow get along with all that by running around mostly like a remote-controlled zombie, jerking off for breakfast and vomiting for dinner.

Or vice versa.

Maybe it wouldn't have hurt to get professional help. In any case, he would have advised everyone else in his situation to do so. However, the world always looked very different when it came to his own ass. The idea of lying on a worn-out couch and lamenting about his distress to a frowning and mildly nodding psychologist didn't seem to be an option at the moment. He'd feel like the last perverted filthy pig.

Basically, he was exactly that!

At least there was hope that it would stop on its own. Just like with the other girl. When he no longer saw her, he quickly forgot her. He had himself under control again. Until Selina appeared … that should not have happened.

Something always has to get us in trouble, right?

On the other hand, it was his own business as long as he kept his mouth shut and was satisfied with his fantasies about Selina. He didn't hurt anyone but himself, but that wasn't a crime. How he was doing was his problem as long as he didn't bother anyone else.

Mark liked that thought.

It made him feel better.

Thoughts were free and he knew he was in control of the rest. There would be no healing for him because (in his opinion) one was powerless against the urges, but he could at least try to live with them in his own way.

If Mark Willis had known that he'd soon experience a very special kind of healing, which couldn't even be compared to his dirtiest fantasies, he wouldn't have left the bed that day.

***

Waking up had become the worst part of Dan's day. It was this short moment between dream and being awake that hurt the most. This moment when he realized every morning that all this was reality.

His little Leila was dead.

Kate had actually died of thirst.

The corpses of Bill and Stefanie in his living room were real.

Just like that horrible girl with the cold heart into which his former princess had turned.

Everything was real.

Relief was brought only by dreams, but every morning they ended with a punch in Dan's face, which made his heart burst and his body numb. With a moan he rolled to his side and pulled the blanket up to his neck. If he lay still and kept his eyes closed, he could continue to tell himself that none of this had happened. He could make himself believe it was that cloudy, coffee-smelling morning again when his world had been destroyed forever.

Only this time it would be different.

The morning would go on without Kate running into the room with that terrible dead bundle. The coffee would only smell and never stink. In a moment he'd get up and go downstairs to get a freshly brewed cup. Because there was no alcohol, only coffee, which his Kate made him every morning.

And that coffee was the best beverage in the world!

He'd enjoy it at the kitchen table, joking with Selina munching her cornflakes while a smiling, beautiful Kate held his sweet baby in her arms.

That's how it should be.

Forever.

A perfect morning for eternity.

There would never be any screaming or wailing. It would never stink of coffee or blood in this house. Never would his own daughter get him to abuse her. Not even in his worst dreams. Leila and Kate would live. He had countless happy hours with them ahead of him. And Selina would always be his dear little girl.

His princess …

Dan closed his eyes. He wanted to hold on to this picture as long as he could. He wanted to lie like that forever, so that the morning would never end.

He wanted his life back!

His family.

He wanted Selina to stop being a monster. Was that asking too much? He just wanted a damn happy ending!

Suddenly someone shook his shoulder.

Someone who wouldn't let him dream on.

Someone who not only wanted to possess his mind and body, but his life, his thinking and feeling … and his dreams.

Dan moaned and tried to turn away. The shaking continued until it hurt. He reluctantly rolled over his back and opened his eyes. He had to rub them first to see at all. The light of this morning was gray and relentless. Outside the rain splashed from the roof gutter. Selina stood in front of him. She was already dressed and had her wet hair tied together.

"You gotta get up now, Daddy."

Dan sat up. The blanket slipped from his naked upper body, and he immediately began to freeze. At the same moment he remembered his mother, who had locked herself in the bathroom. Hadn't they agreed on taking turns at the guard?

"What about Grandma?"

Selina lowered her eyes.

"What …?"

She shook her head. "I'm really sorry, Daddy … but she tried to get away. I had to stop her."

"What have you done?!" Dan jumped out of bed. The magic of the morning was finally over. What came next was the horror of another day in this new crappy life, which he owed to his daughter.

"She really left me no choice," Selina shouted after him.

But Dan didn't hear her anymore. Barefoot and only in boxers, he ran toward the bathroom …

… and froze in front of the open door.

Selina had already wiped the floor so as not to carry the mess through the whole house, but Nora was still lying where she'd died. Her eyes stared expressionlessly at the ceiling, her mouth wide open. An enormous amount of blood had accumulated under her body. Her hands clawed around intestines that were spilling out of her belly.

Dan opened his mouth, but before he could even make a sound, his legs failed and he sank to his knees, trembling.

Images of his mother appeared in his mind. From yesterday and from the past. Also pictures from his childhood. He saw her hands in front of him, as he'd seen them as a child. Those big gentle hands that had always been there when he'd needed them.

He would have recognized them among thousands. He still did this now that they were stuck in this terrible pile of guts, because at the end of her life, they'd had to do something for which God hadn't made them.

Dan thought of holding her in his arms. But in the end he didn't move.

Selina had done that.

His Selina.

She'd done so much that was completely impossible to understand. She'd taken everything from him that he'd ever loved. What was left of him now was small and weak and completely spineless. Nothing more than the broken shell of a man.

What was left of him now belonged to her.

***

Mark was sitting over the third piece of history test he wanted to check. He wondered if he needed to start over again because he'd been far too unfocused when the door opened and Mrs. Johnson, the deputy principal, stretched her fresh perm into his office.

"Good morning, Mark."

"Good morning, Ellie."

"You know you have the first lesson off, right?"

Mark nodded and hoped she wouldn't ask him why he was already here. On the other hand, it looked like he had something to do. There was nothing like keeping up appearances. This could gradually become his motto of life.

"I came earlier to correct these tests here."

She smiled. "All right. Then I don't want to disturb you."

Now, that would really be something, he thought, discontented. "See you later, Ellie."

She left, and Mark tried again to do his job. But his thoughts were constantly wandering. Again and again he fantasized about Selina lying astride on the desk, spreading her legs for him to admire her pink pussy.

Mark was startled and just in time pulled his hand out of his pants when Ellie walked in again.

Again without knocking.

Mark looked at her and hoped his facial expression was somewhat neutral. "What's up? The first hour has only just begun."

"Yes, but we have a problem."

Mark, who was still trying to breathe normally while his cock was pounding painfully, raised his eyebrows. "What kind of problem?"

"It's about Selina Meller."

Mark stopped breathing.

Selina?

"She didn't show up today, and there's no excuse. The secretary called home but couldn't reach anyone. Now I just wanted to double-check before calling the police. If Mr. Smith should ask."

Mr. Smith was the director and was currently on sick leave due to a herniated disc.

Mark shrugged. "Sure."

"I always have a bad feeling about involving the police in something like this."

"But it's the normal procedure," Mark said.

Ellie nodded. "But we all know what this family is going through. We don't help them by sending the police on them now, although the girl probably just overslept."

"But something might have happened," Mark replied.

"Of course, we have to look into it. But for the family it would be a lot gentler if one of us would check the situation first. If, contrary to expectations, the matter cannot be clarified, we can still call the police."

"And that someone should be me?" asked Mark, who was now sweating like a pig. If he didn't wank soon, he'd explode.

"You've got time right now, and you're the guidance counselor."

"That's right, but she never talked to me. She always refused."

"But at least she knows you. Better than me. What do you think, Mark, would you drive there quickly? I'll take

241

over your classes until you come back. I just think we're doing the family a big favor. They've been through enough already. After all, nobody is happy when suddenly the police is at the door because the child didn't show up for class. The headmaster wants to play it safe in this special case. We can arrange that differently."

Mark nodded. In reality he was anything but enthusiastic about this proposal. Ellie was an incorrigible do-gooder and always wanted to do everything on her own. In the past he'd liked exactly this attitude of her, but those times were over. Now he only agreed so she'd finally leave him alone and he could jerk off.

That's how simple the world was.

Sometimes.

"Okay, I'll go. Have the secretary write down the address for me. I need to use the bathroom first."

Ellie smiled. And finally walked away.

Mark quickly Selina as wanking material before heading off to see the real one.

***

Dan was completely distraught, and Selina had trouble getting him back into the bedroom. Showers would probably be canceled today. There wouldn't even be a cat wash, although he smelled strongly of sweat. He trembled and his skin felt ice-cold. Selina brought him his sneakers, a fresh T-shirt, socks, jeans, and a gray hooded sweater. She'd have preferred it if he changed his boxer shorts as well; after all, it was written in the stars when he would have the next chance to change, but the result didn't seem worth the effort at the moment. Selina gave each garment to Dan in turn, even socks and shoes, and he put everything on as she handed it to him. He probably would have worn the pants on his head if she'd suggested it.

Selina liked the idea.

Thinking of the power she had over him excited her, but there was no time for that. They finally had to get out of here. There would be plenty of time to fuck later.

"How much money do we have in the house?" she asked her father after he'd finished dressing and sat on the edge of the bed like an oversized doll.

He shrugged. "A few hundred."

"And where?"

He pointed silently at the nightstand.

Selina checked it. In a cloth bag she found five hundred dollars in fifties. She stuffed them into her pants pocket. "More?"

"The rest is in my wallet."

"The credit cards too?"

He nodded.

Selina knew where his wallet was. She'd stowed it in her bag long ago. At her behest, Dan had also packed a bag last night that was already in the car. It was now shortly after eight, and they had to leave. Breakfast was canceled today as well. After all, it was only a matter of time before someone showed up to inquire about the missing. The battlefield into which the living room had been transformed wouldn't leave much room for speculation.

"You have to pull yourself together," she said quietly as she looked at the little heap of misery that had once been an attractive, charming man, after whom many a woman would have licked all five fingers. Selina had always understood that and hadn't liked it. She hadn't liked Kate either. But she'd always put a good face the matter, until the time had finally come to show her true face. Patience was a virtue. It was good that she'd waited so long. At that time she wouldn't have known where and how a man could best be touched in order to completely make him lose his mind. She couldn't have possessed him as she did today. Because by now she had her hands not only on his cock but his brain.

Dan let his head hang.

"You have to drive later. Can you do it?" she asked. That was one of the few hindrances she hadn't considered. She'd bite her ass for all eternity for not having done the driving lessons back then.

Dan sighed. Mourning for Nora had him fully in its grip. Selina hoped he'd recover quickly. She squatted, put her hands on his thighs, and looked into his eyes.

"You'll make it, Daddy, right? Otherwise they'll catch us and you'll go to jail. Forever. Because now you're not just a rapist." She smiled thinly. "But you certainly know that. And also that I will be sent to a shelter, because there is nobody left who can take care of me until I'm twenty-one. Well, you have to play along so we get our happy ending. Okay?"

Dan said nothing, but when Selina reached out, he took her hand, and she led him downstairs.

***

Dan stood in the living room and watched bloody stains bloom on the blankets he'd just spread over the corpses of his in-laws.

Then the doorbell rang.

His guts instantly turned to water, and he wasn't sure if he'd already had his pants full or if this was going to happen any second.

244

Selina, who stood in the kitchen and had just been about to pack beverages and some food into a bag, looked exactly like her father felt. Only her responsiveness was far better. She immediately dropped the bag and pulled the gun out of the waistband. Their glances met and she made a hectic gesture to Dan not to move.

With her gun held up, she sneaked to the door.

It rang again.

And again.

Then a knock.

And another ringing.

Whoever was out there wouldn't leave on his own.

Selina positioned herself in front of the door.

"Hello? Mr. Meller? Selina? Is anyone home?"

***

Selina's eyes grew big. She knew the voice but wasn't able to recognize it immediately.

"Mr. Meller? This is Mark Willis. I'm a teacher at Selina's school and only want to see if everything's okay."

Selina gasped for air. Mr. Willis, of course! How could she not have recognized him? Probably because she never expected to hear his voice anywhere but in a classroom.

What was this idiot doing here?

Then it fell off her eyes like scales. She'd forgotten to call the school.

She exhaled and wiped sweat from her forehead. She clasped the handle of the pistol with one hand while groping for the door with the other.

"Is anybody home? I'm otherwise obliged to inform the police ..."

Selina pulled the door open, and Mark stared right into the muzzle of the revolver.

He opened his mouth and stared at her in horror. "Selina, what ...?"

"Come in!" Selina commanded. She knew there was no way she could have a discussion outside the door. Around this time, the neighborhood was very quiet and you rarely saw anyone, but you could never be sure.

Mark was far too perplexed not to obey.

"Close the door!"

Mark did as he was told. Then he stood there and could only stare. He'd already caught a glimpse of the living room and saw Dan between two body-shaped lumps of blankets.

"Selina, whatever happened, we can talk about anything. You just have to put the gun down." He looked at Dan nervously again and tried to understand a situation that was impossible to understand.

"I won't, Mr. Willis. Show me your hands!"

"Selina, listen ..." Before he could continue, the pistol barrel hit his temple. Terrified, he pressed one hand against the spot and looked at Selina in bewilderment. His glasses had slipped and were now hanging slanted on his nose.

"No, you listen to me now, Mr. Willis." Selina aimed right between Mark's eyes. "You have witnessed something that doesn't concern you. Now I can't let you go anymore, you know?"

"Please, Selina. I won't tell anyone. I can help you," Mark wailed but didn't believe it himself. Blood came out between his fingers. The girl had given him a laceration.

Selina shook her head vigorously. "All the begging will be useless. Who knows you're here?"

"N-nobody."

Selina struck again. This time on the nose. Mark screamed. He panicked, pressing a hand on his nose and crouching in a corner of the hallway.

"Again, who knows you're here?"

"Mrs. Johnson. The deputy principal. She sent me here," Mark replied with a nasal voice.

Selina nodded contentedly. "That sounds more like the truth. Anyone else?"

Mark shook his head.

"All right. I believe you. Dad and I were just about to leave. We're going on a little trip, and it looks like there's three of us now."

Mark started one last attempt. "You don't have to do this, Selina. I really want to help you."

"I have to do what I have to do," Selina said. "And now take off your jacket, Mr. Willis. Today I'll decide what's on the timetable."

***

There didn't seem to be much going on with Selina's dad today, but at least he managed to tie Mark's hands to his back with duct tape while Selina held the gun at the ready. When he was done, she got so close to her teacher that she could have kissed him. Mark felt her warm breath on his face. She raised a hand and flinched in anticipation of another blow, but she only took off his glasses.

"You have no idea how long I've wanted to do this," she said with a teasing smile.

Mark, who was as blind as a mole without glasses, found the whole thing hard to laugh at. "Please," he panted. "I can't see without them."

"Oh, really?" Selina dropped the glasses, and Mark heard a crunching noise as she stepped on them. She ran her fingers through his back-combed hair until it fell in strands over his sweaty forehead. "Then it's probably a little awkward for you now."

Mark gave off a desperate sob. Without glasses he just recognized the hand in front of his eyes; everything else was blurred. He was completely helpless. Selina's father put something over his shoulders that felt like a jacket. Probably so that nobody could see the tied wrists.

What was wrong with that man? Had he gone mad or had Selina or had both of them?

He was pretty sure there were two corpses in the living room. Bloody corpses. Whatever had happened here, it was something terrible.

Who was under those blankets?

The wife, other relatives? People like him who had been in the wrong place at the wrong time?

Selina went to the kitchen once again while her father stayed with Mark and held him. Mark wondered if he should say something to the visibly unhinged man. Maybe he could somehow get him to turn against Selina. He didn't seem to agree with what happened here. Nevertheless, he made no effort to resist Selina. Mark just didn't understand how it fit together. He was the father and she was the daughter! Why was she the one in command? What had broken this man so much? The death of his little daughter? Mark doubted that was all. It made no sense and didn't explain Selina's cruel behavior in the least.

"So," she said when she came out of the kitchen. There was something in Selina's hand that Mark couldn't see from a distance. As soon as it was at his throat, he knew it was a knife, and not a small one.

He swallowed hard and pressed himself even closer to the wall.

"It depends on you what happens next," said this girl he didn't recognize. "If you're a good boy, you might even survive. Understand?"

"Yes," Mark whispered.

"What's your first name?"

"Mark."

Selina smiled. She took the knife away and patted his freshly shaved cheek. "You do like me, don't you, Mark?"

Mark didn't know what to answer, so he decided to keep his mouth shut. The main thing was that the knife was gone.

"You always looked at me like that. And you wanted me to come to your office." She was very close now. He could smell her. The Selina with the pink pussy in his fantasies was so completely different from the one here.

"But only because I'm a guidance counselor and wanted to help you."

Selina licked his mouth and nose. Mark felt the warm, moist film of saliva she left behind. His cock was moving.

Oh God, please! Not now!

Selina pressed herself against him. She handed her father the gun and he took it wordlessly. She kept the knife to herself. Mark closed his eyes. He just wanted it to pass.

Please, dear God, don't let her notice I have a hard-on!

But Selina had already noticed. That was one of her specialties. She put her hand on Mark's penis, and he couldn't help but throw his head back and moan. This feeling was stronger than pain and panic. He had to give in to it, as absurd as the situation was. How long and how often had he dreamed of it?

Selina massaged him through his pants. Mark felt that she knew exactly what he needed. She gently pulled on his cock and then squeezed it firmly, just to pull on it again. A part of him begged God to stop her. Another part had given in to a much darker power and prayed that things would go on like this forever. If his hands hadn't been tied, he would have freed himself from his pants long ago. The weapon that Selina's father held to his temple was no longer of interest to him. He was allowed to keep aiming at him as long as Selina didn't take her hand from his crotch.

But then she did just that.

Mark clenched his teeth. His penis rubbed painfully on the inside of his underpants. "Can you please …"

Keep going, he was about to say. *God in heaven!*

"Can I please what?" Selina asked and grabbed it again, but this time so brutally that Mark screamed.

"Unfortunately we don't have time for games now. But I know you want me, Mark. Let's see if you'll get me."

Mark decided it was smarter to keep his mouth shut. Selina's father also seemed to have come to this decision.

They went out into the cool drizzle.

Mark was grateful for the fine drops on his sweaty face. Selina sat with him in the back seat while Mr. Meller sat behind the wheel. She now had both weapons with her. First she put the safety belt on Mark, then on herself. Her arm accidentally touched his crotch. Mark's erection immediately awakened to new life. It was pathetic. Selina giggled. Of course she thought it was funny. A little girl with her toy.

The car started to move.

Mark looked out the window and wondered if he'd ever return.

He could only see his Ford as a silhouette on the side of the road as they drove past. When would they start looking for him? And what conclusions would they draw? Surely his cell phone would soon run hot if Ellie tried to reach him.

She'd call the police.

Yes, for sure!

She wouldn't wait long. They'd go to the Meller house and find his car. They would ring the doorbell, but nobody would answer. They'd force their entry.

Immediately? Or did they have to get a warrant first? No, that would surely not be necessary in this case. Probably they'd first send two officers who were nearby. But there would quickly come more after they found the bodies in the living room. Reinforcements would arrive. The house would be turned upside down.

What else would they find?

Or who?

Mark could only speculate.

And what would happen then? Of course, they would start the manhunt. For whom? Selina? Mr. Meller? They would think the latter was the culprit, who else? Mark still wasn't sure if the girl wasn't somehow under the influence of her father, even if it looked different at first glance. Nobody knew how long this lunatic had manipulated and suppressed her. Maybe meanwhile she did things voluntarily that he'd forced her to do a few months or years ago. Possibly a kind of brainwashing or even Stockholm syndrome that sometimes occurred during kidnappings.

But he looks a lot more fucked up than she does, Mark thought as he alternately observed Selina from the side and tried to read her father's gaze in the rearview mirror. The damn nearsightedness didn't make it any easier. Although his eyes had adjusted a little and he could see a bit more, it wasn't enough to get a good picture of his environment. Selina's facial expression was barely recognizable, and it didn't promise anything good. The expression in her father's eyes remained a mystery.

"Well, what do you think now, little Mark?" Selina suddenly scoffed. "Do you regret your wet dreams of schoolgirls?" She clicked her tongue and laughed lewdly. "You almost look worse than my poor daddy. But don't worry, if I could convince him, I can do it with you as well!"

It was enough to drive him to despair. Mark would have liked to cry like a little child, but he pulled himself together. He'd already shown enough weakness. It seemed as if Selina fed on it like a vampire from the blood of his victims. His weakness and helplessness were the essence from which she drew her strength.

That … and the devotion of his damn cock!

Had she known it all the time? Had she read his face like in an open book, or had he given himself away?

But how?

Was it because of the way he talked to her or the expression on his face when he imagined fucking her?

How had she recognized it?

What kind of damn fool had he been?

She was a hard-boiled bitch, a poisonous snake who knew exactly what she was doing. Had she done the same with her father? Manipulated him with that sweet smile and poisoned him with the bitter bile of her wickedness? Mark thought it was possible. The guy seemed to do everything his daughter wanted him to do, even though he looked as if he was about to shit his pants or vomit all over himself, possibly both. He didn't seem to agree with all this, yet he obeyed her every word.

Yeah, I guess that's how it is. Then everything fits together. Not that he manipulated her, but she manipulated him. Somehow she has him in her hand. But with what? Is it about sex? Or is she blackmailing him?

Of course, she could blackmail him with sex. With sex that he'd already had or sex that he'd like to have. Both options were possible. And it made sense, as sick as it was. It was the only thing that halfway made sense if you thought about it a little longer. Of course people seemed to have died, which was damn stark, but somehow it fit the picture, if you looked at it correctly.

Selina obviously had plans with her father, which probably deviated quite strongly from everything normal people considered acceptable. Had she murdered to protect these plans? Or had she somehow persuaded her father to do it? In Mark's head this resulted in a logic as sick as it was believable. It may not have explained everything, but surely a lot. And now he'd burst into this sick rendezvous like a rotten fruit. Had he been someone else, he probably would have been dead already, but Selina seemed to have taken a liking to him. She'd noticed that he could be quite a nice toy. Just like her father. Only she probably wouldn't keep him as long as she would her daddy.

He was just a little pastime. A toy you didn't have to pay much attention to because you could throw it away if it was broken.

Fuck, Mark thought desperately as the gray rainy landscape trailed before his eyes. *I'm really in some deep shit.*

Indeed.

***

"Where are we heading, anyway?" Mark asked suddenly.

His voice cut into the silence like a knife through soft butter. Selina, who had just been nodding off, flinched and instinctively grabbed the gun on her lap.

Without a word, she held it to Mark's temple. "Nobody asked you anything, teacher," she hissed.

"Okay, okay, I'm sorry. I just wanted to have a little conversation. I thought we could—"

Selina cut him off. "You'd better stop thinking. I'm not in the mood for stupid drivel. Dad knows where we're heading. Right, Daddy?"

Dan, who tried to concentrate on nothing but the road, nodded in agreement, even if it wasn't quite true. Selina wanted to go to Mexico, but he didn't think they would make it there. It would take them at least three days, but they certainly already had the cops on their asses. That was perhaps quite good, because then it would be over without him having to make the decision. The cops would do that for him.

For him and Selina.

Meanwhile, they had left the city behind and now drove southwest on the interstate toward Knoxville. From there he wanted to head to Georgia. Simply always to the southwest. The old map he'd found in the glove compartment showed the approximate route to the Mexican border.

Almost two thousand miles.

Dan could have bet they couldn't even make half of it before they got caught. So he didn't think it was necessary to follow an exact route. What role would it have played? Selina was satisfied as long as she felt she was heading in the right direction and holding the reins in her hands. Dan, on the other hand, was just waiting for them to get to a checkpoint or for a police car with a wailing siren to suddenly appear behind them. They were on their way and would drive as far as they could, and that was the main thing. He was almost happy to be on the road, because he couldn't have stayed in the house another minute. Again and again pictures of his dead mother forced their way into Dan's mind, but here it was easier to suppress them. He had to drive and concentrate on the traffic. He wasn't allowed to miss a single exit ramp. The steering wheel and the front part of the car belonged to him alone. He didn't have to look at anyone or talk to anyone.

That was good.

It helped with the suppression, which had become the main content of his life. That's why he was annoyed when the teacher took the floor. Why did the guy show up at all to interfere in things that didn't concern him? Dan didn't believe this was a normal procedure. Teachers didn't make house calls when a student didn't show up for class. Or did they? This one had done it, and instead of just killing him, Selina had decided to take him with her.

Dan didn't really care. Maybe it was quite good when she concentrated on another guy.

A new object of her desire ...

But did he really want that?

Dan had no answer. He'd lost the ability to notice or even understand his feelings and motivations. Selina had probably made him what she wanted: a powerless and soulless being without an opinion. Nothing more than a damned marionette who could basically drive a car and fuck her.

For now, he was just happy that Selina had silenced the guy. The silence was a blessing. Later he might turn on the radio, even though he was afraid to hear the news.

What would they report?

They'd left a house full of corpses behind. Would they put all this on him? Yes, probably. The teacher could confirm that Selina had been the driving force behind his kidnapping, but who knew if the guy would still be alive then?

And even if ... who would fucking believe that?

Selina was a teenager on the road with two adult men who were her hostages. That sounded ridiculous even in his ears. And it wasn't true either. He could have overpowered her long ago, he could have called the police, he could have avoided worse ... the teacher's hands were tied in the most literal sense of the word, but he could have ended it several times already. Instead, he let Selina have her way since this insanity had begun. Did he do this only because he was afraid of prison?

Cut the bullshit! Stop thinking! Just stop thinking!

Dan clasped the steering wheel with both hands and stared doggedly at the wet road. In the rearview mirror he saw that Selina had her head leaned against the window and her eyes closed. Knife and pistol were on her lap. She certainly didn't get much sleep last night. No, she'd been far too busy carving up her grandmother.

Dan swallowed the pain and pushed the picture of his mother aside again. When he was a child, she'd often sung to him when he was sad or hurt, with that deep, soft voice. The song of the little spider in the rain had been his favorite ...

He turned the mirror and caught a glimpse of the teacher, who sat stiffly and stared into nowhere while the muscles in his face worked ceaselessly. He had dry blood on his temples and under his nose. The poor guy wondered what was in store for him. He'd certainly imagined this day differently when he got up that morning.

Dan turned the mirror again to look at Selina. His princess. With her eyes closed, she looked so sweet and innocent.

Why had he let all this happen? He could have saved his mother and the Kruegers, maybe even Kate. Was it all about him not ending up as a rapist in prison? Or could he just not bear the idea of losing her?

His princess.

What would he be without her?

***

They were almost in Georgia when Selina woke up and became aware of the unpleasant pressure on her bladder. She stretched her body extensively. There was nothing out there but gray roads and dark trees. Twilight had set in. She looked at Mark, who was still sitting like before. He avoided her gaze and let his head hang.

Good boy.

"Daddy?"

He'd actually persevered all those hours. Selina was proud of him.

"Yes?" He sounded tired, but he was really not to blame for it.

"We have to take a break."

"Do we? They're certainly already looking for us."

Selina feared that too. "Have you turned on the radio?"

He shook his head. "Probably a manhunt is going on already. They know what car we're in."

"Not everyone listens to the news. And nobody knows where we're going."

"You wanna risk it?"

Selina sighed. Her bladder was about to burst. They had a few supplies and something to drink with them, but that was no substitute for sleep and a toilet. At some point they had to refuel. Besides, Dad couldn't drive all night, it was way too dangerous; he could fall asleep at the

257

wheel. She wondered if it would be an option to let Mark drive. She could sit next to him with the gun so he wouldn't get any stupid ideas. Dad could rest in the back in the meantime. She'd slept a few hours and was now reasonably fit again. She liked the idea.

"We'll drive through the night," she finally decided. "Mark will drive." She looked at her teacher, but he showed no reaction. "But first we'll stop at some rest area. The lonelier, the better."

"Okay," Dan muttered with little conviction.

"I have to pee," Selina added.

It was probably the same for Mark. It wouldn't be easy to get out of the car with him. Whether she let him pee or not. As soon as he was no longer tied up, there was a danger that he'd try to escape. He wasn't as devoted to her as Dad, she had to remember that. Surely he'd do anything to free himself. Of course, he wanted to save his ass.

"Mark?" she said to him.

Mark turned his head and looked at her.

"You heard what I said, right?"

He nodded.

"You have to drive so my dad can rest."

"I could have—if you hadn't broken my glasses," he replied.

Selina froze. Shit! Was he serious?

"You'll probably see well enough!"

Mark laughed dryly. "I told you I was practically blind without glasses. I'm very nearsighted, Selina, that was no joke. You can force me, but we won't get far."

Selina felt her heart drop into her guts. "Why didn't you say that right away, you stupid asshole?"

"I did! But you didn't care."

Selina nervously ran her fingers through her hair. "Shit!"

"Yes, shit," Mark agreed. "I'd feel better if I could see something, too."

"Can't we buy glasses somewhere?" Dan intervened. "Maybe not perfect, but better than nothing. You get them everywhere."

"You're talking about reading glasses. But I'm short-sighted. I can't see anything in the distance, which is quite important when driving a car. I'm not talking shit, guys. I can't drive like that."

"So, what now?" Selina sighed. She would have preferred to beat Mark, but then she thought of the cracking when she'd stepped on his glasses. Only because he looked better without them. Now she had to deal with it.

"I guess we'll just have to find a place to sleep after all. In the car, if necessary," Dan said, shrugging.

Selina didn't like the two options very much. But they had no choice.

"We'll leave the interstate at the next opportunity and look for something in the middle of nowhere."

"Okay," Dan said.

Mark was silent. He'd said enough anyway.

***

It was dark, and Selina's bladder was throbbing when Dan stopped in front of a rundown motel. There were only two other cars here: a rusty Ford pickup and an ancient Buick. The flat building looked uninviting, even in the dark.

Selina hoped the people staying here would have little interest in calling the cops. That was one reason they had decided on this sad flophouse. The other reason was that they could park behind the house between trash containers and bulky garbage, where the car would be well protected by wild weeds and crippled bushes.

"Go inside and get a room for two," Selina said. "Mark can sleep on the floor."

Although Mark wasn't to blame for losing his glasses and even less his shortsightedness, she was damn angry at him and just wanted to make him pay for her messed-up plans.

Dan unbuckled and opened the door.

"And don't forget to use a false name. You can pay with this." She handed him a fifty. Dan took the money and got out.

Selina turned to Mark. "When we get out of the car, it might spark your imagination, but I'll tell you right away that if you try to escape, I'll shoot you without hesitation. I'll shoot you in the back; I don't give a damn. And out here it won't be of any interest to anyone. Do you believe me?"

"And I thought I was your favorite teacher," he replied with a thin smile. A touch of humor she didn't expect him to have.

"You'll remain that if you're a good boy."

"I'm not running away," assured Mark.

Selina knew she shouldn't believe him, but for the moment she had no other choice. At least he was as blind as a mole, which surely restricted his zest for escape. She could only guess what it was like not to be able to see properly but suspected that this circumstance seldom produced heroes.

LITTLE GAMES

Starlight Motel was the name on the sign. Even Dan couldn't help smiling as he crossed the dusty parking lot. The sign was supposed to glow or perhaps twinkle, but the only thing it did was flicker. The rooms he passed were dark, but there was light in the reception area, so somebody had to be here.

Dan climbed two rotten steps. When he opened the glass door, it rattled in such a way that he feared it would fall off at any moment.

A shrill bell above his head announced his arrival. The sour aroma of old sweat dominated the room. A fat man with an unkempt full gray beard looked up from a magazine. He was sitting in a small dusty cone of light behind a counter that had seen better days—like everything here. Next to him was a portable TV. Dan hadn't seen such a device since childhood, except in old movies. Fortunately, there was no news on, just a talk show. Dan noticed the magazine the guy was reading was a cheap pulp mag.

The guy inspected Dan with distrustful, piggy little eyes. He had an obnoxious brown wart on his upper lip.

"A room?" he asked with a dragging southern accent. He didn't seem to have a single tooth in his mouth.

"Yes," Dan replied. "For thr… for two, please."

The guy kept inspecting him at the same time he took a brown book out of a drawer and opened it. The pages were full of grease stains. He pointed a stubby finger at the next free line. The last entry was from today, so they wouldn't reside here alone.

"Register here. Twenty dollars a night. I don't care how many people you are and what you do as long as you don't mess up my room."

What else can you mess up here? Dan thought. He took the pen from fingers suffering massively from nail fungus and scribbled the first name that came to mind: Ron Peterson. One of his former classmates in junior high. Dan had hated him like the plague. He returned the pen and tried not to touch the guy's hands.

"Fine," he said and closed the book.

He probably didn't need it too often because he put it away immediately. "And now the cash."

Dan gave him the fifty.

Hopefully this motherfucker can give change.

The guy grinned at him. In slow motion, he rummaged through his old-fashioned cash register and finally produced three tens, which he solemnly handed over to Dan.

"The beverage dispenser is broken," he said. "But we have ice cream if you need to cool anything." He laughed as if he'd just made the joke of the century. "If there are no more towels, you can come here and get some. If the TV doesn't work, you're out of luck, it's not the Ritz."

He laughed again.

"Yeah, all right," Dan said. "We actually only want to sleep. Can I have the key now, please?"

"Yes, of course, my son." The guy stood up sluggishly. He wore yellow-stained boxer shorts and a crumpled shirt—nothing else.

Dan swallowed and warily looked forward to the room. It probably didn't look any better than this rancid guy. Selina would freak. She was meticulous about such things.

"There you go. Room number eight." This time their hands touched.

Dan shuddered.

"Have a nice stay." The sleazebag winked at him. "And if you need some pussy, I'm friends with the owner of the next brothel …"

Dan shook his head. "No, thanks. I'm only just tired."

The guy nodded earnestly. "Tired, yes of course, I can understand. Have you been on the road longer?"

"And I don't want to talk about it," Dan said quickly.

The motel owner remained calm. He probably heard the sentence quite often. "All right, boy. Then good night. Check out tomorrow at eleven."

"Yes, good night."

Dan looked around nervously as he went back to the car. The parking lot was deserted. There was light in one of the rooms, but the curtains were closed. People probably preferred to stay to themselves here.

That was good.

When he reached the car, he opened the door and sat behind the wheel again. He held the key card so that Selina could see it from the back seat. "We have room number eight. The best thing is I drive right in front of the door. It's safer."

"But you'll hide the car afterward, right?" Selina wanted to know.

"Yeah, sure."

Dan didn't know how he managed to function just like that. He only realized it was good for him to follow a clear plan. As long as he could cling to something that made sense to him, he felt better. The trick wasn't to think of his mother and the others who had died—especially Leila.

Right now, it almost felt like he was on vacation. With his daughter. Why not? He took care that she was provided for and that she was well. That was his job as a father, right? Of course he wasn't allowed to think of Mark if he wanted to keep up the illusion. But he was here and real and therefore not as easy to fade out as Dan would have wished. It was nevertheless worth a try.

He parked the car as close as possible to the door of number eight, then got out and took the bags out of the trunk. Selina took care of Mark. She walked close behind him and drilled the barrel of the pistol into his back while she held the knife in her other hand. Mark behaved calmly. He didn't even look around. He wouldn't have seen much anyway.

Dan pushed the card into the slot and the door opened with a tired click.

A musty stench hit them, and Dan knew it would be bad even before the light revealed the ugly truth.

The floor and walls were covered with stains, most of which appeared to be human liquids. Over the bed lay a dirty bedspread you didn't want to touch. Dan preferred not to think about the bathroom.

"Oh, that's really bad," Selina said next to him.

Mark, who in this case could be happy to be nearsighted, remained silent.

Dan entered the room and threw the bags on the bed.

"We can't change it."

"Hopefully the toilet isn't too disgusting," she said disdainfully. For the moment she was nothing more than a moaning teenager.

She was the Selina Dan knew from before. His mistake was to draw hope from it. "Don't expect too much, Princess," he said automatically.

Selina gave him a doubting smile. "Hurry up with the car, Daddy! I urgently have to pee and don't want to leave him alone."

"I can't go anywhere anyway," Mark threw in.

264

Selina shook her head. "You'd like that, but I'm not taking that risk."

Mark sighed when he was supposed to sit on the floor, while Selina sat on the bed with a disgusted expression on her face.

It didn't take long for Dan to come back, and she finally got a chance to check out the sanitary facilities—Dan had preferred to pee outside. He heard her curse several times, but then she stayed in there for quite a while.

Dan sat on the stained bedspread with the weapons next to him.

Mark put his head back so he could look at him. "What's the matter with her?"

"Shut up!" Dan snarled. He didn't want to talk about Selina, especially not with this guy!

"I just want to understand what's going on and why I'm here."

Dan jumped up and grabbed his daughter's teacher by the collar. He had strength, but didn't know how to use it. If his hands had been free, Mark would have had a realistic chance. But he was tied up and couldn't defend himself against the blows that rained down on him.

Dan beat his head and neck uncontrollably because Mark had instinctively bent forward, his hands protecting his face. As he tilted sideways, Dan grabbed the teacher and sat him down again, just to continue hitting him. Dan's anger blazed like red lava in his head. Actually, he was only angry at himself and Selina, but Mark was an easy victim.

That was reason enough.

Mark endured the beating silently.

At some point Dan stopped because his hands hurt and he realized he was completely out of breath. Sweat dripped from the tip of his nose. He raised his throbbing fists and saw the skin on his knuckles had burst open. Mark just sat there with his head bowed, as if not much had happened. But he trembled, and as he raised his head, Dan saw that he was crying.

So it hurt after all.

Fine.

He looked at him madly. "You shut up from now on if you're not asked a question, understand?"

Mark nodded. Tears ran down his cheeks.

At that moment Selina came out of the bathroom.

"Did you start without me?" she asked with a grin.

***

When Selina saw that her father was beating Mark, her heart jumped. Finally! He was now 100 percent on her side. She'd known it was only a matter of time.

"Did you start without me?"

Dad looked back at her like a dog trying to please his master. Mark, on the other hand, grimaced and glanced at her angrily. For the next few hours, Selina wanted to make sure that this gaze broke as much as her father's. Tonight he'd be the pupil and she the teacher. She could hardly wait, but first she had to eat something.

She was dying of hunger.

She pulled a pack of disinfectant wipes out of her pocket to clean the small table in the corner from the legacies of former guests and thought about using them later to disinfect the toilet. She'd only just removed the worst dirt with toilet paper. This motel was a disaster, but she couldn't afford being choosy.

In the meantime, Dan turned on the dusty TV, which actually worked. He decided on an episode of *The Walking Dead*. Selina didn't like the series very much. She found zombies stupid. Dan liked it. Kate had given him the sixth season for his birthday, and so far he hadn't missed a single episode. He just liked to escape into fantasy worlds.

Selina decided it could run in the background as long as it didn't distract Dad too much from the essential. Still better than any newscast.

The essentials were her and her plans for the night. But first they had to eat and drink. Selina fetched a water bottle and a pack of chips from the bag she'd brought with her. It wasn't a sensation, but it had to be enough for today. She'd also packed wine for Dad, who wouldn't need anything else. Fortunately, it was a bottle with a screw cap. Dan looked relieved and drank directly from the bottle. Selina sat at the table with her water. She noticed Mark watching her.

"Look to the TV!" she ordered brusquely.

He obeyed.

Dan took off his shoes and made himself comfortable on the bed with the bottle. Suddenly the disgusting bedspread didn't seem that bad anymore.

She didn't have to order him to watch TV.

Selina wondered if she should offer Mark something, at least water, but then decided not to. She was curious whether he would ask for it. Or for the toilet? Everyone had to go to the toilet sometime. But Mark didn't ask. The beating had probably been a lesson to him.

After she'd eaten and drank, Selina went over to the bed. She forced herself not to look too closely and not to think about what was hiding underneath and cuddled up to her dad. Somehow he'd changed in the last few hours. This morning she'd thought he wouldn't recover so quickly and was afraid he might end up stabbing her in the back without worrying about the consequences. She'd have to accept this risk, because without him she wouldn't be able to make it. Without him she wouldn't even have made it this far. Apart from that, it wouldn't make any sense without him.

It was time to say thank you. Selina grabbed her father's hand and gently pressed it. Dan turned his head and looked at her. He was beautiful. Selina bent over him and kissed him on the slightly open lips. "I love you, Daddy."

Dan stiffened for a moment, but then he grabbed her hair with both hands and held her head to return her kiss. His warm, firm tongue tasted of wine. He licked her lips and teeth. His breath was hot. Selina sat on him and fiddled around with his pants. He was already hard. Suddenly everything seemed so easy and natural to her. Dan's penis jumped out of the open zipper. He hadn't had a shower for a while, and you could smell it, but that didn't matter now. Selina took a deep breath and took his cock in her mouth. His taste filled her. She licked, sucked, and swallowed. She sucked every single drop out of him, and Dan twitched and moaned under her. He arched his back and lifted his pelvis toward her.

She knew she should take everything he could give her. And she did.

***

After he'd shot his load into his daughter's mouth, Dan's penis was useless for now. It hung down limply, dripping on the blanket. Selina wiped her wet mouth with the back of her hand and smiled. While Dan was naked from the hip down, she was still wearing all her clothes.

He grabbed her pants, tried to help her undress, but Selina shook her head. "Sit back and enjoy the show, Daddy."

Dan did.

Selina undressed next to the bed so Mark wouldn't miss a thing. He could have gawked right between her legs and certainly would have done so in other circumstances, but instead he kept his gaze down.

"Look at me," Selina ordered.

That fucking bitch!

Mark was wondering if he should obey her orders. At the moment she was stark naked and unarmed. But the knife and pistol were lying on the bed, right next to her father, whom she'd just milked with every trick in the book.

That greedy little slut!

Mark still couldn't believe it! Of course he'd tried not to look, but in the end he hadn't been able to turn his eyes away—he'd been so horrified and fascinated at the same time.

Who would have thought that? Daddy didn't make any effort to stop her either. Quite the contrary.

But she's his daughter, damn it! His own flesh and blood! Would you do that with your own child?

Well, the truth was, he didn't know. Anyway, he'd been about to do it with his own student, which wasn't too praiseworthy either.

But his mind resisted desperately. The same mind that had allowed some wet daydreams just a few hours ago.

Was that any better?

Well, first of all it had been only daydreams and secondly in his case it might have been the seduction of a protégé, but not inbreeding or even abuse.

No?

Shit, she's so damn sexy!

Selina now stood in front of him in all her splendor, stark naked and with her legs apart. How often had he seen her like that in his dreams?

Now everything was real.

Within reach!

Her sweet scent, her plump breasts (so rosy and tender), her little navel, her slender, well-shaped legs.

She was here, right in front of him.

He'd only have had to reach out his hand …

Which, of course, didn't work.

Long before his mind could grasp it, he'd already devoured her with his eyes, and she just stood there and enjoyed it. Mark's thoughts overturned.

What was she going to do with him? Would she touch him? Just like she did with her father? Was that what she wanted? Making the very men submissive who were supposed to be an authority?

Because she liked to feast on their weakness?

Selina gave him enough time to look at her from top to bottom, then she bent forward and Mark thought at first she was going to kiss him. Instead, she reached over him for the knife. Dreamily, she looked at him as her fingers moved slowly and very carefully along the blade.

"Would you like to fuck me, Mark?"

Mark swallowed hard.

"How many times have you imagined that, huh?"

Mark felt caught and hated her for it. What should he say now?

"Come on, you can admit it."

"No," Mark replied. "I didn't imagine that."

"Oh, really?" Selina mocked. Suddenly she pushed a foot between his legs, which didn't hurt much because she was barefoot. Mark cried out in torment, though. The pressure of her toes made his penis twitch.

"And what is that, then?" Selina massaged him with nauseating serenity.

Mark gritted his teeth and somehow tried to suppress his arousal.

It was impossible.

He had a giant boner, which she hadn't even had to strain herself for.

It was enough to make you weep.

"You're a liar, and you know it."

Mark closed his eyes. He was going to cum at any moment. But then Selina stopped abruptly.

"Hold his head, Daddy."

Mark started a pointless attempt to slide away from the bed when he already felt two hands on his temples. Meller's grip was firm and relentless.

What is she up to?

Mark felt panic in his chest.

Selina stood with both feet between his legs. With her left hand she grabbed Mark's sweaty hair and pulled his head back. Her father held him in this position.

"Liars are supposed to get their mouth stuffed," she whispered and smiled. "But today I feel much more like cutting." She pressed the blade against Mark's wet lips, which he instinctively pressed together. Desperately, he tried to squirm out of Dan's grip. The blade slid vertically several times through his upper and lower lip.

Mark sobbed hoarsely. The blood running down his chin and into his shirt collar was warm. Finally, Selina took the knife away and put the index finger into the fresh wounds to smear the blood like lipstick.

The pain was dull and burning.

"So," she said when she'd finished her work. She looked at him in a disdainful way.

Mark didn't see much, but she was close enough that he could see his blood on her skin.

"That was the punishment, sweetie. But there is also a reward." She was still smiling and came so close that his face was right in front of her pussy.

"You can lick me."

"W-what?" Mark sighed to his own surprise.

"I want you to lick my pussy! And do it real good! I don't want to hear any complaints."

"But I ..." *I'm bleeding!* Mark wanted to say, but then he realized that this was exactly what she wanted. He closed his eyes and stuck out his tongue.

"Just a moment," Selina said cheerfully. "First lick this." She held the knife in front of his face.

"Selina, please ..."

"If you play along, you might survive," she explained dryly, as if it was actually a game.

Mark hesitantly licked the blade, but Selina made sure that he developed the necessary passion to make himself bleed. She helped him by turning the blade over and over.

When he was finally allowed to stop, his tongue was a painful bloody rag. But it wasn't over yet, for Selina Meller expected nothing less than a climax.

At first, Mark concentrated fully on the pain and the blood that flooded his mouth and ran down his throat. He swallowed a few times and had to cough. In return, he received a few powerful blows to the back of his head. Finally he decided to give the bitch what she wanted. He pushed the maltreated tip of his tongue deep into her crack.

Selina moaned and grabbed his hair. She set the rhythm for Mark to follow. Finally she lay down on her back and her father helped Mark find the right position between her thighs. His cock pounded painfully while Selina seemed to be on the verge of orgasm. She lifted her twitching abdomen toward Mark, and he did his very best, even though he was nauseous from all the blood he'd swallowed, and the pain almost made him lose his mind. He suspected that this was the last night of his life, but he wanted to do everything to prevent that. He was actually clinging to the miserable life of the perverse high school teacher. He'd have liked to fuck the little bitch as if there was no tomorrow. Just like in his dreams. After all, his cock was doing much better than his mouth, and he'd have given everything to finally get rid of that pressure.

Daddy seemed to have other plans. This show wasn't exactly to his taste.

Selina's breath came faster and faster in the last seconds, and Mark could only think of his pulsating member in this prison of fabric from which he couldn't free it without help when he was suddenly grabbed and torn back.

Dan now occupied the place between Selina's bloody thighs, desperately trying to shove his half-erect penis into her.

Fucking shit, have they lost their minds?

Mark would have laughed if the whole thing hadn't been so tragic.

"Are you crazy?" Selina was outraged. She sat up and pushed her father away.

He immediately crawled toward her again. Sobbing, with his penis in his hand.

"I did all this for you," he cried. "And now you push me away? I've given you my fucking life!"

"I love only you, Daddy. But that doesn't mean you are the only one I fuck! And now I want him!" She pointed at Mark, who had meanwhile gotten up. Thick blood dripped from his disfigured lips onto the front of his shirt.

"Put him on the bed and take his pants off."

Dan gave Mark an evil glance. His face was a grimace of sheer madness. He looked from Mark to Selina and then back to Mark, and he seemed to be ponder something that probably only made sense to himself. Mark noticed that Dan's penis was now completely flaccid. Quite contrary to his own. Selina's father was, of course, older than he was, so the virility could wear off if you overdid it. Dan would have to come to terms with the fact that he alone would never be enough for her.

And what makes you think about that?

That was indeed a very good question.

Selina smiled contentedly when her dad finally moved toward Mark. He grabbed him under his armpits and tore him to his feet. For a brief moment the eyes of the two men met, but neither could make sense of the other one. Dan unbuttoned Mark's jeans and pulled them down to his ankles. Mark gasped for air with relief as his penis finally jumped out and stood up to its full size. All he wanted was to be freed from this pressure. For the time being, any remedy would have felt right.

Dan pushed him onto the bed. Mark dropped onto the mattress, loudly exhaling. He wished his hands hadn't been tied; he would have grabbed the damn slut long ago and impaled her on his cock. Perhaps it would be possible to thrust a little bit of reason into her.

Reason that had long since left him itself.

Selina didn't hesitate a single second. She sat on Mark's dick, which disappeared in her bloody vagina with a smacking noise.

A pleasant heat shot up from his loins. Mark groaned.

That little bitch knew exactly how to move. Mark closed his eyes and enjoyed the show. If this was really the end of his life, then at least it ended with a fucking bang!

***

While the two seemed to have the fun of their lives on the dirty bed, Dan slipped into his pants, crying. He forced himself not to look at his moaning daughter riding her teacher.

The noises were bad enough. That moaning and the dull clapping of meat on meat. Not to mention the smells. If he'd once believed that the smell of coffee in his house was the worst of all evils, then he'd probably not yet known how his daughter's sweat would smell if mixed with that of another man. The motherfucker with the bloody face seemed to have the time of his life here!

In the end, Dan couldn't help it. He just had to look. Selina squatted upright on her former teacher and moved lasciviously up and down. The gentle play of her muscles under the smooth skin was breathtaking. Dan would have liked to drag her away from this guy to fuck her himself, but his cock was useless for now. Did she do this on purpose?

His gaze fell on the bloody knife and his father-in-law's pistol, which had fallen to the floor in the heat of the moment. He bent down and thoughtfully looked at the gun for a few seconds before picking it up.

With his eyes narrowed, he aimed at Selina's back.

He could put an end to all this, here and now.

First Selina, then the teacher, and finally himself. That wouldn't be the wrong thing to do. They all were guilty.

He and the teacher might have been bewitched by Selina, but that wasn't an excuse that would apply in court or at the gates of heaven. They had let the damn instinct prevail over their minds, for which there was no apology. So many people had died because he'd been too weak to stop this girl. Instead, he'd had nothing more important in mind than to shove his cock into his daughter.

Who deserved death more than he?

Without any further thought, Dan walked around the bed. From the corner of his eye, he realized the serial hero Rick had just taken on a horde of zombies on TV. He shot their skulls off. One by one.

Bang. Bang. Bang.

There was nothing to it. Blood and brain splashed on the asphalt.

Dan turned back to the hustle and bustle on the bed. Selina bounced around like a whore on this Mark, who had turned his bloody lips into something like a grin.

That was enough now!

Dan pressed the barrel against the teacher's left temple.

Selina paused.

She seemed confused.

The teacher turned his head and looked directly into the muzzle.

"Dad!"

The teacher made a noise like "*Argh*," just like the zombies on TV, and then his eye was gone.

There was a little smoke, and blood splattered on Selina's breasts. As if stung by a tarantula, she jumped back. Mark's penis slipped out of her. Milky sperm seeped from it.

"Are you crazy?" Selina screamed. She tried to wipe the fresh blood from her breasts but only smudged it.

Dan shrugged and aimed at her.

"Drop the gun," she screamed.

"It's better this way, Selina. Believe me."

"You don't really want that, Daddy! I love you!"

"Close your eyes," Dan said and cocked the gun.

"Do you really want our baby to die?"

Dan froze. "What? What baby?"

Selina slowly approached him. One hand she'd stretched out, the other lay on her stomach. Was there a small bulge?

Impossible!

"I did a test," she whispered, sobbing. "If you don't believe me, I'll do another one. It must have happened right in the beginning."

Dan shook his head. His hand trembled so much that he could no longer aim. He lowered his arm and stared at his daughter.

"I'm pregnant, Daddy. You know we never used contraception."

Did he know that? He should have known. However, he'd been far too busy to get a grip on what was going on between him and his daughter. He'd never have thought she could get pregnant.

I'm such a sick asshole!

"This shouldn't have happened." The barrel pointed to the ground.

Selina was with him now, but she wasn't as naked and helpless as she appeared. While Dan was still staring at her belly, trying to understand all this, she'd already grabbed the gun from his suddenly powerless hand.

She took it without any effort but didn't aim at him.

Dan shook his head as if he could drive the madness away.

"Why did you do this?" he finally asked.

"I didn't, at least not alone."

He took a hasty look at the teacher's corpse. Only a little blood ran out of the empty eye socket. Most of it had accumulated on the pillow under the head. He didn't have to worry about his shortsightedness anymore.

"It doesn't have to be mine, does it? You've certainly done it with others."

Selina smiled and shook her head. "What do you think of me, Daddy?"

He rubbed his mouth, a gesture of absolute helplessness. "You know very well what I think of you," he whispered.

"Too bad, because it's not like that. I wasn't a virgin anymore, but I always used a condom. I still had my period after the last guy I slept with. But I haven't had it since we started. It was supposed to happen, Daddy. It's our destiny."

Now he rubbed his hands all over his face. His knees became weak and he had to sit quickly to not collapse.

Dan staggered backward and barely managed to flop onto a chair. He slumped like the biggest pile of misery the world has ever seen. Without much overstatement he probably was.

"You've never used a condom with me," he lamely said. Dan raised his head, which seemed to weigh tons, and looked at her, this sweet girl who had once been his beloved princess, for whom he'd give the shirt off his back.

He didn't know her anymore.

He didn't even know himself anymore.

278

I should have shot her while I still could. Baby or not, maybe she's lying. In any case, I should have shot.

"We'll soon be a family," Selina said dreamily, patting her belly.

"Are you completely crazy? Don't you know what happens to such babies?"

"Most of them are healthy. Ours is surely healthy and beautiful."

"Are you listening to yourself?"

"Yes. That's the baby I want." She stroked her belly and said the intangible, "Our child of love."

"This has nothing to do with love, Selina. Absolutely nothing."

"Oh, really? Then why do you behave like a jealous lover?"

She looked over at the dead man. Dan followed her gaze.

He didn't answer.

A thousand thoughts rotated in his brain, yet they couldn't find any connection. Maybe that was the way it should have been.

Everything could still be all right.

With God's help.

Somehow.

Selina came to him and snuggled up on his lap. Her body was warm; most of the blood had already clotted. She stroked his face with one hand and held the gun to his neck with the other.

"Do you really want to be dead? Like that guy over there? Do you want to feel nothing anymore?" She let the muzzle slide down his upper body, into his crotch.

Dan flinched. He was hard.

Selina kissed him and she tasted good.

As good as always.

Dan put his arms around her.

She felt the same as always.

Whether she lied to him or not.

Whether she carried his child under her heart or not.

Whether she was his daughter or not.

Whether he would die or not.

Whether he wanted it or not.

She'd be his princess forever.

***

A little later, Selina got off Dan's sweaty lap and went to the bathroom without paying attention to the dead body on the bed. Dan did the same by concentrating on the TV while he dressed. He should have taken a shower or at least washed himself a bit, but he didn't feel able to at the moment. He was completely exhausted and dead tired. He urgently had to sleep, otherwise he'd go crazy.

But there was a corpse lying in his bed.

All the pillows and sheets were dirty.

Dan tried to make himself comfortable on the chair.

No chance.

With burning eyes he stared at the screen. Instead of *The Walking Dead* there was now another series he didn't know. Something like a thriller. Possibly the five thousandth episode of the hundredth season of *CSI Fucking Whatever.*

It didn't matter.

Dan had his own little psychodrama here. A bloody corpse on the bed and a freshly fucked daughter in the bathroom.

Welcome to the most bizarre movie script of all time!

Dan's eyes fell on the gun and the knife. Selina had left both on the table. She trusted him, even though he'd almost shot her an hour ago. Somehow she seemed to know that he wouldn't hurt her.

But was it really like that?

Dan stared at the gun as if he could hypnotize himself with it. Was she right? He closed his eyes.

She had a baby.

His baby.

Possibly.

Dan thought about Leila. She'd smelled so sweet, and her little head had been so soft. He missed her. Her chuckle and her laughter. The little hands in his face. The little head with the soft fluff on his shoulder. Dan wiped a tear from the corner of his eye. What would it be like to have such a small creature around again? As a father (as well as husband and son) he'd failed all along the line, but this would give him one last chance to make up for everything. The idea was crazy, but basically he had no choice.

Maybe he'd have somehow managed to kill Selina to put an end to all this.

First Selina and then himself.

But that wasn't possible if she was pregnant. He could never kill a baby—unborn or not.

No, he wasn't such a person.

So, on with the show?

Selina wanted to go to Mexico, and maybe he should actually try to get her there. If they made it, it could be a new beginning. They just had to find a place where people didn't care what their fellow men did. A place where no one asked questions. And if they didn't find it in Mexico, they could keep searching.

Somewhere in the south.

They could go as far as Brazil or even to the end of the world, where no one cared who did what, when or with whom …

Selina came out of the bathroom and distracted him from his thoughts. She was completely dressed and wore a towel like a turban on her head. This wasn't the first time Dan wondered how women managed to keep those things in place.

"We should get away from here." She looked at her dead teacher and then at her father.

"But I don't know how much longer I can drive."

"Just a bit. We'll sleep in the car, somewhere."

"But that's ..." Dangerous, Dan wanted to say when he realized it was absolute nonsense.

What was he afraid of?

Of people like them?

ROLE SWAP

By that time, the nationwide manhunt had been going on for several hours. Photos of Dan, Selina, and Mark circulated through all forms of media.

The filthy motel owner had recognized Dan on television but had no interest in a horde of cops on the property. The local dealers and pimps paid him well to keep his mouth shut. Sometimes they brought the women here to serve the customers on the spot. Some were young. Children in garish makeup and cheaply dressed baby hookers who often screamed and wailed loudly as they were being fucked in the dilapidated rooms.

Motel owner Erwin also liked them young. His favorites were those who didn't have tits yet and were so tight that they literally ripped apart when you shoved your cock into them. There was no hornier lubricant than warm virgin blood. But he rarely had the privilege of breaking in such a horse, at most once or twice a year. Otherwise that, he had to be content with "normal" hookers. Some at least had tight assholes.

Erwin was a swine with no scruples. After seeing Dan on TV and knowing he was travelling with a damn hot girl who was supposed to be his daughter and another guy for whom he didn't give a shit, he grabbed his cell and called Mario, the most fucked-up pimp in that sad area.

He answered with an annoyed grunt. "I hope it's important, man."

"Mario, listen. A guy just checked in who's wanted for murder by the cops, and he's got his daughter with him.

She seems to be a real piece of gold, if you believe the pictures on TV. Looks fucking awesome."

"Sounds like a pretty hot potato, man."

"Nobody knows they're here, or the motel would be swarming with cops by now. We could get the guy and his companion out of the way, then the girl belongs to us."

Mario gave a skeptical snort. "Did you just say companion? So there are two guys?"

"Yeah, man. But what the hell? We'll wait a while and then surprise them in their sleep. That—"

At that moment there was a loud bang that made the rotten walls vibrate. Erwin flinched. "Holy shit!"

"What's going on?" Mario asked.

"A gunshot," Erwin whispered, instinctively reaching for the double-barreled shotgun from under the counter.

"Somebody was shooting."

"You mean one of these guys?"

"Think so." Erwin felt the sweat on his fleshy neck. Goosebumps spread on his arms. "Shit, man, what do I do now?"

There was only one other guest that evening: a junkie who came here regularly to shoot up. No help would be expected from him.

"Stay where you are! I'll drop by with some of my boys."

"Hopefully they didn't kill the girl," Erwin muttered. "That would be a real shame."

"Stay out of this, understand? We'll hurry."

"M-maybe I should call the cops."

"No, man! Are you crazy? Doug didn't bribe the sheriff for nothing. And don't forget the girl! I thought you wanted her."

Erwin hesitated. Yes, he wanted the little bitch, that much was certain. Even if she didn't quite meet his expectations of age. A new little pretty horse for Mario's stable. And the one who found it was allowed to break it in, that was the rule. Hopefully the assholes hadn't just killed her. Although Erwin didn't want to exclude that he'd still be interested in her. As long as no one had shot her pussy or ass off, it would still be fun with her. Even if it would be a bit more boring then. Erwin had already seen so many stubborn looks breaking under him. Most of them gave up after the first load of sperm that was shot up their ass. The more stubborn ones were allowed to play "toilet" for him at the end, and that killed the strongest fighting spirit.

Only one had swallowed several loads of shit to finally understand who was the boss. After that she automatically spread her legs when he entered the room. If he didn't come in, it was one of the dozens of others who were fucking her every day. It shouldn't matter to her anymore.

Because she was broken.

Just like all of them.

Owning such toys was great, but nothing could top that one sacred moment when the will and strength disappeared from their eyes to make way for that endless emptiness that filled them from then on. Every new chance of such an experience was worth the risk. But Erwin wanted to wait for Mario and his boys.

Better stay on the safe side.

After all, they were dealing with at least one murderer here, even if the guy in the photo didn't look like a tough guy but rather like a fucking momma's boy. The kind of guy Erwin would almost fuck if it wasn't a guy.

He grinned stupidly. It was time for the news again, and this time he looked very closely at the photos of the three. The curly guy and the girl were supposed to be father and daughter, both blonde and blue-eyed. Dan and Selina Meller from Roanoke, Virginia. The other guy was allegedly the girl's teacher and probably served Meller as a hostage. Just like his own daughter. According to news reports, this harmless-looking Dan had killed at least three people, including his wife and mother.

"Holy shit," Erwin mumbled as he clasped his rifle even tighter. "The guy doesn't look that mean."

So this Dan had kidnapped his own daughter. What else did he do with her? He wouldn't have believed the snooty guy to do that. Erwin wondered if the girl would still be as tight as he liked it. Unfortunately, she was too old for him, and Daddy had likely been on her for too long. But then he'd come up with a few other things to give the girl an experience or two. His cock, which was short and thick and rarely washed, throbbed joyfully at the idea. Maybe he'd even come up with a role for Daddy if he lived long enough.

But first, Mario and his bums had to show up!

That takes forever!

Erwin took his shotgun and looked out the window. Everything seemed quiet and peaceful. There was no car in front of room eight. They'd probably parked it behind the building so the car wouldn't be seen from the road. Not so stupid at all.

"Man, this is taking long ..." Erwin wanted a cigarette but didn't want to take his hands off the gun for a second.

Where the hell are they?

He wondered if he should call Mario again when a car finally turned into the parking lot. The headlights were turned off and five armed men got out.

Finally!

286

Erwin opened the door and ran toward them.

***

"What's going on out there?" Selina sounded nervous. She went to the window and pushed the curtain back a bit. When she turned back to Dan, her face was white as a sheet.

"There's some guys with guns."

"What?" Dan had been stuffing supplies back into the bag. He walked past her and took a look. His heart stopped for at least two beats when he saw the men gathering in the parking lot. One was the guy from the check-in.

He let go of the curtain as if he'd burned himself on it and took a step back. "Shit!"

He grabbed the pistol and stood with his back to the door.

"What are they doing?" Selina was close to tears.

"Hide in the bathroom!" Dan ordered. His stomach contracted painfully. It felt like the evil wolf the hunter stuffed with stones. He swallowed to suppress the nausea.

How much ammo is actually in this damn gun?

In any case, there were no spare rounds.

"You think they're coming for us?" Selina's eyes were huge. Her fear was real. For the first time in so long.

Dan nodded. "I'm pretty sure. Lock yourself in the bathroom! But stay away from the door!"

Not bad advice.

Dan moved along the wall. He was now in the narrow space between door and window. If someone shot at it blindly, he wouldn't get hit here. And if the door opened, he'd have a chance to shoot back.

But the ammunition wasn't enough for six men.

Probably not even for three.

Dan trembled. He could hardly hold the gun. How was he going to shoot?

Please, God, make them go away! Make them come here for someone else. Please, don't let them come in. Oh God, please!

Selina looked the way he felt. Her gaze spoke volumes.

"I'm trying to protect you, Princess. Please go hide!" With that came the tears.

Selina finally understood and disappeared into the bathroom.

At that moment, there was a knock on the door. Dan buried his teeth in his lower lip and raised the pistol to eye level. He trembled so intensely that he would hardly hit if they came in.

"Hello? This is Erwin from check-in. I have fresh towels."

Yeah, right!

Dan held his breath. He felt his pulse in his temples and ears.

"Hello? I'll put the towels outside the door."

What's he saying? Why doesn't he just come in? He surely has a spare key.

Even before Dan finished his thought, the door broke open and crashed into the wall with a loud bang. He was alert enough to pull the trigger, but the shot went blank because no one had come in.

Shit! Shit! Shit!

Dan tried to find any target, but there was nothing. The door was wide open, and the smell of smoke and dry leaves hung in the air. Dan didn't move; he hardly dared breathe. He felt the presence of the men who were less than three feet away.

"You'd better put the gun down, boy. Somebody might get hurt," a voice Dan didn't know said.

"Forget it!" he yelled back.

"We just want to talk," the voice continued. "We know who you are, Dan Meller. You're in a lot of trouble, right? Maybe we can help. We don't like the cops either, you know."

"I just want you to go away. Leave us alone!"

Dan's throat felt sore and scratchy. However, he couldn't stop shouting. His lips were wet from his saliva and from the tears running down his face.

"Your daughter is here too, ain't she?" asked the voice, which almost sounded sympathetic—in its own, lulling way.

"You want to protect her. I can understand that. I'm a father myself. My daughter is now eleven. Just before puberty."

A dry laugh.

"Your Selina is still in the middle of it, right? She probably thinks she's an adult, but we all know that at eighteen, you're still a long way from being one. I know that from my niece. It's not always easy. As a father, you want to do everything right, but sometimes it just doesn't work. I know that, Danny. Can I call you Danny? My name is Mario."

"Please, go away," Dan begged. "Just let us leave!"

"We will. Later. First, I want to talk to you in peace, Danny. So now you have to put your gun on the floor and push it through the door with your foot. Understand?"

Dan felt as if two huge hands were squeezing his chest from both sides.

Had he ever been so desperate?

What was he supposed to do?

These guys were up to no good. But it was also clear that there were six of them, probably armed to the teeth.

And he was alone and had almost no ammo left. If they wanted to kill him, they would.

Either way.

"Why should I?" he asked anyway.

"Because you can't beat us alone, boy. And because it makes me angry when I have to talk until I'm blue in the face. When I'm angry, it usually ends up pretty painful for the other person. You should not only think about yourself but about your girl. You certainly don't want anything to happen to her. Right?"

"How do I know you're not gonna hurt her anyway?"

"You don't. But you have no choice."

Dan closed his eyes and pressed the back of his head against the wall. He was scared like never before in his life.

"Okay," he finally said. "I'll do it."

"Good boy."

Dan bent down and put the gun on the dirty carpet. Then he straightened up again, pressed himself as close as possible to the wall, and pushed the gun toward the threshold with his right foot. A polished black leather boot appeared in his field of vision and kicked the gun out.

"And now it's your turn. But nice and slow, with your hands behind your head."

Dan gasped for air. Maybe one of his last breaths. His heart somersaulted as he put his hands behind his head and slowly walked to the door. Four men stood in front of him, including the fat guy with the ugly wart on his upper lip, to whom he owed all this. They pointed their weapons at him.

One stood on Dan's pistol—or, rather, Bill's. The guy had a southern accent. He was small and very slim, a guy around forty in a colorful shirt and black leather jacket. A triumphant grin played around his thin lips.

Mario.

"Danny boy," he said satisfied. "It wasn't that hard, was it?"

Before Dan could answer, the barrel of Mario's gun hit him on the chin. His lower face immediately went numb. He felt something wet on his throat, and blood poured out of his mouth. Like a wet sack he fell to his knees, but Mario grabbed him by the hair and tore him back to his feet.

Two other guys, both tall and broad-shouldered, grabbed his wrists and pulled them behind his back, twisting his arms painfully. They forced him back into the room where Mario stepped in front of the bed, grinning, and bent over Mark's body.

He sniffed like a dog and then turned to Dan, baring his teeth. "So you killed him, huh? Right through the eye. You're a tough bastard, right? Why are his lips cut up?"

Dan didn't answer. His mouth was full of blood and his shoulder joints throbbed. He couldn't think clearly.

"Was that you?"

What should he say?

What should he do?

What was right and what was wrong?

"Answer me, you motherfucker!"

Dan nodded. "It was me." He spoke as if his mouth was full of cotton.

"And why does his dick hang out? Who did he fuck with? You?"

Dan shook his head.

"With the girl? Did you force her? Shit, what kind of perverted asshole are you?"

Dan burst into tears. So far, he'd been trapped in a vacuum of madness. Alone with all the horror. But now that this strange son of a bitch was saying the unbelievable, Dan realized the full extent of his hell.

Mario stepped in front of him and put a finger under his bloody chin. "It seems to me we've caught a true psychopath here. You cut your daughter's teacher's lips and watch him fuck her? And while he's still at it, you shoot his eye out? Man, I've seen a lot, but that's really sick!"

Dan swallowed his own blood and had a coughing fit. Meanwhile the rest of the men had entered the room and closed the door. The room was dark, and the crime series was still playing on TV.

"Where is she?" Mario asked.

Dan's arms were turned upward until black dots danced before his eyes. He wasn't far from fainting.

"In the bathroom," he gasped. What should he have done? He could no longer protect her.

His princess was lost.

Just like him.

Mario nodded to Erwin. "Check that!"

With a grin and a visible bulge in his shorts he walked to the bathroom, only to stupidly realize a short time later, "The door is locked."

"Then ask her to come out," Mario said. "Tell her Daddy will lose an eye if she doesn't." He pressed the muzzle of his .45 against Dan's closed eyelid.

Erwin tried his luck, but nothing moved behind the door.

"You're probably not a nice daddy at all, and she doesn't give a shit what happens to your damn eye. Could that be it?" Mario snarled at him.

Dan nodded and thought, *Please, God, I hope she's escaped already! Let her get away. Her and the baby!*

Mario's men forced him to the floor. They let go of his arms, giving him a moment of enormous relief until he felt Mario's foot on his neck. Dan's face was pressed into the smeary carpet.

"There's blood on this knife," someone said.

And another one: "Give me that!"

Then Mario: "Further down. I want him alive for a while still."

The next moment, there was a dull, stabbing pain in Dan's back. The blade was driven deep into the lower part of his spine, turned around a few times and finally pulled out again.

Dan cried. He couldn't feel his legs anymore. All the blood in his mouth made him gag, and he lost the sparse contents of his stomach in a hot gush.

"Gosh! Such a mess." Mario laughed.

And another one giggled hoarsely. "Oh man, now he's pissing, too!"

"I got the right point. You can let him go, Mario. He's not going anywhere."

Mario took his foot away. Dan felt that, but everything below his navel was like cut off. He hadn't even noticed his bladder emptying. The bastard had severed his spine.

"And because it's so funny right now, you can break his arms too," Mario declared with a laugh.

Dan screamed with all his might. Two tall men bent down and tampered with his arms. His bones broke with the nauseating cracking of rotten branches.

Finally the fainting came.

Dan welcomed it with gratitude.

***

Selina didn't even try to hide. The only possibility would have been the dirt-encrusted shower. A hiding place for children. She could just as well close her eyes and hope nobody could see her as long as she couldn't see them herself.

Little children believed that, but Selina Meller wasn't a child anymore. She'd pushed the memories of her childhood deep into the back of her consciousness.

But they were there. Memories of the time in the trailer park and of her mother, Clara.

Dan didn't know there were memories.

Nobody knew.

Selina had buried them inside herself like a black stone with sharp edges.

Sometimes this stone cut into her heart.

Even today.

Weird images flickered through her mind. Pictures of a little girl with matted hair who was hungry but got nothing. How she searched the garbage in the camper for something to eat while her parents were drooling in their delirium. Sometimes she even found what she was looking for: sour milk, rotten fruit, moldy bread, and a few cookie crumbs could already be dinner. Often it was just thirst that almost made her lose her mind until she'd learned to drink from the garden hose, because there was no water in the trailer. Before Selina had become smart enough to use the hose, she'd regularly drunk the leftovers from some bottles and cans that stood around everywhere. The taste had been so bitter that her small stomach had somersaulted, but after that, a quite pleasant feeling of warmth, security, and safety quickly set in. Selina could then fall asleep without crying. That's why she used the alcohol leftovers of her parents when she already knew how to get water.

Dan didn't know about this. He'd always told himself that he had everything well in hand, while Clara was the one who got completely out of control. But he subconsciously blanked out everything that had gone wrong and finally only remembered the more or less clear moments in which he'd at least tried to take care of his child. When Selina was a baby, he'd actually saved her life, even though his care had been poor. Compared to what Clara did, he performed quite well, but this comparison was a joke.

Clara would have let her daughter die.

Dan let her vegetate.

He thought he could be proud of that.

Selina saw it differently.

She often thought it might have been better if he just let her die when she was still a baby. That would have saved her the memories of what happened to her mother that morning. Dan had been sound asleep when Clara suddenly started panting and coughing. Selina stood right next to her and hadn't noticed urine running down her legs as she watched her mother die. Clara wasn't conscious, but her body fought nonetheless. She kept rearing up, tossing her head back and forth, and twitching uncontrollably. Vomit splashed out of her mouth, her face turning blue and then purple. She already had too much stomach contents in her windpipe to cough it out. How could she, when she was unconscious?

Dan had always believed his wife had died quietly. Otherwise he'd have woken up, right? But, in fact, her death struggle had lasted several minutes and little Selina had to watch everything.

She still didn't understand what that had done to her. Like every child, she loved her mother. And like every child, she loved her father. Although she knew he was weak, which made him both guilty and innocent.

Little Selina was confronted with this weakness early on. For example, on that gloomy afternoon when she was sitting on the tattered couch in front of the trailer together with her dad and one of his buddies, the men had smoked joints and drunk beer while Selina sat between them with a lollipop and enjoyed the closeness of her daddy. She'd already been his princess then and was proud of it. The other guy was called Shawn and was probably what Selina today would call a horny asshole. At some point he pulled her on his lap and stroked her legs with his rough hands. She didn't want that, even less when she felt something hard under her.

She cried and looked at her daddy, begging for help. But he just rolled a fresh joint and made no effort to help her. Then she cried even louder and stretched out her arms to her father.

He'd just giggled like a lunatic and asked without much interest what was going on again.

And Shawn?

He shrugged with a grin and said, "Oh nothing! You know the women. Always bitching. Will you get me another beer?"

Her father laughed and got up to get some new beer.

He left her alone with this Shawn and his hard cock.

Selina remembered how she cried and called for her daddy, but he just got up and left.

When he came back, he was still laughing. He didn't seem to understand that she no longer wanted to sit on Shawn's lap. After all, there was only one way out.

"Dude, now she's pissed all over me, the little pig!" Shawn had shouted and finally let her go.

It wasn't always as easy as that day.

Was that the reason she blamed her dad?

Nothing really bad had happened.

Or …?

No, she'd never reproached him.

At least not directly.

She only recognized his weaknesses, and the older she got, the more conscious she became of how to take advantage of them. Her daddy had always meant well. He'd never been evil, just a jerk. He'd always loved her but still let her down, never realized or even understood how she was doing. All his life he'd only seen the beautiful glimmer and had been blind to what lay behind it. Just like on the mangy couch in front of the even mangier trailer.

He'd seen the curtain move and had known something bad was hiding behind it, but he'd never opened it.

Because he was a coward.

A master of suppression!

Later, Selina seemed to grow into a normal and happy teenager. She kept her nightmares and nightly tears to herself. She kept her fears, doubts, and insecurities to herself. Just like the hatred that slumbered so hot and deep inside her.

But whom should she hate?

Her mother was dead.

And she loved her daddy so much.

Herself? Society? Shawn?

In the end, she had to make a decision. How could you hate the person you loved the most?

It wasn't written in any textbook, not even in the damn Bible. Selina was on her own to realize that. And finally she found a way to let her father feel both at the same time: love and hate.

She wanted him to sacrifice his life for her without dying. So she could possess and love him as well as make him repent and suffer. For he'd finally made her what she was, had dropped her and held her in the same moment.

It was crazy, but it was exactly these thoughts that shot through her mind as she desperately searched the narrow, dirty bathroom for a way out that had been denied to her for a lifetime. Her only chance was the window above the toilet. It was small, but probably just big enough to squeeze through.

Dad wouldn't have had a chance.

He probably never had one.

Selina heard a shot first, then soft voices.

Was he already dead?

Her heart pounded in her throat as she climbed on the toilet seat. The window could be opened easily, and cool evening air streamed in. Selina took a deep breath.

She'd have to pull herself up by the window frame. Fortunately, she'd always gotten high marks in gym class. Nevertheless, her muscles trembled and ached with exertion when she was finally out in the fresh air with her upper body. Now all she had to do was get her legs outside and it was done.

Panting, she struggled through the narrow window opening. No part of her body didn't hurt.

For a moment she paused for breath, one leg still in the bathroom, while the other was already dangling in the air. She heard screams that clearly came from Dad. On one hand it meant he was still alive, but on the other he was suffering worse than she'd ever have expected of him.

Her father's screams pierced Selina's bones down to the marrow, but she jumped outside. Away from here!

She was no longer a little girl peeing her pants to escape the pain.

Not that it would help here.

Selina landed safely on both feet in the knee-deep weeds of the overgrown motel and listened into the night.

What now?

She looked hectically around. Daddy's car was standing behind a big dumpster, but Selina had not been able to drive nor had the key.

What was she supposed to do?

They'll kill him!

Yeah, probably. But what was she going to do about those guys she didn't know anything about? She didn't know how many there were, or whether they had guns. She'd only heard one shot that her dad could have fired.

Who could help her?

She couldn't call the police …

What about the owner of the motel?

Selina couldn't know that he was one of them. She considered sneaking behind the motel to the front desk. Maybe she could persuade him to leave the police out of it and help on his own. Of course, he wouldn't do that for nothing. She could offer him a blowjob. More if necessary. Selina would be willing to do anything—no matter how disgusting the guy was—if she could save her dad.

Not that she felt sorry for him. But without Daddy, she wouldn't get to Mexico.

That much was certain.

I can't just run away without him.

This option was no longer available.

Selina hadn't moved a foot away from the window when two dark creatures came out of the darkness. She already saw herself turning around and running away, but in reality she didn't move an inch. Her pulse accelerated when she realized that both men were pointing their weapons at her. Selina instinctively raised her hands. She wanted to beg for her life, but her voice failed and all she brought out was a helpless cawing.

"Well, there's our little girl," one said.

Both were tall and broad and wore black leather jackets. Their weapons looked scary. Much more dangerous than Bill's. There wouldn't be much of her head left.

"Stay cool, sweetie, and nothing will happen to you."

One aimed at her, while the other let his gun disappear under his jacket and pulled out a pair of handcuffs.

"Just a little security measure," he explained with a grin.

Selina swallowed. The light from the bathroom reflected off the shiny metal.

"What do you want from me?"

"Oh, actually quite a lot," the man said cheerfully.

As he approached, Selina smelled his aftershave. He was young and could have been considered attractive if there hadn't been this long, bulging scar across his cheek.

"Stretch out your arms!"

Selina had no choice but to obey. The other guy aimed right between her eyes. He was about Dad's age, but far less attractive. The handcuffs snapped shut with one click. Selina tried to make eye contact with the younger one, but he didn't respond. Instead, he grabbed her by the arm and dragged her with him.

"Please," she pleaded and hoped for a way out. "I'll do anything you want if you let me go!"

The man laughed. "You're gonna do whatever we want anyway, baby."

"What's happening to my dad?"

"My boss only needs women, so your dad's gonna bite the dust. Sorry, sweetie."

Selina could hardly get these words into her mind. Everything had worked out according to plan, but now? "You can't do that! Please!"

"Stop whining! It's not my decision." He pushed her forward while the other man drilled the barrel of his gun into her back.

They reached the front of the motel, and Selina looked desperately for help. She couldn't see anyone, just the car belonging to the men.

The door to her room was wide open. Selina could hear the TV and then she saw it.

Him!

Four men crowded the small room. Only when two stepped back did she see her daddy. He lay on his stomach, bleeding from a wound on his back.

"Daddy?" Selina screamed and tried to break free. But the young man held her effortlessly with one hand.

"Well, who do we have here?"

A dark-haired man came up to her. Under his black leather jacket he wore a colorful shirt. Compared to his buddies, he was small and slim.

Was he the boss? He wasn't much of a gorilla or a stooge.

Next to him stood another man who didn't really fit the picture—fat, stained, and smelly.

Selina turned her head away when the smaller man stroked her cheek. That didn't seem to bother him.

"Erwin didn't promise too much. You are a true beauty. I'm Mario, your new daddy. Will you tell me your name, too?"

New daddy? What was that about? And who was this Erwin? Did he call these guys?

"What do you bastards want? What about my dad?" she yelled.

Mario looked at Dan and then at her again. Selina noticed that her father's arms were twisted strangely and the sleeves of his sweatshirt were bloody.

That doesn't look good!

"I don't know what your relationship is like," Mario said slowly. "After all, he's a murderer. All I can tell you is that I'm going to kill him. Whether he was a good daddy or a bad daddy doesn't matter to me."

"Please don't do that! Let him go! He won't say anything!"

"Yeah, I believe you, actually. But every girl can only have one daddy. And you have me now."

"I'll do anything …" Selina whimpered. "Really anything!"

"Well, I've heard that before, but the human body has limited resilience, my darling, so please don't talk too big. You'll soon do a lot for me and others, but it won't be possible for you to do everything as long as we need you alive."

Selina didn't know what to say. Every word seemed to be wasted here. For the first time she had no plan, no way out, not even the idea of one. With an empty gaze she stared at her dad and prayed her mind would start working again. She had already met some bad guys, but these obviously knew no mercy.

"Somebody get some cold water! Then we'll see if we can wake this guy up again. He should have a chance to say goodbye to his little daughter," Mario called, turning to his men.

One of them grabbed an empty bottle and hurried to the bathroom. When he came back, it was filled to the top with water. He kneeled next to Dan, grabbed him by the shoulder, turned him on his back, and poured the water over his face.

Dan's eyelids fluttered. He coughed and choked. Finally, he was awake. When he saw Selina, his face contorted. He didn't move. Selina realized his arms had to be broken and something was wrong with his legs as well. His jeans were wet at the crotch, and she imagined herself as a three-year-old for a horrible moment, with wet panties on the lap of Shawn, that scumbag.

Only she'd pissed on purpose back then.

"What have you bastards done to him? Daddy!" Again she tried to tear herself loose, but this time they let her. Selina fell to her knees in front of Dan and touched his face. His eyes filled with tears.

"I'm so sorry, Princess."

Selina shook her head. Her tears dripped on his face and mingled with his.

This time they were real.

Of course she'd wished he'd be punished for his cowardice and ignorance.

But not like this!

She tenderly stroked his pain-contorted face as far as the handcuffs would allow.

"It's okay, Daddy," she whispered. "It's not your fault."

"I … did … not … protect … you …"

He wasn't wrong about that, but Selina shook her head again. "You did what you could."

"Forgive … me?"

She nodded. "Yes, Daddy. I forgive you. I love you!"

"I forgive … you … too."

Selina lowered her gaze. She would have liked to reach for his hand, but there wasn't enough time. The two men grabbed him by the arms and legs. Dan roared in pain.

It was as if Selina suddenly felt everything he suffered. Her throat closed, and she gasped for air while her eyes followed him until he was out of sight.

She turned to Mario when he pulled her on her feet. "Where are they taking him?"

"None of your business, bitch!" the nasty guy named Erwin grunted. He came so close that his stench covered Selina's senses like a thick cloth. Then he grabbed between her legs and pressed his bulging lips onto her mouth. A slimy tongue licked over her teeth.

Selina felt his ugly wart rubbing against her upper lip. She gagged and caught a slap in the face for it. Erwin dug thumbs and index fingers into her cheeks and pressed against her jaw joints until she opened her mouth. Again he licked over her lips and her face and shoved his tongue deep into her throat.

Selina closed her eyes and held her breath.

"I'll get you first, bitch, did you know that? You'll be at my service all night long. And once you've tasted my shit, the rest of me will taste like vanilla pudding." He moaned in her ear and laughed scornfully.

"That's enough now, Erwin," Mario intervened as Erwin's sweaty hands were already busy under Selina's sweater. "You'll have plenty of time for that later."

With a disappointed grunt, Erwin let her go and took a step back.

Selina looked at Mario and wondered if it would be clever to thank him. She had to pull herself together and try to get him on her side if she didn't want to go down completely.

Finally, she decided it was worth a try. "Thanks," she whispered while perfectly batting her eyelashes.

Mario grinned. He seemed to like that. "You're a quick learner, child. Or what did your old man call you? Princess. Can I do that too?"

She nodded devotedly.

Mario ran his fingers her through her tangled hair and she let it happen.

"I'm looking forward to you, Princess."

"What are they doing to my dad?"

Mario sighed. "I hate to tell you, but they'll kill him. They have orders to take your car away and burn it somewhere. Daddy will go down with the sinking ship, if you know what I mean."

Selina swallowed her tears. "Is there anything I can do to prevent that?"

Mario shook his head. "I'm sorry, sweetie. Basically, we're doing him a favor. He'd be a cripple forever and would never be able to fuck his little princess again."

Selina was silent.

"But don't be sad. You won't lack cocks in the future." He laughed dryly.

At that moment his cell phone rang. He pulled it out of his pocket and listened nodding.

Selina lowered her gaze. For the moment there was nothing else to do or say. She was trapped and had to give in if she wanted to survive. Maybe later there would be an opportunity to escape this nightmare.

She'd remain vigilant.

And strong.

As strong as a girl could be who had grown up in a rancid trailer between a whore and a drunkard. She'd had to endure so many torments in her life and had locked them in her broken heart. She could take quite a lot if she had to.

Mario put his cell phone away again. "Take the body and whatever else is lying around and get everything into the car," he told the two young men who were standing bored in the corner.

Apparently, they felt relieved to finally have something to do, so they set to work immediately. One checked the bathroom and then put Dan's and Selina's few belongings in the two bags. The other one wrapped Mark's body in the dirty bedspread until only his feet stuck out.

Mario turned to Erwin after the men had disappeared with the body and the bags. "You take care of cleaning the room."

Erwin seemed anything but enthusiastic. "What? But not now, right?"

"When else?" Mario barked. "It's your fucking motel, so it's your fucking responsibility!"

He's the owner of the motel? Now everything makes sense, Selina thought and watched the hustle and bustle as inconspicuously as possible.

Erwin pouted like an insulted toddler. "But I can lock the room and not rent it out for the time being. It's no problem ..."

"The risk is far too big. You clean it, and you do it now! I'll come by tomorrow and take a look. Take some bleach and burn anything you can't get clean."

Erwin looked around the room and snorted. The carpet was dirty, as was the mattress and all the sheets and pillows.

"That will take hours," he complained with a disgusted expression.

Mario's gaze remained hard and uncompromising.

"I was supposed to get the girl," Erwin lamented. "She's mine first ... you said that—"

"I don't give a shit!" Mario yelled. His dark complexion turned red. He grabbed Erwin by the collar of his torn shirt and contorted his face because of the stench.

Selina couldn't blame him. Soon this disgusting guy would come at her like a rutting bull, and she didn't know if she could bear it without losing her mind (or without killing him). But first she'd probably spend a night with Mario, she was pretty sure about that. He was just as disgusting deep inside, but at least you didn't smell it. She could try to manipulate him somehow, maybe even wrap him around her finger. The main thing was that she manage to be his girl only. Most of the men she'd dealt with so far had been easy to handle. Why should Mario be an exception?

"You'll get the girl when you've done your job," Mario explained, letting go of the creep and wiping his hands on his pants.

"But there's brain on the wall," Erwin complained.

In fact, some suspicious lumps were hanging on the wall above the bed that looked like it.

"If you don't get to work right now, I'll splash yours against the wall too, if you got any at all!"

Mario grabbed Selina by the arm and dragged her toward the open door. He added, "We're going back to town. Two of my men stay here and take care of the car. You lend them yours for the way back, understand?"

Erwin grunted reluctantly. "I'll get you, baby. I swear to you."

Selina didn't even look at him. Silently, she let Mario lead her away and was for the moment only happy to leave this terrible room.

***

On the edge of consciousness, Dan noticed how they hoisted him viciously onto the back seat of his car. When they dragged him out, he'd hoped to catch a last glimpse of Selina, but she stayed inside the motel while he was quickly carried behind the building. The pain in his arms drove him to the threshold of unconsciousness again and again. He knew his legs were in much worse condition, even though they were currently the minor problem because he couldn't feel them. They would kill him, which was perhaps not the worst. He'd have to face a life in a wheelchair otherwise—and only if he was lucky enough to still be able to sit.

A life as a cripple in jail.

Where's the fanfare?

The thought of losing his life didn't sadden Dan. But he was scared. He was afraid of what would happen to him now. The question was why they didn't finally finish it. Dan would have liked to ask, but his tongue was so thick and heavy that he could scream but not speak.

Despite his fear, he could accept his own death. He only hoped the pain wouldn't be too bad. The only reason he couldn't let go yet was Selina.

The guys didn't seem to want to kill her, and that was a big relief.

Somehow.

They surely didn't have anything nice in store for her. Probably they would force her into prostitution.

Would she be able to cope with that?

Probably.

She was basically like her mother.

But what would happen to the baby?

His baby!

Would they even let it be born?

And then what?

Would they kill it or just give it away?

Or would she be allowed to keep it?

Crazy!

Life was a goddamn vicious circle!

It was for sure that he wouldn't find out. All fighting was in vain. Hope, fear, and guilt had lost all meaning. What remained was a deep, stifling sadness.

Dan felt it like a heavy boulder on his chest and in his throat. This all-embracing sadness was stronger than any pain.

In the past, he'd often been angry and disappointed.

He'd hated himself for his weakness and Selina for her unscrupulousness. But now, so close to the end, he knew they would both atone for their mistakes.

He had to think back to that day in front of the trailer when Selina had been an innocent three-year-old and he himself was nothing more than a stupid, boozy junkie. He'd never been as stoned as Clara, but he hadn't covered himself in glory either. On that memorable day, he'd already taken his first line in the morning, and then there had been countless joints and, of course, this goddamn booze, which was his worst vice. Clara had woken up for a moment to get her next dose. Selina walked around and had to take care of her meals herself—as usual.

Sometimes Dan remembered to give her a bowl of cornflakes.

Sometimes not.

Many times they didn't have any cornflakes or milk on hand.

Somehow, though, he'd saved her from death, taken her in his arms from time to time and kissed her on the tip of her nose when she came to him (although he was often totally stoned), but he wasn't a father to her.

That came later.

Although a proverb said it was never too late, it was never mentioned whether what had happened before was so easy to smooth out.

There was no proverb for that.

Right?

Except maybe the one that said that time would heal all wounds.

But does it really?

Or did time create scars that more or less healed?

And what if one of these scars was in the wrong place?

In the heart, for example.

Maybe you tried to hide them somehow, but you used the wrong material. So perhaps it became inflamed afterward, and the consequences of such an inflammation could be devastating.

Just like with Selina.

His princess.

Everything had always looked so beautifully well on the outside, but pus and rot spread on the inside and poisoned her soul. All the love of the world couldn't reverse such a process once it was in full swing.

Dan hadn't known that.

Until now.

He hadn't wanted to know either and had preferred to spend his life on a pink cloud on which someone had scribbled "happy ever after."

Shouldn't he have known better?

The past couldn't be undone. It ate through our hearts and souls like acid. And the younger we were, the deeper it could penetrate. It didn't depend on what our mind remembered but only on what settled in our subconscious.

In these last minutes of his life, Dan's subconscious opened like a long-forgotten cellar door, but what he saw

310

wasn't a gloomy landing but a sultry, cloudy autumn afternoon in his personal horror park. There was the worn-out couch on which they had sat for an unnecessarily long time and got drunk with all sorts of things. Dan was sitting with Shawn, who wasn't a buddy but an asshole who was only tolerated for supplying drugs.

Shawn was a douchebag, but he always made a good price. Sometimes he even bartered. When there was no money at all, Clara gave him a blow job. She'd already fucked him. So Dan knew how to turn around and look the other way. But that afternoon it hadn't been Clara that Shawn had been fiddling with, but Selina.

Of course Dan had noticed the arousal in Shawn's voice and the bulge in his pants. And Selina's fear because she had to sit on his lap although she didn't want to. Dan had seen how much she begged him to get her out of this predicament.

But they needed the stuff badly.

Especially Clara, who could become extremely uneasy if she didn't get her daily dose. Unlike Dan, who could comfort himself quite well with booze. That didn't work for her anymore, since she was hooked on the needle.

So he had to consider very carefully how he'd behave now—on the couch that afternoon—and had come to the conclusion that nothing bad could actually happen as long as they both were sitting completely dressed on the sofa.

Selina didn't understand what was going on. Well, okay, she cried. But at that time Dan had thought there was no reason for that. Sure, Shawn was a disgusting guy, but he didn't hurt her. He just enjoyed having her sit on his lap. Even if she didn't like it. Life wasn't always easy—you couldn't learn that early enough.

So Shawn visited more often.

Dan looked away every time.

Just because of those fucking drugs.

Was that guilt?

Oh yes, and it was the biggest and most disgusting load you could ever burden yourself with!

He shouldn't have left her with Shawn for a single second …

Dan jerked in horror when the car door opened. They threw the teacher's body into the footwell and slammed the door shut again. He heard the trunk lid being opened and closed. Even though Dan couldn't move, his other senses worked perfectly. He smelled the dead teacher's blood and wished to be dead as well.

They probably wanted to get rid of the car and its contents. Maybe they would sink it in the river. That's how Dan would have done it. He realized he would drown like a damn rat in the trap.

Not a very nice prospect.

A quick head shot would have been a mercy. He hardly dared hope they would do him this favor.

And Selina?

Once again Dan wondered what those bastards would do to his princess. Maybe she'd be able to free herself. His princess was strong. Stronger than he'd ever been.

He'd take this hope with him to death and perhaps to hell … as long as he managed to keep it up. Despite all the bad things she'd done, Selina wasn't the one who deserved to pay for it. Dan would have gladly spared her from this, but he had no choice but to accept his own fate.

It was too late for everything else.

Silently, he watched one of the men get behind the wheel.

For a while, they just drove. Dan gritted his teeth at every bump. He wouldn't have minded if his arms had been as numb as his legs. When his bowels emptied, he smelled it but felt nothing. The guy at the wheel noticed it too and cursed loudly.

Dan didn't care.

After all, he hadn't made himself a cripple. He thought of Kate, who had been in a similar situation before she died.

Now he knew what it felt like to be without dignity, having death right in front of your eyes and being at the mercy of a person who didn't give a shit.

For Kate it had probably been even worse, because her tormentor had been her own man who actually should love and protect her.

Dan, on the other hand, only had to deal with a primitive and criminal asshole, just like Shawn had been.

Shawn.

He hadn't thought about that motherfucker in a long time.

It all had started with him.

Or even earlier?

With a young, primitive Dan, who had fantasized about following his heart when he fell in love with Clara, who was already pretty fucked up at that time. For her he'd exchanged his boring average life for the miserable existence in the trailer park. His mother had warned him, but he hadn't listened.

That's why Nora was now dead, slashed by her own granddaughter.

Action and reaction.

Dan felt the wetness of his tears on his cheeks. Snot ran from his nose, but he couldn't wipe it off.

All he could do was lie there and wait to be redeemed. Suddenly he thought of the prisoners on death row and that he'd sometimes wondered what it would feel like if you knew exactly when and how you would die. As an inmate on death row, you could at least be more or less sure that it wouldn't be too painful and that they wouldn't let you suffer, whether you deserved it or not.

Here and now there was no certainty and no last meal. Not even a last wish. He had no choice but to wait and hope.

Or he could pray.

Didn't they all do that when the end was near?

Dan thought about it, but he couldn't think of any prayer.

Dear God, please let it happen quickly. And please let Selina and the baby get away. Amen.

That was all?

And please forgive me. I know now that it's my fault. Forgive me. Do what I can't do.

What else was there to say or think?

Action and reaction.

Either way it was time to die now.

It was better to accept it.

Amen.

***

Back in town, Mario led Selina through the back door into his brothel. They climbed a dark staircase to get to his apartment on the second floor. The elevator didn't work, as Mario explained. His men disappeared somewhere in the guts of the large brick building.

Upstairs, Mario took off her handcuffs. Selina rubbed her aching wrists while she looked around. The apart-

314

ment was tastefully furnished, although a bit kitschy. In the middle of the spacious living and dining area was a white leather couch with colorful cushions. A huge flat-screen TV hung on the wall. The polished floor tiles looked expensive. Mario's business was apparently doing quite well.

Too well!

Selina couldn't imagine that it was an ordinary brothel, like dozens of others in every big city. After all, these guys' methods were anything but ordinary.

She wondered if the other women in this house had been kidnapped too. How did that work? The building didn't look like a prison so far. It would be easy to run away from here as soon as you were without surveillance.

Mario led her from the living room to the bedroom. A huge round landscape of pillows probably represented the bed. Chains with handcuffs were mounted to the walls. On the bed lay a long black object, which looked like a whip, and a black leather collar, as was used to restrain big dogs. Cameras on black tripods stood in every corner of the room. They were directed at the bed but could certainly be turned in any direction. Selina looked up at the ceiling and recognized a strange cross-shaped device, which was also equipped with chains and shackles.

"It's a privilege to be up her," Mario said proudly, looking like a little Napoleon.

"What's all this?" Selina asked quietly. She felt an unpleasant pressure in her stomach.

The worries about her dad had long-since given way to fear for herself. He was probably dead by now and could consider himself extremely lucky.

"Oh, what you see here is solely for my own pleasure," Mario explained while he strutted across the room. "Most girls do their best to get here. They're not allowed to sleep in my bed, but it's definitely better to hang on the chains here than on those in the basement."

He laughed hoarsely.

"In the basement?" Selina asked, although she didn't really want to know more about it.

"Oh, yeah. I have a very big basement, sweetie. It's also pretty well equipped. I had to dig deep into my pocket for that. I dare say that there is hardly a perversion that gets a raw deal."

He laughed again. "The people who enjoy themselves in my basement pay a lot of money for it. Ordinary guys visit the brothel and the strip bars on the lower floors. The women who work there are all over twenty-one and do it of their own free will. They also make some good bucks, but in comparison, it's not worth mentioning. It just makes the camouflage perfect."

Selina didn't dare look at him. It slowly dawned on her.

"I have to admit the girls in the basement aren't volunteers. But we treat them a little better now, because too many died last year. It's not always easy to get new suitable goods. A girl like you is a real lucky shot. From time to time my men catch girls from surrounding states, but this is dangerous. The last one was about your age. Also very pretty. A redhead. The boys caught her somewhere in Florida on the way to school. She didn't have any experience, so I had to prepare her for a few weeks. Unfortunately, she didn't even survive a month in the basement. A customer was too good with the anal punishment, and she bled to death."

Now Selina turned her face to him. It didn't bother her that he could see her tears. "Why tell me?"

Mario shrugged. His eyes sparkled mischievously.

At least Selina knew what she had to do to avoid ending up in the basement: she had to convince this man that she was the best toy he'd ever possessed. She had to make sure he wouldn't give her away—no matter what his customers were paying.

Could she do that?

At least she wasn't a naïve schoolgirl who didn't have a clue. She forced herself to raise her hand and stroke his smooth cheek. "Just tell me what you want, honey, and I'll make sure you get it."

Mario grinned. At the same moment, his slap in the face threw her astride on the bed. "Let's start with you shutting up, *Princess*. Now get undressed!"

***

The car finally stopped. Dan closed his eyes. However he would die, now was the time.

Still swearing at the stench, the driver got out. Dan heard the sound of another vehicle coming to a stop somewhere behind them. The men talked in a muffled way. He couldn't understand what they were saying. They sounded excited. Probably because of the stench in the car. Dan didn't smell it anymore. He had other problems.

What would happen now?

Where were they, anyway?

The ride had been quite bumpy, so Dan guessed it was an unpaved road that could have led anywhere. He didn't know this area.

Suddenly Dan heard a wet splashing noise. Somebody poured something over the car. Thoroughly and from all sides.

He noticed a peculiar smell.

Gasoline?

Shit, those bastards are gonna burn me alive!

Dan screamed even though he knew it didn't make any sense. He yelled until his lungs burned and the wet splashing stopped. He desperately threw his head back and forth. That was all he could do.

For a moment everything was quiet, and he heard nothing but his own hoarse wheezing. Then the interior of the car was bathed in bright yellow-red light.

Fire!

He screamed again. He screamed until he couldn't make a single hoarse sound anymore and his lungs were bleeding. There was a taste of warm copper in his throat. Now he also felt the steadily increasing heat. Horrified, he noticed that the teacher's skin was already blistering.

Dear God, please let it be over!

Still, Dan desperately gasped for air that was far too hot to breathe. The heat swallowed him up. One last time he screamed out all his pain and fear through lips that had already melted.

Finally his lungs collapsed and shortly afterward his heart failed.

Dan Meller was finally allowed to die.

His last thoughts were of his children: the dead, the living, and the unborn.

EPILOGUE

SELINA OR WHAT REMAINED

She tried hard to win him over. For this purpose she let herself be humiliated in a manner she never would have thought possible. Smiling, she drank Mario's piss and licked his asshole. She showed maximum flexibility and swallowed anything that fit into her sore mouth. She was allowed to stay with Mario for one week. At night and when he was away, he chained her to the wall.

Naked and on her knees.

He regularly gave her to drink and fed her a gray slimy stuff that might have been oatmeal. Once a day she was allowed to use the toilet under his surveillance. It wasn't easy getting used to sleeping against the wall, and Selina tried everything to get Mario to let her into his bed at night.

But Mario wasn't Dan, even though he wanted her to call him Daddy.

He wasn't manipulatable.

On the seventh day he was fucking her in the ass as she lay over the table when one of his men came in with a naked woman with huge breasts with dark, saucer-sized areolas. Mario looked at her while he pumped his juice into Selina's now-stretched asshole and then wiped his wet cock clean on her back. He dressed, grabbed Selina by her hair, and threw her to the floor, where she lay trembling.

"Who's that?" he wanted to know from the very over-weight man.

"A runaway. Wanted to hitchhike. Allegedly comes from California," the fatso replied with a grin.

The young woman, who was actually just a girl no older than Selina, made a suffocated sobbing sound. Mario went to her and pinched her breast.

She whimpered.

The girl's face was swollen, her body covered with bruises. Mario grabbed between her legs, eliciting a tortured scream from her throat.

Angrily, he looked at the fatso. "Who fucked her?"

"That was me," the guy admitted sheepishly. "Her tits are so amazing, I just couldn't help it."

"You'll get your punishment later. Now I want you to take this fucked-up piece of shit downstairs and tell Erwin. He's been waiting the whole week for this moment."

He kicked Selina in the ass. She panicked and realized he was talking about her.

Her thoughts revolved as the fatso pulled her to her feet. She hadn't thought of her father for days, but now she did.

She missed him and envied him.

"You little bitch didn't really think you could turn my head, did you?" Mario mocked her and spat in her face.

Yes, that's exactly what she'd thought.

Until the end.

Her anus was painfully throbbing from his kick and the countless times he'd raped and humiliated her in the last days.

And for what?

Had everything been in vain?

"Your old daddy probably made you think you're something special, Princess. But now I'm your daddy, and with me you'll learn that you're just an ordinary bitch like all the others!"

He laughed and massaged the thick breasts of his new toy.

"Think about it, please," she begged, although she knew it was pointless. "I'll do anything for you, Daddy! Things she doesn't even know exist!"

"Forget it, bitch. Tonight you belong to Erwin, and he has enough ideas of his own."

He dragged the girl into his bedroom and closed the door.

The fatso grabbed Selina by the arm to take her to the place that was to be her home from now on.

***

Two months later, Selina suffered a miscarriage while she was just strapped to a fuck machine, a thick black plastic dildo in her ass and the cock of a masked customer in her mouth. This one had previously bound her breasts so tightly that they turned purple-blue.

The guy behind the camera gave a cheerful scream and came closer to film the bloody mess at close range.

Selina, who had given up crying, began again, where-upon the customer silenced her by ramming his dick up to her tonsils. The machine drove the dildo powerfully into her while her little secret flowed out of her in short painful cramps.

"Who knocked her up?" the customer wanted to know.

"I have no idea," replied the guy with the camera. "Could have been anyone. But fuck it! None of the girls stay pregnant here for long."

The two men laughed and withdrew for a moment to fetch the electric cattle drover and the nipple clamps.

Today's filming had only just begun …

***

At night, when Selina lay half naked and tied up on the cold concrete floor, she sometimes dreamed of Mexico.

In her mind's eye she saw a small cozy kitchen in the glistening sunlight. Dad was sitting at the table. His gaze was warm, and he looked happy. In his arms he held a baby that resembled Leila but wasn't Leila.

It was their child.

His child.

It was exactly what made their little family perfect.

Selina stepped behind him and put her hand on his warm neck. She massaged her daddy while he rocked their little daughter to sleep.

Everything was bright and warm and felt right.

But then dark shadows appeared in the corners and crawled like greedy monster fingers over the floor of their perfect little kitchen. They reached Dad's feet and crept up his legs. He stiffened, and his neck became cold.

At that moment, Selina realized the child in his arms was dead.

Dead and decayed.

It had rotted holes instead of eyes and gray mold where its mouth had once been. Selina wanted to scream and shake her father awake so that he could see what he was holding, but then he turned his face toward her. It wasn't a face anymore but an inflamed red mass of craters and blisters. He said, "I forgive you, Princess."

Then she woke up, sweating despite the cold and trembling like a leaf. Sometimes she was even happy when a new customer maltreated her body so badly that she had no strength left to think of that dream or of Dad and Leila … or of that tiny piece of happiness that had been in her belly.

Selina Meller had been proud and selfish.

She thought she could have everything.

She'd been vain … and naive.

She'd used and destroyed her dad to make him hers forever. In a way, she had. When he died, he'd only belonged to her.

But she now belonged to Mario and would pay for her sins.

Every single minute of her miserable existence.

Some will say she deserved no better.

Maybe they're right.

THE FAVORITE GIRL

BONUS STORY

He sipped from his whiskey, couldn't keep his eyes off her.

What a woman! Fucking hell!

The thick blonde mane almost reached her ass.

And that was some ass! My God!

Plump and heart-shaped. Something to touch.

Or bite.

And she'd packed it into these incredibly tight jeans!

If he'd given a fuck about Christmas or birthdays, that would probably have been the gift he wished for …

John licked his lips.

A lump formed in his throat that no whiskey in the world could flush down.

His jeans slowly became too tight.

He scratched his crotch and drank. His greedy eyes remained on the woman. They were gliding over her taut body like slugs.

And she just sat there. Straight as a pole. A glass of wine stood in front of her. She wore these brazenly tight pants and a short red top.

Red! Goddamn!

And she was alone.

Wasn't she in the mood for some company?

What was a girl like that doing in a fucked-up bar like this? Weekdays and after midnight?

Who was she and what did she have in mind?

Usually there were only workers from the nearby factory here. They drowned their after work worries in booze, and on weekends one or the other bitch came here in search of a quick fuck.

Cheap sluts with fat asses and too much makeup in their swollen faces.

John was one of the guys who worked in the factory, and not a day went by without him wondering if that had been everything already …

He approached his forties and had been divorced for two years now.

His two daughters were now teenagers and only talked to him when they needed money. His ex had a new stud who didn't seem to mind her wobbly thighs and the wrinkles around her eyes.

She'd been beautiful.

And horny!

John had forgotten when that was.

Today she was a ridiculous fat cow who pestered him about alimony payments. The kids were in college now. And who had to pay for that?

John seldom thought of his daughters or the past. They had been cute pudgy girls with cute pigtails and round eyes. They had adored their daddy. And he would have done anything for them.

Anything!

Now they were bimbos with garish makeup and bleached hair who didn't give a shit about their daddy.

As long as he gave them enough money.

And he did, as long as he was working himself to death at the factory.

What had become of his family?

They had been happy once.

Or …?

Nowadays John had a beer belly and too much fat on his hips, his chest was already wobbling, his beard was gray, and his hair would follow soon.

He spent the evenings here, drinking whiskey to ease the pain in his back … and to forget.

Tomorrow morning at six he would have to struggle his way out of bed again, stretch his stiff limbs, and try to cover the disgusting taste in his mouth with toothpaste.

He'd drink liters of black coffee and smoke one cigarette after the other, get into his old pickup and drive to work, thinking of the evening, the bar, the next whiskey.

That's what he was living for now.

There was nothing else for John anymore.

While staring at the blonde woman (and he wasn't the only one to do so), he wondered when he'd last seen a pussy up close.

Months ago.

And the pussy in question hadn't necessarily been what a man in the prime of his life was longing for after a hard day's work.

Its sour and fishy smell had expanded John's limit of disgust by a few nuances.

He'd fucked the slut nonetheless.

You didn't always have a choice.

He wondered how this pussy would smell?

And taste?

Even the thought of it made John breathless.

It would be sweet. And juicy.

What was that girl doing here?

He couldn't stop asking himself this question.

If she were his daughter …

But she ain't, man! And you should thank God for that.

Had she come to make him lose his mind?

His colleagues apparently had the same problem.

Even the bartender had an expression on his face that seemed horny and transfigured.

The woman surely knew all eyes were on her. It didn't seem to bother her. Maybe she even liked it. Why else would she be sitting in such a bar at this hour?

She's waiting for it! John thought in his heated skull. *If you don't seize the opportunity, someone else will.*

But who?

He was by far the youngest and (as far as John could judge) the most attractive man in this bar.

After all, there had to be a reason why the sluts loved to throw themselves at him!

He was nothing special and had long since passed his best days, but he was still the best piece of man this sad honky-tonk had to offer.

Would the woman think the same?

Didn't she look over at him a few minutes ago? Hadn't she winked at him?

Why don't you try your luck?

That was a good question. What did he have to lose?

If she was here to seriously pick up a guy, she was eventually just a slut and he should have felt sorry for her …

Why wouldn't he take advantage of the situation?

In a life that no longer had much to offer, that was a very special treat.

To refuse it wouldn't only be stupid but almost a sin.

So John took his glass and walked over to the woman who was still sitting stiff and silent on her bar stool.

When he stood next to her, he could smell her.

Her perfume was too tangy for his taste, but a look into her neckline simply compensated for everything.

"Hi!" he murmured and raised his glass. "I'm John."

"Hi!" Her voice sounded deeper than expected. A little hoarse and damned wicked.

John's cock wanted to dance.

She closed her long fingers with the red lacquered nails around the stem of the wine glass.

Red!

"Cheers!" she whispered. A soft smile played around her full lips.

"Cheers!"

They drank without taking their eyes off each other.

"What's your name?"

She batted her eyelashes that were too thick to be real.

"Angel."

John suspected that was a lie, but he didn't care.

His gaze was trapped in her neckline.

At the rosy edge of her nipples!

Good Lord, she really was an angel!

Their glasses were empty and John was happy to provide supplies.

He ignored the bartender's disparaging gaze. That guy was just jealous!

Angel's deep blue eyes drilled into his.

John imagined kissing her sweet little snub nose. And these lips …

She was hardly any older than his daughters, but that didn't matter.

"Where you from, Angel?"

The answer was obvious. This wonderful being must have fallen from heaven …

"I'm not from around here," she whispered.

Was there and bit of sadness in her voice?

"Passing through?" John had noticed a black travel bag standing next to her on the floor.

She shrugged. "Something like that."

John was satisfied with that information. After all, he wasn't a psychiatrist or social worker, just a horny guy with a hard cock!

"Do you know where you're sleeping tonight?"

Again she shrugged.

Bingo! Surely she didn't have any money! She was probably running away from something or someone; she was helpless and on her own.

It couldn't be any better for him!

I'll fuck you tonight, baby!

"You can come with me if you want."

She looked at him and seemed to think about it. She frowned and played with a strand of her long hair.

Finally, her face brightened. She grinned and suddenly looked like a twelve-year-old. "Sure! Why not?"

John grinned too. He had every reason to. "Then let's get outta here!" he hastily suggested.

He'd forgotten his morning shift and the fat on his hips.

He'd forgotten all his worries and doubts.

For tonight, an angel had fallen from heaven.

***

On the way to the parking lot, John carried Angel's bag, which was surprisingly light.

He wondered if she was really on the run.

On high heels? Only with a small bag and a thin leather jacket?

Or maybe she was just a traveler looking for happiness and for a real good man?

Well, she found him now, John thought and smiled.

Who cared anyway?

The looks of the other men had been worth their weight in gold when they left the bar together.

His angel.

John had deserved that.

After all these years of deprivation between flabby thighs and fishy pussies.

He stared at Angel's ass.

How her ass cheeks bobbed …

John already saw himself grabbing between them and pulling them apart. A sweet little revelation. He'd stick his tongue in first and then maybe a finger. He'd …

They had arrived at his pickup.

John wanted to touch Angel. No matter where. Right now!

He reached out and helped her get in the truck.

Angel gave a dreamlike, sweet smile.

She was a real piece of candy!

Oh man, he'd fuck her brains out …

John was dizzy with happiness when he started the engine.

Now she was sitting right beside him, filling the stale smell of his car with a fresh scent.

His angel.

John set off.

Ten minutes.

He would have liked to drive even faster.

Too risky.

He pulled himself together but still could only think of his throbbing cock and Angel's pretty little butthole. Most girls didn't like it when you took the back door, but John didn't care about that.

Not tonight.

***

The stinking old skank that John had fucked last had been up for anything. Even today, he still shuddered when he thought of her worn-out holes and wrinkled

330

grayish skin. Nevertheless, he'd kept her for a few days before he chased her away, for his cock was by no means as picky as he was.

He to admit that her blowjobs had been pretty good.

And it was a good thing having a woman in your apartment when you came home after a long day at work. John had canceled a few evenings in the bar to enjoy her macaroni with cheese instead. Together they had eaten, drunk, smoked and most of all fucked their brains out.

If only she'd been a little younger and prettier …

In the end, John got tired of her.

What would it be like with Angel?

He could well imagine keeping her forever. She could cook for him and massage his cock. She could clean the apartment and let him fuck her ass.

Every night.

Then it would finally make sense again to struggle yourself out of bed in the morning and drag your aching carcass to the factory. The thoughts of Angel would sweeten John's days and turn his nights into fireworks. He'd never have to go to a bar again to get pointlessly drunk.

But Angel was so beautiful … so young …

Whoever or whatever had driven her into his arms tonight, she certainly wouldn't want to stay.

Absolutely not!

What's a girl like her supposed to do with a guy like him?

It was crazy to imagine that at all.

Completely crazy!

Although … she wasn't a local. Nobody knew her. And she was already making quite a secret of herself, which probably suggested that she sure had a skeleton in the closet or at least something to hide.

Girls like her were rarely missed.

His colleagues and the bartender had seen her leaving the bar with him, but was that of any importance? They would believe him if he claimed she'd left him the next day.

Why not?

They must have thought she was a hooker anyway.

What pretty young woman would wear a provocative outfit to sit in a bar full of horny factory workers?

And she'd left with John without batting an eye, even though he was a stranger.

What decent girl would do that?

She was either totally desperate or just as horny as he was.

Only that she could have picked better guys than old Johnny, who had to make an effort to see his dick while peeing.

Well, he'd make a special effort to make her happy tonight.

He'd do his very best for his Angel.

Even if it was the last thing he did, ha-ha!

She now sat on John's worn-out couch, her long slender legs crossed, a glass of whiskey in her hand.

John had put on music (Aerosmith, good old-fashioned shit) and dimmed the lights. His pants got tighter when he sat next to Angel.

It had to be clear to her that this was about sex, but she smiled sweetly and seemed very relaxed.

Because she wanted it too or because she didn't know what he was up to?

Well, we'll find out pretty soon.

John put his glass down and bent over her. Her mouth tasted of whiskey and was sticky from her lip gloss. She returned John's kiss and didn't fight back when he grabbed her breasts.

Everything was perfect!

But the world was spinning a little too fast.

Had he drunk that much?

John grabbed Angel by the wrist and led her hand to his crotch.

She massaged him.

Ah, good, that was so awesome!

He tugged at her top, tore it down, and freed her big breasts.

Great! Those nipples!

John sucked on them like a toddler.

Too bad he got a little nauseous now.

Maybe he shouldn't have eaten yesterday's burger for lunch today after all.

But damn, that felt so hot!

Was his zipper open already?

All of a sudden, Angel's hand was deep in his pants.

John greedily sucked on her nipples, her neck, her mouth …

Or was it her chin?

He could no longer see clearly, and his sense of touch seemed to have left him.

Damn booze!

That had to stop!

Angel covered his face with wet kisses.

Her tangy scent turned John on.

He lifted his hands to grab her, wanted to push her down and turn her around, take off his pants, knead her ass …

But his limbs were suddenly so heavy …

John moaned.

The sounds he made ranged from lust to pain.

What was she doing with his dick?

That hurt!

Fuck!

He wanted to push her away but instead slumped down like a wet sack.

What the fuck?

What was she doing with him?

Why did that hurt so much?

He tried to yell at her, but instead of words, a gush of vomit came out of his mouth. At least that made her let him go.

John wanted to look at her, talk to her.

Her face was blurred.

Not an angel anymore.

He felt a burning pain in his crotch.

What had she done?

He wanted to get up, grab her, beat the shit out of her, and then fuck her soul out of her body …

He couldn't. He seemed paralyzed.

All he could do was puke.

What had she given him?

Poison? Drugs?

What did angels bring from heaven?

John couldn't think anymore.

The pain pulsated red in his brain.

Red.

Shadows twitched before his eyes.

And somewhere in the background Steven Tyler was singing, "And then at times I'm so weak from lovin', I couldn't even carry a tune …"

John was weak too. Just not from making love. Or was it somehow …?

Take me with you! John thought desperately. *Get me outta here!*

But Steven didn't even think about it.

Nor did anybody else.

***

When John regained consciousness, it was cold and quiet.

He looked down at himself and realized he was naked.

His penis and testicles pulsated painfully.

Angel had used shoelaces (presumably his own) to bind his genitals into a grotesque object. The skin was bluish and swollen where the blood was accumulating. It felt as if it would burst open at any moment.

Please don't! Dear God! Please, please don't!

The pain was terrible.

Compared to that, the whirring in John's head and the tingling in his tied limbs felt almost pleasant.

Angel had dragged him from the couch to the floor and tied him up there. John could see duct tape (probably from his kitchen) on his ankles. She must have also used it to tie his hands behind his back.

"Angel?" he croaked hoarsely. "Where are you? Angel?! Damn fucking bitch!"

He couldn't see her.

That fucking slut!

She was completely crazy!

This was kidnapping!

And torture!

What was that bitch thinking?

"Angel?! Please, let … let's talk about it! Hear me? *Angel!*"

Considering what that bitch had done to him, her name was pure mockery.

Now John was sure this wasn't really her name.

That miserable whore!

Had she planned this from the beginning?

Probably!

Now it made sense.

John wriggled in his shackles and threw his head back and forth, which only made him nauseous again.

Don't vomit! Not again!

He retched dry. Nothing happened.

Again he screamed her name.

Angel! This damn spawn of hell!

Maybe she was long gone. And maybe that was the best thing that could happen to him. He'd have enough time to free himself. And if he didn't manage that, sooner or later someone from work would come by to check on him. An embarrassing situation, for sure, but still better than to die here, killed by this devilish woman ...

And what if my dick rots off by then?

John had no idea if that was anatomically possible. He didn't know anything about such things. But the thought scared the shit out of him.

Could he lose his cock?

Or his virility?

Again he fought against the shackles, but the tape wouldn't move an inch.

In any case, he hadn't bought any shit!

Even if he now wished he'd ...

"Angel!"

Did he really want her to still be here?

Maybe she wasn't finished with him yet ...

On the other hand, he might be able to talk to her and convince her to let him go.

She was just a stupid bitch! How hard could it be?

"Angel? Please talk to me if you' re here! Don't leave me like that!"

And then she actually showed up.

The long hair framed her face and added a deceptive softness to her features. She was naked and she moved with the gracefulness of a Greek goddess.

Angel.

John almost didn't notice the carving knife in her hand. She'd taken it from his kitchen.

Just like the tape.

Angel came closer.

John panted breathlessly. He'd be hyperventilating in a minute. Desperately, he tried to free his hands. Panic and nausea raged in his guts, stealing his breath. He knew exactly how well this damn knife could cut! He'd sharpened it only a few days ago.

Dear God, you can't let that happen!

But why not?

What would he have done to that woman if he could?

Did someone like him really deserve mercy?

Even now, with all the panic and pain, he was still gawking between Angel's legs.

She was shaved.

"P-please!" he stammered as she squatted next to him. "Don't hurt me!"

Tears ran down his cheeks now. He hadn't even cried at his father's funeral five years ago.

Angel's hair hung down to his upper body.

Like gold.

Then she grabbed his crotch and John screamed in pain.

"Is that good, Johnny? Pretty tight?" She didn't sound mocking but strangely serious.

"Take it away!" John whimpered. "Please, remove it!"

Angel smiled and squeezed again.

John roared until everything turned black before his eyes.

Finally she let go.

"Please, Angel, let me go!"

"But where do you wanna go, you sad old man?"

She lifted the knife, turned it around, looked at it from all sides. Finally she stuck it tip first into John's belly button.

A stabbing pain shot through his abdomen.

Angel grabbed the handle with both hands and slowly turned the knife.

John felt the blade drill into his flesh. He tried to pull in his stomach and hold his breath. "Stop it! Please!"

But Angel didn't stop. She leaned all her weight on the knife, which finally disappeared up to the handle in John's belly with a smacking noise.

The pain was as sharp and pointed as the cursed blade that John had sharpened himself.

He felt warm moisture and knew it was his blood.

Red! Red like her fingernails.

He gasped and stared at Angel's rocking breasts. Her flowing hair glided over his skin.

She let the knife stick in John's belly and beamed at him.

This smile made the sun rise.

John would have given anything to wake up next to this girl only once in the morning.

After a long night of happiness and sex.

But that wasn't the reason she was here for ...

"Soon you'll have it done," she whispered.

"W-why are you doing this to me?"

Angel's bright white teeth flashed when she laughed.

"'Cause you're one of them, my darling."

"Who are you talking about?" John shook his head. "You're wrong!"

338

The warm liquid spread, running over his chest and thighs.

The pain was even bearable.

For the moment.

She straightened up. Only now did he notice the scars on her otherwise flawless body. There were a lot of them in the pubic area.

"Who hurt you?"

Angel just smiled.

"Angel, please! I can help you!"

"You're dying, Johnny. That's all that's left for you to do in this life."

"Tell me who hurt you! We can go to the police, we—"

"I was his favorite girl." Suddenly her voice sounded younger. "His princess."

She sighed. Her gaze drifted into nowhere. Lost in thought she played with her breasts. Her fingers were stained with blood.

His blood.

Red!

"But he couldn't save me either. Nobody can."

"But I can, Angel! Please believe me!"

"He's dead now. They're all dead. And I'm still their favorite girl."

"Please, Angel, listen to me! You have to pull the knife out of my stomach! Very carefully! And then …"

Angel massaged her nipple with one hand while the other slipped into her shaved crotch.

Her lips formed an O.

John thought of the women in the sex commercials who apparently brought themselves to orgasm with their own fingers.

A typical male fantasy.

But this was nothing but a nightmare that had come alive!

Whatever that girl had experienced, she was crazier than a shithouse rat and he was so fucked!

Angel moaned and pushed her pelvis forward.

Suddenly she paused and stared right in John's face. Smiling, she reached for the knife in his stomach.

John flinched, trying to prepare for the pain. No important organs seemed to be injured yet, although the blade stuck deep inside his body.

"You would have love to fuck your favorite girl, right?"

John's mind was spinning.

What should he say?

What was the right thing to do?

Was there even a right or wrong?

Angel slowly moved the knife handle back and forth. The pain intensified.

John tried to be strong. He knew this was his last chance.

"Y-you're a pretty woman, Angel. Beautiful. And I admit that I wanted to sleep with you. What man wouldn't? But I … I'd never have hurt you. Do you understand? Never! I just wanted to be tender and—"

"You would have fucked me hard, right, old man?"

"No!" John sobbed. "I would have been very tender."

"Oh, tender?" Her face distorted into a grimace as she grabbed the knife and shoved it up to John's sternum.

He felt his flesh gape apart, and he screamed his head off.

Angel now looked like a fury gone wild, speckled with his blood.

Red!

She left the knife stuck, turned around, and held her ass in front of his face. "That's what you wanted, right?"

John fought for his consciousness. He opened his eyes and stared at Angel's scarred flesh. God alone knew what had happened to this woman.

If she hadn't just slit his tummy open, he might have had the chance to think about it a little more. But all he could do was moan and whine for mercy. He only subconsciously realized she was peeing in his open abdominal cavity and that her hands were now stuck deep in his gaping wound.

John looked into her sparkling eyes and saw bliss.

Black dots danced in front of his field of vision.

His body shook violently as Angel rummaged in his guts.

Suddenly he remembered his daughters, whom he'd never see again.

"I have kids!" he rasped with his last strength.

Angel had just pulled a bowel loop out of his abdominal cavity and wrapped it around her wrist like a grotesque bracelet. It stank of blood, fear, and excrement.

John's innards were glued to Angel's body, which had been badly battered by life.

And again she plunged very deeply into him, dug up to the elbows in his guts, tore and pulled …

John's heart rate slowed. He could no longer lift his head, and it took great effort to keep his eyes open.

His younger daughter Jennifer had been his favorite. Angel could have been. He only would've hurt her a little.

Not as bad as the men whose darling she'd been before.

But it was too late for all that now.

Angel looked like a monster, full of blood, slime, and shit.

A favorite girl to run away from.

An angel from hell.

John's tied hands twitched behind his back, looking for a hold they wouldn't find anymore.

Angel's delicate fingers squished his pancreas. That hardly hurt.

John's last thought was that he probably deserved it.

He wasn't any better than all the others …

But in the end, it wasn't him sticking in her but her sticking in him and maybe he still had a bit of luck, because he was allowed to look at those beautiful golden hairs and those pretty big tits until the end, which trembled to the beat of her lust.

And this one promise she gave him on his way into the darkness: she'd be his favorite girl.

Forever.

EPILOGUE AND ACKNOWLEDGEMENTS

Dear readers,

It's been almost a year since I had to withdraw *The Princess* from the market after two very successful years.

In the meantime, I've learned that the term "artistic freedom" doesn't mean much. The original version of the book ended up being canned, because unfortunately, some people were unable to deal with what they'd read or to distinguish fiction from reality.

But there are many more people who love my Princess and I would like to thank all my readers, colleagues, and friends for their active support at a time that made me doubt a lot. Thanks to you I didn't have to despair completely but managed to stay true to myself.

Thank you very much, dear Michael Merhi and REDRUM BOOKS, dear Marion Mergen, one of the best editors ever, dear Klaus Schidzick, who always stood by me with help and advice, dear members of my Facebook fan group, and dear REDRUM-non-pussies!

And last but not least, as always, thanks a million to my family.

What would I have done without you?

I don't even want to think about it.

But let us look forward together.

My princess is back! The way she's allowed to, not censored at all—that's what my name stands for.

Finally, I managed to edit the story about Selina and Dan in such a way that it didn't lose any of its horror but can still be sold. So before you pay huge amounts for the original on eBay, you can devote yourself to this new version without hesitation.

I hope you will like the new Selina and that it will send a shiver down the spine of every reader. Because that is my job and always will be.

Where it says Simone Trojahn "Hardcore" on it, there's hardcore in it!

Thank you for appreciating it so much!

Simone Trojahn, October 2018

PUBLISHING PROGRAM

www.redrum-verlag.de

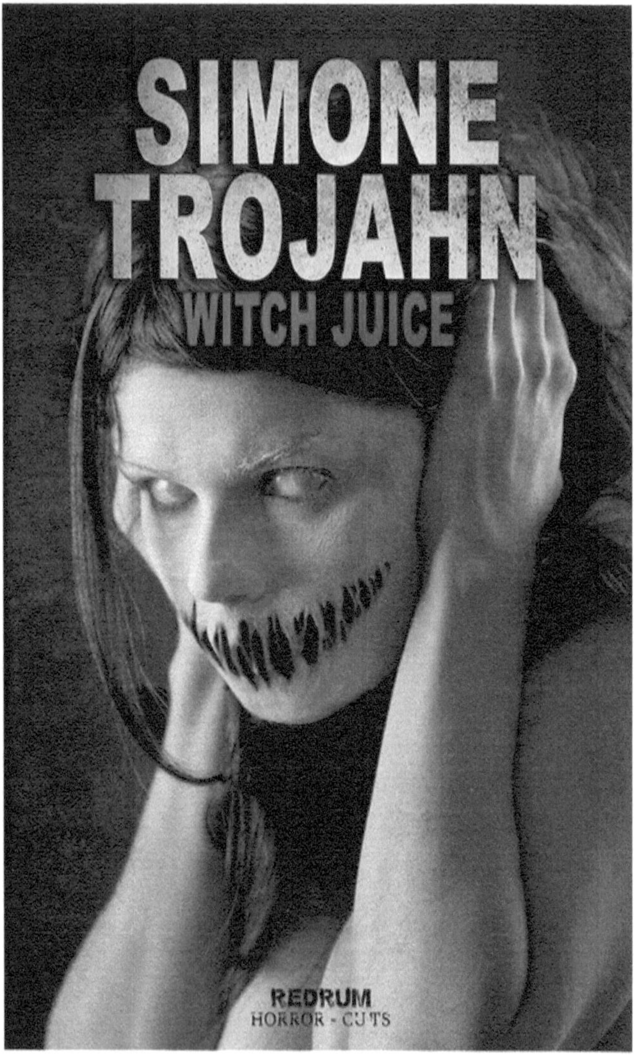
SIMONE
TROJAHN
WITCH JUICE
REDRUM
HORROR - CUTS

SELINA'S
WAY

Psycho   Thriller

SIMONE TROJAHN

REDRUM

SIMONE TROJAHN

BAD FAMILY

THRILLER

REDRUM

REDRUM loves you!

REDRUM liebt dich!

Visit our facebook group now:

REDRUM BOOKS - Nichts für Pussys!

www.redrum-verlag.de